THE HIDDEN CITY

Also by Charles Finch

The Last Enchantments
What Just Happened

The Charles Lenox Series
A Beautiful Blue Death
The September Society
The Fleet Street Murders
A Stranger in Mayfair
A Burial at Sea
A Death in the Small Hours
An Old Betrayal
The Laws of Murder
Home by Nightfall
The Inheritance
The Woman in the Water
The Vanishing Man
The Last Passenger
An Extravagant Death

THE HIDDEN CITY

Charles Finch

**MINOTAUR
BOOKS
NEW YORK**

This is a work of fiction. All of the characters, organizations, and events portrayed in this novel are either products of the author's imagination or are used fictitiously.

First published in the United States by Minotaur Books, an imprint of St. Martin's Publishing Group

EU Representative: Macmillan Publishers Ireland Ltd, 1st Floor, The Liffey Trust Centre, 117–126 Sheriff Street Upper, Dublin 1, DO1 YC43

THE HIDDEN CITY. Copyright © 2025 by Hampden Lane LLC. All rights reserved. Printed in the United States of America. For information, address St. Martin's Publishing Group, 120 Broadway, New York, NY 10271.

www.minotaurbooks.com

The Library of Congress Cataloging-in-Publication Data is available upon request.

ISBN 978-1-250-76716-5 (hardcover)
ISBN 978-1-250-76717-2 (ebook)

The publisher of this book does not authorize the use or reproduction of any part of this book in any manner for the purpose of training artificial intelligence technologies or systems. The publisher of this book expressly reserves this book from the Text and Data Mining exception in accordance with Article 4(3) of the European Union Digital Single Market Directive 2019/790.

Our books may be purchased in bulk for specialty retail/wholesale, literacy, corporate/premium, educational, and subscription box use. Please contact MacmillanSpecialMarkets@macmillan.com.

First Edition: 2025

10 9 8 7 6 5 4 3 2 1

For the marvelous, magical, mysterious

Annabel,

with her permission, and a father's deepest love!

THE HIDDEN CITY

CHAPTER ONE

Thousands of years had passed since the Romans turned this small English harbor into a port city, and she had never for even an hour since ceased her maritime activities—yet still, after all this time, when a ship appeared on the horizon, Portsmouth's eyes turned in unison to the sea.

Charles Lenox observed this fact from the window of his rooms on the second story of the Bosun's Arms. This was a public house and inn facing the waterfront, with old crossbeams on the ceiling, its walls scratched with sailors' names and darkened nearly black with pipe and fire smoke.

He was a Londoner himself, but had been comfortably installed here since his arrival late the evening before. What was left of breakfast lay on the table nearby, encircled by badly folded newspapers. There was a cup of strong tea in his hand.

"*Marie Grace* ahoy," a deep voice rumbled from downstairs, just lagging the bell that had been struck quayside at the sighting of the sail.

On the cobblestone street, people peered out to sea. As for Lenox, he couldn't make out the ship, in the sheared-up misty distance, unless—yes, there it was after all, he saw, with a little leap in his heart. He studied her distant approach for a long minute before turning back in to the small room. A coal fire was burning in the grate; a stubborn white frost lingered on the windowpanes of the carriages outside. It was the early winter of 1879, nearly the end of November. He could only imagine how cold it must be on board.

He opened the door and called for the porter who was posted in the inn's upper hallway.

"Yes, sir?" said the boy, a wiry, undersized person of fifteen or so.

"Is that very definitely the *Marie Grace*?" he asked.

"Yes, sir," the lad replied, barely glancing. "You'd recognize her foremast at twice the distance."

He spoke with such confidence! "Have you sailed upon her yourself?"

"Oh, no, sir. I've never left Portsmouth, sir. Never been on a ship, for that matter."

Lenox paused at this surprising information, then said, "And how long till she's here?"

The boy, who was in a double-breasted navy blue jacket with a long row of rubbed-down vaguely maritime golden buttons bisecting it vertically, squinted expertly at the sail.

"Fifty-one minutes, give or take," he decided. "The wind ain't much."

Lenox nodded. "Thank you. It amazes me to hear that you have never been on a ship."

"No plans, either," said the boy with satisfaction, pleased to have amazed a customer. He was clearing away dishes as they spoke, with the inveterate usefulness of his type. Downstairs the tremendous row of the ship's appearance continued, stevedores and businessmen shifting themselves away from the comforts of the bar and toward the stations of their various trades, in preparation for the arrival.

"Are you not curious, living and working so close to the sea?"

"Not curious enough to fall in and drown, sir."

"Not everyone who sets foot on a ship immediately falls into the water."

"Enough do to have put me off it."

"Fair enough."

"Not a waterborne fellow, you see, sir—haven't learnt to swum yet, and don't intend it."

There was the sharp ring of a bell at the other end of the hallway, and the lad's eyes brightened. Lenox knew that the opposite room was taken by an openhanded merchant who bought silk from India directly at the wharf each month.

"Is there something else, sir?"

"No, that's all, thank you. Oh—but do please see that the room I reserved is ready for the stay of a young woman."

"Of course, sir," said the boy, lenient with the nervousness of those who didn't see ships come in every day. "Margaret will look it over again."

Lenox gave him a shilling, which the boy deposited into the cloth of his soft cap—for in this city, more than any other he had visited across Great Britain, there was no such thing as an implicit later gratuity. You tipped when the person was in front of you. Perhaps it was growing up amidst the tales of so many drownings and piracies and vanishings at sea; the shilling was for that day.

When he was alone again, Lenox returned to the window. So she would be here soon! Not more than forty-five minutes now.

He was a man just past the milestone age of fifty, and still not quite sure how to comprehend that blunt reality. Generally he felt rather spry. He was tallish, trim of build, with hazel eyes and a short, dark beard. As was his custom, he wore a dark gray wool suit, well-cut, and a shirt of the soft, snowy white that would have been enough for any English man or woman, with their unerring eye for class, to place him no lower than the level of gentry.

In his figure and his face one saw great energy, but his eyes at the moment were bloodshot, and his expression both a little wary and very weary. The truth was that it had been a hard year; perhaps his hardest. Lenox was a detective by trade, and that spring, while traveling in America in the line of work, he had been stabbed, an ugly brute of a hunting knife piercing the muscle between two ribs on his right side.

For a few strange, bitter, terribly real seconds he had been sure his life was over. When he had awoken, it was much later, having already been operated upon. Not even a dream survived to him of the intervening hours. The quick work of that Yankee surgeon had saved his life, but in the days immediately afterward he had suffered from strange hallucinations, chills, fever, and terrible pain in his right ribs.

The other symptoms had eventually gone. But that pain lingered obstinately still, the muscles gnarled and incensed, some days seemingly as far from healed as ever.

There was a rap at the door. "Come in."

It was Margaret. "Here is some fresh tea, sir. Alfie said you wanted to see me?"

"I wanted to be sure the room I hired was ready."

"Yes, sir. For one guest besides yourself, a cold lunch to be set, hot waiting? I did it this morning."

"But the guest is a young *woman*," said Lenox, with special emphasis on the last word. He halted there, suddenly unsure of what it was that made a room suitable for a young woman. He had two daughters, but neither was yet ten years old. "What is the cold lunch?"

In a single-breath monotone, Margaret repeated what must have been the daily menu. "Cheese bread roast beef sliced tomatoes hot cross buns young onions and oysters, and the hot is brown potatoes and lamb pot pie. With anchovy sauce."

Lenox nodded. "And there's a mirror, I suppose?" he asked, feeling a bit foolish. "And a basin of water and soap, and all that kind of thing?"

"Oh, yes, sir."

Margaret, who had a big, blank face with two pigtails framing it, stood there looking prepared to answer equally stupid questions until sundown, if it was required of her.

"Thank you," said Lenox. He peered out the window. "How long until the ship's here, do you think, Margaret?"

The girl followed Lenox's gaze to the ship. "Forty-three minutes," she said after an instant. She departed with another of his coins.

There was a great deal Lenox could have done with forty-three minutes. For a start there was his correspondence, neatly prepared by a footman into a packet tied with heavy string at his house in London the day before.

But he couldn't quite face it—for the first time in his life, he was hopelessly behind in letter-writing, and it filled him with a grievous fatigue to think of untying that string.

Then there was the agency. Lenox had done his work alone for almost twenty years; when he started, he had been the only detective of his kind on this side of channel. These days, however, there were dozens like him in London, and the agency, which he had established with two friends, had to keep a keen edge to stay atop the business. Thus, with him he had, in a small leather traveling portfolio the notes from four cases currently puzzling his partners, one of them a particularly nasty blackmail. He knew he ought to look at them. Certainly Polly and Dallington would appreciate it if he pitched in.

But here, too, he found himself beset by the unwonted lassitude that had characterized the months since his injury—and instead of picking up the portfolio, which he had also ignored the night before, and the several days before that, he took a small bowl of apple slices left over from the breakfast and sat down by the fire.

What was it? His exhausted heart thumped, thumped; and as he ate the apple slices, his thoughts turned to home, to his wife, Lady Jane, and their two daughters, Sophia and Clara; and with a little longing, to his comfortable study overlooking Hampden Lane, where he could be assured that no matter how many letters he left unanswered, how badly he let down Polly and Dallington, he would still find his books, his fireplace, and the soft brown chair where he had his best sleep these days.

A quick, whipping sort of rain was beginning to fall outside, barely enough to mark the street. A typically English greeting for the passengers arriving on the *Marie Grace*. Lenox went to the window and stood motionless, watching the faces of the people passing below. Over the years he had learned faces, and with an old, almost unconsidered skill, he began to study these, most of them turned down against the rain. He saw what he would have bet money were two blatant liars; any number of innocent men and women hurrying along to workaday tasks; a new mother with that peculiar luminosity that meant it was her first baby; a gang of cackling sailors whose leader's dark restless gaze signified no good to the captain of the ship he sailed on; and dozens more, including at one point Margaret, who rushed outside to deliver a pot of ale to a man in a little hut across the quay.

After several minutes of this surveillance Lenox's eyes heavied, and he went and sat. Thirty minutes or so and a new person would enter his life. He felt the warmth of the room's little fire on his outstretched legs. An evanescent sense of ease at last was restored to him just before he fell asleep. He was awoken only when another bell announced that the ship for which he was waiting had arrived.

CHAPTER TWO

But not his passenger.

The *Marie Grace* tied on to the wharf at just after ten in the morning and let down two gangways, one for first-class travelers, one for steerage. Lenox stood with some nervousness at the first-class gangway, accompanied by Alfie, who had a cart for the luggage.

A dandified curate and his family led the descent of the first-class passengers. They were followed by an elderly gentlewoman on the arm of a naval officer, with a small barking dog that must have been heartily glad to say goodbye to the sea, and a procession of families, couples, and single gentlemen, many quite chummy with one another, hallooing their goodbyes around the wharf.

But Lenox was waiting for a young woman, and he didn't see any among the disembarking crowd.

He hailed a foremast jack up on deck, who was securing a large crate with deftly woven knots. "Is anyone left in first class?" Lenox asked.

"No, that's the lot of them, sir," said the young fellow.

"Not a girl of about twenty?"

"No, sir," said the sailor, with a cheerful grin that suggested he would have been least likely to miss that sort of passenger.

Alfie with the luggage cart gave Lenox a suspicious look.

Where could she be? He surveyed the scene with a critical eye. Even down at the second- and third-class gangway it had cleared out a good deal, families reunited, seamen hoisting rucks up onto their backs. There were jolly boats crowding the hull of the ship, trying to entice the nearly liberated sailors' accumulated pay away from them in advance. One had three or four women in it, unblushingly proposing various acts to the men on the rail, a steady young lad with a cask of wine by the tiller steering them. Another boat promised to whisk the sailors straight to the gambling parlor, a third to a "clean and sober young gentlemen's hotel"—though this proposition was attracting less attention than the other two.

Lenox felt in his breast pocket for the letter that had brought him here, even though he knew its contents by heart. It had arrived three weeks before.

22 August 1879
Messrs. Coutts, Jejebhooy, and Spear
Wellington Pier, Bombay, India

Dear Sir,
It is my duty to write you with the unfortunate news of the death of Lieutenant Jasper Lenox (ret.), aged fifty-one, on July 9th of this year. The cause was cholera. As you will see from the enclosed report, registered by Dr. Reiter with the governors here, the illness was mercifully brief.

Please also find enclosed the last will and testament of Lieutenant Lenox; of which he has named you sole executor. His estate is to be settled in England. At the discretion of the consistory counsel, he has been buried in the Officers' Cemetery of Bombay. His final three months' pension from the army has been used to pay for his funeral and the future maintenance of his plot.

The few funds left to Lieutenant Lenox's name after the fulfillment of these obligations have been used to defray some of his outstanding debts; what remain of his movable goods have been packed and will arrive in England by the steamship Cortlandt before the end of this year, where they may be claimed using the enclosed receipt.

A subscription has been raised by the Friends of Her Majesty's Guards, and with the funds, first-class passage has been booked for Miss Angela Havens Lenox to return home to England. The details of her travel aboard the Marie Grace are the final document enclosed.

Any questions you have may be directed toward our branch office in Claridge Street, London, or by letter to Bombay.

I am honored to be, sir, with condolences and best wishes,

Your servant,
William J. Coutts, Esq.

Lenox folded the letter. The girl must have missed the ship, he realized—or, just as likely, dodged it. Perhaps she'd stayed behind for some young gentleman. Or simply a wish to remain in the country where she had passed her whole life.

He had never met Angela Lenox; he knew nothing about her.

Poor Jasper! His sweet cousin, buried five thousand miles away, interred in that strange soil, forever. Lenox had come to loathe the letter for the sad implications between its lines—the lack of money ("few funds," "some of" the outstanding debts) and the lack of friendliness. Every favor to Jasper, down to his burial, had been performed out of naught but duty.

And now, though he felt the responsibility of caring for this young cousin of his so solemnly, he had failed before he even began.

But just then there was a tap on his shoulder. "Mr. Charles Lenox?"

It was a young dark-skinned girl of perhaps eighteen or nineteen. Indian, he was all but sure, and not only because the *Marie Grace* had posted from Bombay. She was small, neat, with even white teeth, and warmly dressed in an oversized heather-gray sweater that looked as if it had been made for someone else, possibly a sailor. But a goodwill radiated out from her bright, appealing eyes.

"That is I," he said.

She pointed down the dock, which had cleared with remarkable speed; two months at sea, and now, not fifteen minutes after arrival, the passengers nearly all gone, already scattering to different parts of these isles.

But one young lady was left. Lenox had missed her because she was sitting low on a trunk, in such a forlorn posture that she seemed to sink in on herself—and of course because she was at the other gangway.

When she glanced up, however, Lenox saw instantly, in her willowy frame, her long blond hair, and even the faintly absent look in her pale blue eyes, his cousin Jasper.

So this was she. He smiled and lifted a hand, his heart in his throat. He had a profusion of cousins, Lenox, and he was loyal to all of them, even the criminals and cads. But there was none he had ever loved as dearly as Jasper, the only child of Lenox's father's own first cousin.

Charles and Jasper had spent at least four weeks and often longer together during the summers of their childhoods, adventuring, swimming, riding. Jasper had been blithe, happy, so distractible and softhearted that it was a running joke among the servants, just faintly ugly, with an open, cordial expression, and enviable long blond locks. The same hair that this girl had, and Lenox saw, too, the same long, slender fingers.

Jasper's supreme trait in those days had been an almost uncanny physical grace. There was no horse he couldn't ride on sight; no game he couldn't master to a first approximation after ten minutes; no dance at a ball, however dreary, that he could not endow with the beauty of its original design. He had played fives at Eton and once received a note complimenting his skill from no less august a retired athlete than the Prince of Wales.

In the end, alas, those were to be the happiest days of Jasper's life.

Like all the men in that branch of the Lenox family, he had gone into the army from school. Certainly he had seemed bound for glory then. Lenox could remember the exhilarating goodbye dinner for his cousin at the Army and Navy Club in Pall Mall, the champagne, the speeches by various related generals and colonels. The eve of a great career.

But once Jasper had gone out to Ceylon, he had changed quickly, first in his letters, which became stilted and formal, and then in his silences, which grew long.

On the only occasion he had returned to England, for the funeral of his father, he had struck Lenox a different person. Much inclined to drink, for starters. Throughout every social occasion he had stood to the side, with a gin lime whenever it was decently possible and at certain moments when it wasn't quite, rarely speaking to anyone, his once-lustrous hair still long but lank, his uniform clean and pressed but hanging in ungainly billows over an even slimmer frame.

One of the few things he had said to his cousin on that occasion—and not for lack of effort on Charles's part—was that he would never return to England once he had left again. In this prophecy he had proved correct.

There had been a moment shortly before Jasper left when he and Charles had stood together for five minutes, and all the warmth and affection of their boyhood had revived—Jasper himself again, briefly. They had been talking about the horses of their youth, a subject in which he could apparently still lose himself.

"Is it awfully bad in India?" Lenox had asked at last, at a lull.

It was the sort of thing he would never have asked anyone but a brother. "Oh, no," said Jasper lightly, and in the reply Lenox heard all of his own hard-bought stoicism, the value his family held in higher regard than any other. "It's not so bad."

"You don't miss England?"

"I suppose at times."

Lenox had been too avidly involved in his own career those days to spare more than an afternoon's thought to Jasper. And suddenly, the years rushing past, it was too late to gather anything more from his once beautiful cousin himself. The memories they had made were all they ever would make. The grief of that was so sharp, and sunk in somewhere very deep: not to be avoided. And in it was grief, too, for himself, his parents; for all of them, busying their ways around Portsmouth that morning.

CHAPTER THREE

"Are you with the ship?" said Lenox to the Indian girl.
"I? No, I am Miss Lenox's companion."

"There are two of you," said Lenox dumbly.

"Yes," she said. "My name is Sari. Forgive me having to make my own introduction."

"Not at all, no," he said, bowing. "I am Charles Lenox. I'm very pleased to make your acquaintance."

Lenox's cousin had risen from the trunk and started hesitantly toward them. It took him only a few quick strides to reach her first.

"Angela?"

She bowed her head in shy assent, and he took her offered hand and pressed his lips to the back of it. "How do you do, Cousin?" she murmured, curtsying with the old-fashioned stiffness of the colonies, where the manners were frozen in the '40s and '50s.

"I am so very happy to meet you. I hope that your passage—it is so very cold even today—but here, the inn is just across the street there, you can see the window of your room. There will be plenty of time later to tell me your tale. Alfie, the trunk please!"

Alfie was already levering the trunk onto his cart. Angela said to

Lenox, "May I please introduce you to Sari? She has been like a sister to me—and—and—"

Sari saved her friend more stammering. "We would not dream of parting from each other," she said.

"No, never," said Angela.

There was an absolute firmness in the declaration that went against everything shy and quiet about the girl. They were still with brave fright as they waited for his response.

"If she is like a sister to you, she must logically be as a niece to me," Lenox said, with a formality which he hoped these girls, so far from home, would recognize as friendship.

Their faces eased.

In the room at the Bosun's Arms were tea, the luncheon, a chaise, a warm fire. These comforts seemed to give the young women back some of their composure. Sari was more alert and less wearied than Angela, though neither looked as if the voyage had done them much good. Both were too thin. They ate and drank so eagerly that Lenox wondered how bad the food had been.

Angela's pale cheeks grew pinker. She sat very upright. It must have been a source of constant worry to them these last five months what Charles would *be* like, whether he would accept Sari's presence, indeed whether he would be kind in any way at all—and all three remained very formal.

It was Lenox and Sari who kept up the conversation over the next few minutes.

"I hope it was not a hard passage," he ventured.

"We have little with which to compare it, sir," Sari said. "It was cold and long, certainly."

"I presume you traded in your single first-class ticket for a pair of third-class ones?"

Both girls glanced at him in surprise, Angela quickly looking away toward the window again—neither used to a detective's skills of surmise being turned upon them.

"Why, yes, sir."

"Were you well fed?"

"Oh, yes, sir. It wasn't all bad."

"Please, you must both call me Charles, or if you prefer, Cousin."

Both girls nodded. With her teacup in her hand, Angela gazed away from them and out through the window at the sea, its gray sweep wind-cut with ragged strips of white. Lenox, so sensitive to the moods of others, guessed her thoughts: that she couldn't quite believe she had traversed all that water.

He was in a difficult position. As a strange gentleman, even a relative, it would be inappropriate for him to ask many direct questions. The rest of their story would have to wait until they met his wife, Lady Jane.

He wondered whether he ought to leave them alone to recover. Perhaps he would go out for a wander, even stop into the bookshop he had seen up the lane, a street or two inland.

Yet there was a great deal he would wish to have known of his cousin and her friend. What had their lives been like in India? How bad had it gotten for Jasper before the end? What were their hopes now that they were in England? That was just for a start.

"We shall not trespass upon your hospitality long, sir," said Sari, as if anticipating the third of these questions. "We received four pounds in addition to our tickets from the committee, and we have another ten pounds put aside. And I shall work."

"Oh, no," said Lenox, with alarm. "Please, you certainly must stay with us as long as you can. We have a busy household already. Two more will scarcely be noticed."

"Well—thank you, sir," said Sari, a little guarded.

The *sir* pained him. "I do hope you shall both call me Charles," he said again. "Or Cousin Charles, if you prefer."

There was a long silence. That was the name he had imagined Angela might use. Then again, he had imagined a strong, sturdy girl arriving with a hatbox and a head full of plans for the conquest of London. Why had he pictured her so? Not at all like Jasper.

He studied her surreptitiously. Her blond hair fell neatly to her waist, pinned to the side, and her dress was proper, a quiet blue muslin. But it was worn away at the collar, the wrists, the hem. From this and a hundred other small signals, Lenox could begin to guess at the worry and poverty of the last months. It was too easy to imagine the tiny cabin, the rough hammocks swung up in the dankest corner, the disquieting sound of rats' feet whispering through the hold, the coarse manners of their shipmates in third class.

For if one thing was certain, it was that Angela Lenox was well-bred; and her friend's manners, her posture, her mode of speech, equally refined. Whatever Jasper's circumstances at the end, he had been raising his daughter, now Lenox's responsibility, as a gentlewoman.

"You have known each other a long time?" he asked.

"Since we learned to talk," said Angela.

"You must have been a comfort to each other at sea."

"Yes," she said. "Yes, Cousin, I should say."

Lenox smiled broadly, hoping to reward the effort, but met only silence in response. There was a long pause, and finally, standing, he said, "I am going to take a turn outside, to let you two catch your breath alone. I had not calculated for how wearing your journey must have been—you may even wish to sleep. The only question before I go is whether you should like to stay the night here in Portsmouth, to gather your strength, or travel straight to London."

The girls glanced at each other. "I think both of us should be very happy to bring our travels to an end," said Sari.

"Yes, why shouldn't you? There is a train at two forty-one—let us plan to travel by it. Until then I shall leave you. Please tell the girl in the hall if you would like something more to eat. Her name is Margaret."

"This luncheon is perfect—after the sea, sir," said Sari.

"Then I shall return at a little after two o'clock."

He left the room and then the pub. Outside, the rain had steadied, intensified. He found that he was relieved to be alone. He opened his umbrella and walked up the narrow Portsmouth streets with mild interest, past a naval outfitter's, a costermonger, a draper's. He found the bookshop again, but a small sign told him it was closed for lunch. As he was wondering how he would pass these two hours, he saw a different pub and realized that he, himself, was hungry.

Luckily he had brought his correspondence, and thought that he might tackle it at last. He found a little nook in the front window of the place, which was called the Lady Hamilton, after Nelson's mistress, whose rosy-cheeked young face beamed out from a portrait hung above the mahogany bar. He ordered a simple meal of cheese, dark bread, pickle, ham, and salad, and asked for a glass of sherry with the food.

This business concluded, he cut the string of the little bundle of letters. Most of the names on the envelopes were familiar. One did surprise him, however: Huggins, of 12 Conduit Street, a busy London thoroughfare, comprised mostly of shopkeepers living above their establishments.

He had known several Hugginses over the years, but this handwriting was strangely familiar, and he was filled with curiosity as he cut the letter open with his penknife.

CHAPTER FOUR

9 November 1879
12 Conduit Street
Dear Mr. Lenox,
Though it has been many years now, I hope that you will remember your former housekeeper Elizabeth Huggins. I hope very much too that this letter finds you and your young family well.

Did he remember Mrs. Huggins! A whole panorama of images from Lenox's early twenties returned to him—his earliest cases, his comfortable set of bachelor rooms near Green Park, he and Graham cutting up newspapers on the polished dining-room table. His entire education as a detective, much of it self-directed, had taken place with Mrs. Huggins at the head of his household. A stern mob-capped candle-carrying woman, fully good.

He read on.

For my own part, I am happily residing here in London, having recently returned from the country. I am still very active. Perhaps you will know by reputation the Lady Isabelle Bliss Hill Home for

Retired Soldiers, to which I dedicate many happy hours of knitting. Their continual need for good blankets and sweaters is my excuse to indulge in this favored pastime.

There is one blot on my happiness since I returned here last year from the country, however. To state it plainly, the resident of these rooms before myself died in a suspicious manner. The incident took place on the stairwell just outside my own little rooms.

I have prayed upon the matter, attempting to retire it from my mind, but I cannot. Moreover, recent events, small in themselves but troubling, have led me to fear that I may be in danger myself, silly and old womanish though it sounds.

At last my nephew counseled me to write you, in the hopes that you might lend me some assistance. For the police will do nothing.

At that moment, a girl of ten or so approached with Lenox's lunch, setting it down next to him with a "good day." Lenox, picking up a piece of cheese and taking a bite, considered his old housekeeper. He knew her in fact to be the least anxious of women: upright, capable, proud.

Should you find yourself free, I am here between ten and twelve each morning, and three and five in the afternoons. It would be my pleasure to give you a cup of tea and a slice of my homemade cake—which I recall (without conceit I hope!) as being to your taste.

If you are too busy, I shall understand, and in either event I remain, yours faithfully,

Elizabeth S. Huggins

Lenox read the letter twice, then folded it and put it back in its envelope.

Only then did he really attend his food, and begin to eat gratefully, feeling immediately better. A sip of sherry gave a sweet following tang.

Mrs. Huggins must be a few good years past eighty now, he supposed, for even then she had seemed old to him—seemed! He had himself been twenty-two, twenty-three, and in a weak position to analyze the question of age. She had been a direct representative of his mother, who had hired her for Lenox more or less without his permission. He felt a pang at the thought. When someone had been dead a long time, there was sometimes as much grief at the distance of their memory as in their loss.

Certainly he would go see Mrs. Huggins, he thought. The next morning, if possible.

He put the letter together with the one from India in his breast pocket. Looking through the window at the thin rain, he had the sensation of knowing that from now on the two letters would remain together in his memory. Funny that he should have opened this one while attending to the first; for even if Mrs. Huggins's worries proved to be nothing, it was the kind of call upon his loyalties that he knew he must answer, in this sense just like the arrival of Angela. He had declined all other matters since the attack in America, but these were not to be declined—important enough to rouse him from the sadness and half-voluntary indolence of the past months.

The hours passed, and soon enough Lenox found himself again at the Bosun's Arms, settling his bill, seeing to the girls' trunk, arranging a hansom to the station. Then at last they were off.

The two girls passed the train ride very differently. Angela read throughout the trip, from a small volume of Scott, while Sari spent the whole time staring through the window, unable to tear her eyes from the countryside of her new nation.

They did speak a little. Sari told their story quite beautifully, making gentle fun of the hard details in some place—eighteen hours with nowhere to sit or lie down in an Indian shipping office on a remote peninsula, the mercury at a hundred ten degrees; on ship, rats the size of ferrets; every conversation with an English person a "little strange" in Sari's view, as she laughed about it, in Angela's face fear, for they didn't understand nine-tenths of the references the English people took for granted, even having read so many of the novels; and with the looming prospect of a stranger to greet them in Portsmouth when they arrived.

That stranger smiled at the story, and marveled at how Sari's young mind had already advanced beyond these hard months enough to tease them. His own volume of Shakespeare, the only writer he had been able to read much from since America, sat forgotten by his side.

At King's Cross they hired one of the cabmen waiting on the platform. The drive home took only twenty minutes. Lenox watched it from the newcomers' point of view, however, and could see how overwhelming it must have been, London, all its centuries still standing block by block, the blazing windows of the coffeehouses, the immense stone churches. So drastically different from India.

As the brougham from the station started on to Hampden Lane, where he lived, Lenox felt the day's uneasiness dissolve. If he was not quite master of himself, right now, he knew that the house would be full of people willing to take up the slack.

Lady Jane was there to greet them at the front door. Lenox had wired her that there were to be two girls, not just one, and Jane, with impeccable nonchalance, took Sari in just as she did Lenox's cousin, leading the pair upstairs and depositing them into adjoining guest rooms at the top of the house's west stairs, just as if she had been expecting them both all along. In fact Lenox knew that a different room had been prepared for Angela.

Lady Jane Lenox was a woman of exactly her husband's age, plain but pretty, with light brown curling hair. Her gray eyes were calm, quizzical. In person she was serene, self-assured, and often funny, qualities born aloft by deep reserves of decency and discretion. She was the daughter of an earl and the sister of another, and of the couple, it was she who belonged to fashionable London; his profession was too eccentric, for one thing, while her closest friendships reached into the highest spheres of British life.

While she showed them to their rooms, Lenox retreated, tired, to the drawing room, idly thumbing through his book. ("Pause there, Morocco," he read, with a flash of schoolboy recognition.) At last, an hour later, the two girls emerged, chatting more freely with Lady Jane, freshly scrubbed, wearing their threadbare best.

"You must come to the nursery before you do anything else and meet the girls—our girls, your young cousins," Lady Jane said.

They found Clara and Sophia in their schoolroom. Their lessons for the day were apparently over, for they were busy arranging their dolls and animals in rows along the room's front bench.

"Girls, listen and be obedient," said Lady Jane, as they entered. "This is your cousin Angela whom we told you about and her particular friend Sari—and you must meet them and curtsy, and be extremely polite, for they are special visitors, who will stay here at home with us for quite a while, perhaps even forever. Do you understand?"

Both girls turned and stood. "She has brown skin," said Clara, the younger of the two, staring at Sari. She was not quite four.

"You have forgotten to curtsy," said Lady Jane.

"It's true, though, I do," said Sari, with such sweetness that both Sophia and Clara moved toward her a step or two, gravitationally—and Lenox sensed it would be she, not Angela, that they favored.

"I hope your voyage went well," said Sophia, who was five years older than Clara and a little more civilized. "Do you like England thus far?"

"It is very cold," said Sari, but smiling, without any tone of complaint. "I was enchanted by the meadows and pastures we passed. Just like in the books! What are your dolls doing? How I loved my dolls when I was little."

"They are in school, minding their lessons," Sophia answered.

"Just like you," said Sari.

"Yes," said Clara—smiling shyly, highly gratified.

"Marjorie is in trouble," said Sophia. "She didn't know two plus two."

All of them turned to look at a cloth horse that stood with its face ignominiously angled into a corner.

"I hope she can get out soon," said Angela—the first comment she had ventured.

Sophia and Clara looked at her a little crossly, as if they hadn't expected her to take the part of the disgraced Marjorie so soon into the acquaintance; their schoolchildren were subjected to the strictest discipline if they answered questions incorrectly, Lenox knew. He wasn't sure where they had formed this impression of the strictness of other schools—their own governess was so tenderhearted that she had burst into tears once when Sophia called her a muttonhead.

"She can only come out tomorrow," said Clara.

CHAPTER FIVE

The first meeting between the children and the new guests went well on the whole; and supper better still. There was white wine with the soup course, and after dessert and cheese, a dusty bottle of Tokay, which Kirk poured into tiny crystal glasses. Lenox doubted the wisdom of strong drink for the girls still not yet a night's sleep past their long voyage, but Jane had called for the bottle herself, and after a glass both grew flushed, convivial, and happy in spirits, indeed happier than at any time since they landed.

They talked broadly of their upbringing, which at least in its early years sounded as if it had been a typical one for English children in the colonies, with visits among the other British expatriates and a regular schoolmistress. The two had been educated side by side.

"My father was partial to cheddar," Angela observed as she nibbled at a last piece of the cheese. It was the first time she had volunteered any information about Jasper. "It was fearfully hard to get hold of. It is so very strange to be here. It is as if everything the English at home imitated about life were real now—the real England."

The clock struck ten, and soon the girls' mood shifted from giddy to tired. Sari managed to get off a last wry comment about the ship ("We would have given quite a lot for biscuits like these rounding

Africa!") before at last the immense fatigue of the trip showed in the girls' faces.

"Come now," said Lady Jane. "I will take you to your rooms."

A maid was dispatched to put lemon water at their bedsides; and as the girls went upstairs, Lenox heard them laughing and laughing about something. He felt a softening of the tension around his mouth at that. Such a happy noise was welcome in his heart.

The question of Sari—of whether it was possible that she could be introduced into society with Angela, of how people would greet the idea of a young Indian girl living on equal footing in Lenox's house—remained to be solved. But there was a young Indian lad at Oxford now, after all, and another standing for Parliament. Besides, no one who had seen the two girls together for a moment could contemplate separating them.

At breakfast the next morning, Charles's older brother Edmund came to meet the new visitors. "Hello, hello," he said, entering the breakfast room hard on the heels of the footman who announced him. "But where are they?"

"Still sleeping," said Lady Jane, giving Edmund a kiss on the cheek.

"Ah, I see. Look, breakfast! Lord, I was up half the night starving away."

Edmund went to the sideboard and scooped some eggs onto a plate. He was half an inch taller than Charles and wore a sober black suit to his younger brother's gray one, but otherwise they looked very alike.

It was no surprise at all that he had been up late. After thirty years of refusing advancement within his party, holding firm to his status as a backbencher, he had at last accepted Gladstone's entreaties that he take a cabinet-level position.

His reward had been unstinting labor since, and to Charles, who had known him from birth, the strain and exhaustion in his brother's face was obvious.

More subtle but equally present was a new eagerness there. Edmund's wife, Molly, had died suddenly a few years before—there had rarely been a happier couple when she was alive—and this was the first time since her death that he seemed to his younger brother to have found any distraction from the loss.

"How is Parliament, Your Lordship?" Charles said.

"Stop that," said Edmund irritably, sitting down and placing his gloves by his plate. A maid poured him a cup of tea. "It is rotten, as you well know. How are you, Jane?"

"Very well, thank you. In fact Charles and I were just discussing Angela's welcome supper on Saturday."

"Ah, yes," said Edmund, nodding to show he understood the importance of the subject. "I should like to hear. But tell me—what do you make of these two girls?"

"I like them a great deal," said Charles.

"It must have thrown you to find two of them."

"Oh yes. And Angela is—well, very quiet. Fortunately the friend talks."

"Did she tell you anything of their circumstances in Bombay?"

"Only a little," said Lady Jane. "Apparently Jasper had a small house up in the foothills, which had deteriorated a great deal in recent years."

The brothers glanced at each other. "Poor Jazz," said Edmund.

"Angela and Sari thought of staying there after he died, but the local English wouldn't hear of it. Busybodies. They told me last night that there were some very lean years. I'm afraid your cousin was unhappy toward the end."

"I supposed as much," Charles said.

"He was down to two servants by the time of his death, which Sari implied to me was nearly inconceivable for an Englishman there. A cook and a housekeeper. Angela and Sari themselves did all the shopping and the cleaning, and looked after themselves. They sent the laundry out, but besides that had to be quite self-sufficient. The local officers' society provided a governess when they were younger, apparently, but she stopped coming when Angela was fourteen, and she refused to teach Sari at all."

"It sounds rather bleak," said Edmund. "Tell me, who is coming to dine on Saturday?"

This they discussed for some ten minutes, as Charles sipped his coffee, Edmund his tea. There were to be thirty guests, and it was vital to balance the number of men and women. A dozen old necessary relatives would have to be leavened by some jolly younger guests, Lady Jane told them. It was she who understood society better than either of the brothers—better indeed than any woman in London, it was sometimes said.

The conversation moved easily until the subject of Charles's close friend Thomas McConnell came up. It was Jane who mentioned it. "I had thought to invite him and Toto, of course. But they are going to be in the country."

"Strange," said Lenox.

McConnell was a doctor, a gallant Scotsman, and Toto the daughter of a duchess; both were quite social, and it was odd that they should leave London during the season.

Edmund had gotten a guarded look on his face. Charles, who knew his brother, said, "What is it, Ed?"

Edmund set down his fork. "I don't know if you've heard the rumors. But I may as well tell you, since people are talking. They say Thomas has begun drinking again."

Jane whitened, and Lenox knew he must have shown his reaction, too. Besides being one of his closest friends, McConnell had helped him on more cases than he could count. It had been years now since he had touched alcohol—ever since he had begun practicing medicine full time again, a good seven or eight years. Lenox had thought the problem was in the past forever.

"Perhaps it is only a rumor," said Lady Jane.

"I had it from Tallulah Carleton, who is no idle whisperer."

Lenox's heart fell. "Oh no."

At that moment, the door cracked shyly open, and the two arrivals from India appeared. They wore morning dresses, these, too, patched, faded. Jane would have to take them dress shopping.

"Angela and Sari," said Edmund, rising, his face beaming. He bowed deeply. "I am Sir Edmund Lenox, your cousin. How very happy I am to see you. Welcome to England."

Both girls curtsied, and Angela said, "How do you do, Cousin?"

"You must know how sorry I am about your father—the salt of the earth, Jasper. And I hope you will swear to me that though you may stay here, I shall have an equal share in your company as Charles. I have never been able to bear him getting the better of me. Jasper would have told you that. But please, I am sure you are far too hungry for speeches. Here is the dish of scrambled eggs before me—would either of you care for some?"

CHAPTER SIX

At ten o'clock, a pleasant breakfast behind them and Edmund having departed for Parliament, Lenox felt confident enough in the girls' comfort to make a trip out into the city, leaving them in the care of Lady Jane. He stepped into his carriage, which was waiting for him out in the brisk, clear morning, and some twenty minutes after leaving Hampden Lane arrived in front of a pretty yellow row house with blue trim and flowers in the windows at 12 Conduit Street.

This was the address Mrs. Huggins had given in her letter. Already standing there, tidy in a heather-gray suit and dark gloves, was a compact, sandy-haired gentleman.

"Graham!"

"Good morning."

Graham was perhaps Lenox's most intimate friend, and the two of them had agreed by wire upon this rendezvous quite early that morning. Graham was famously always one of the first members into Parliament; as for Lenox, he had been unable to sleep, and so their communication had fired back and forth before the sun was up.

"How are you?" Lenox said, as he came down from his carriage.

"Well enough," said Graham. As ever when he spoke to Lenox, an implicit *sir* lay just beyond his words. "How are you?"

Friends—it was true that Lenox and Graham were friends, but the word did not quite encompass their standing with each other. For many years, indeed since Oxford, Graham had been Lenox's personal servant, or valet—yet this was not all of it either, and indeed perhaps there was hardly a word to describe all that Graham had done in Lenox's employment.

As a person he was quiet and thoughtful, invariably respectful, but with a quick and original mind. It had made him useful in ways a valet would never usually be.

This had first shown itself in the ways he helped Lenox in his detective work. But it was not until Lenox had entered politics that they had discovered Graham's real vocation—for in politics he was a born tactician, with a workingman's understanding of the issues, yet also, from living beside Lenox, an aristocrat's understanding of how they were resolved in the great rooms by the Thames.

His acuity had made it inevitable that he become Lenox's chief political secretary—a job that would traditionally have fallen to a promising young Oxbridge graduate. Later, against longer odds still, he had dared to run for Parliament himself and won. Once he was in his seat, he was, despite his birth, so obviously useful to his side, so obviously an impediment to the other, that it forced all men to greet him on his own terms.

There had been years when Lenox and Graham scarcely left each other's company except to sleep. But days and weeks and even months passed these days between their meetings. Such was the price of a friend's success.

Still, they looked a pair in front of Mrs. Huggins's building, together scrutinizing its arched vestibule, large enough to shelter two or three people from rain, four from a storm. It led through a glass-fronted door up a dim stairwell.

"Shall we go in?" said Graham.

Lenox stood still, gazing critically at the vestibule. "Someone slept here last night."

Graham glanced at it again. "Slept here?"

Lenox pointed to a small grouping of black semicircular smudges on the wall at foot level. "Look. These are fresh." He glanced up and down the street. "Whoever it was put out his cigar and relit it twelve or thirteen times in the night. No one could remain so long unobserved in the day. And it rained yesterday, so these must be from overnight."

Graham shook his head, studying the marks. "Just so. I am out of practice."

Lenox shrugged. "I may be wrong. Come, let's find out from Mrs. Huggins what this is all about."

They went up the stairs where the murder had taken place, according to the letter—nothing very remarkable here, at least that Lenox could see in the shadowy light—and knocked on one of the two doors there. The other led up to a rooftop by a rickety-looking continuation of the wooden stairwell.

Seeing it, Lenox immediately reckoned that there was a nine-tenths chance the death was closer to misadventure than murder.

It would be good to see Mrs. Huggins nonetheless.

She answered her own door. She looked the same as ever, perhaps a little older but in truth not much to Lenox's eye, a short woman with fine bones, white hair pulled back, and intelligent eyes. She wore a simple day dress and an intricate white lace bonnet, in the old fashion of the 1830s.

"Hello, Mr. Lenox," she said, a genuine smile brightening her rather severe features. "And hello to you, too, Mr. Graham! I had wondered now and then if I should ever lay eyes upon either of you again in this lifetime. Well, come in, come in! A pretty year or two has passed, hasn't it, since you incorrigible paper gatherers were young men?"

"Indeed it has, Mrs. Huggins," said Lenox, returning her smile and taking her outstretched hand.

She led them into a clean and spacious pair of rooms. In the main one was a small fire burning in the grate, with a rocking chair next to it and a pot of tea warming over the coals. Lenox could see a partially knitted garment on the arm of the chair. The second room overlooked the street. A black cat prowled the windowsills, only briefly turning to look at them.

"That is Isaac. He won't be very friendly. I'm glad I made a cake yesterday!" said Mrs. Huggins. "Come in, won't you, please. Take these chairs and I shall pour you some tea. I said to my nephew just yesterday that I think this is a colder November than usual."

Mrs. Huggins had not always been so amiable—to either of them. When she'd come into Lenox's service, some twenty-five or more years before, she had just retired as the housekeeper of a larger, more illustrious household. Only her age, sixty, had forced the retirement. (And here she was, a lively and presentable eighty-five, knitting away for the retired sailors, looking very much as if she could still competently handle a great household again in a pinch.) She had been a mortal terror to Lenox on matters of leaving his messes about and probably worse to Graham—conscious of the angle of every fork upon a table, the shine of each windowpane, as if they reflected upon her personal chances of entry into heaven.

Still, the congenial mood of the room and their chatter showed the affection they retained for her—and that perhaps it was not too much to imagine that she felt the same for them.

"To think, Mr. Graham, you're in Parliament!" Mrs. Huggins poured the steaming tea into three delicate lady-pink cups. "I knew you would be respectable when you grew up, but I didn't anticipate that."

"I had you figured for a country dweller, Mrs. Huggins," Lenox said, taking a teacup from her. "Your Christmas cards came to us from Dorset."

"I passed most of my life in London," Mrs. Huggins pointed out, offering him sugar. "It was the country that felt odd."

It took a few minutes for her to assemble the gathering to her liking, and just when she did, and Graham and Lenox each had an armchair by the fire, a piece of tulip cake, and some tea, there was a knock at the door.

"Who could that be?" Mrs. Huggins said. "Unless it's Ernest."

It did prove to be Ernest. This was her nephew, whom she informed them owned the Coach and Horses, a pub a few doors down on the corner of Conduit Street, at number eight. The two small buildings at ten and twelve belonged to him, too: so this was his property.

Ernest Huggins was a large, scowling man, with little tenderness left over for Lenox or Graham once he had bestowed quite a lot, in fairness, on his aunt. He seemed to be here to convince himself that this was not a plot to rob an old woman of her money, apparently forgetting that it had been his aunt's own letter that initiated the meeting.

Only Mrs. Huggins lived here, they learned. The ground floor of the building was closed, he told them, used as storage for the pub.

"I was most concerned to receive your letter, Mrs. Huggins," the detective finally said. "I hope you do not mind that I have shown it to Mr. Graham, too."

"Of course not. You always worked hand in glove." She turned her gaze to the other room for a moment, troubled. "And I am glad you came."

"I do have a question," Lenox said.

"Oh?"

"There has not been a murder on Conduit Street in five years. And that was at number seventy-four, three streets away. Are you quite sure the person who lived here before you was murdered?"

"Quite sure," said Mrs. Huggins. "But my! How do you know that?"

"Yes," Ernest Huggins said suspiciously, "how did you know that?"

"Shush now, Ernest, eat your cake."

"I wrote my agency last night," Lenox said. "I asked the librarian to dig up any articles about recent incidents here in Conduit Street. We have assembled a geographical index of newspaper articles about crime in London, you see."

Ernest had the good grace to look impressed by this. It was a system based on one Lenox and Graham had devised many years before, in fact; Lenox hoped in time to turn it into the most comprehensive reference library for crime in the metropolis, one that outlived him.

"At any rate, the answer is simple enough," said Mrs. Huggins. "The murder wasn't five years ago. It was seven years ago."

"Seven!" said Lenox, amazed.

"Yes, seven years ago—but still unsolved."

"Yet you also said that you are suffering from some current difficulties, I believe?"

"Perhaps I had better tell you and Mr. Graham the story from the start—as I heard you ask a client to do once, Mr. Lenox."

"That would be ideal, Mrs. Huggins."

CHAPTER SEVEN

So this was what she did. Lenox, who was tired from his short night of sleep, and who had felt all morning the great weary pain in his right rib—a complicated inhaling pain made up of both emotion and muscle—noticed his symptoms fleeing as she spoke. He was pure attention again. He remembered in some part of his mind that he loved his work.

"This building has been empty for four years," Mrs. Huggins began. "That was when young Ernest here bought the pub, and he told me in the first letter he wrote after he bought it that this might be a home for me. He himself lives up in Belsize Park with his young wife, Christine."

"Just up in Belsize Park," repeated Ernest into his mustache.

"I did not anticipate leaving the country. But when my brother's widow Ethelina died—"

"My mother," Ernest said, holding the fragile porcelain cup carefully in his huge knobbed hands.

"After she went, bless her memory, I felt the loneliness of the countryside. I tried to occupy myself with the church, my works, and my friendships. But I found the hours hung heavy on my hands. At my age solitude is no simple gift.

"Silly perhaps, but there you are. At last I fancied I might move back to London after all. I have relatives here, and friends from my time in service.

"The shop next door was previously occupied by a chemist named Martell. He lived here, in these very rooms. Austin Martell, to give him his full name. He was a bad sort. Ernest has heard about him an awful lot at the pub."

Ernest nodded. "One of these very tall, bony fellows, apparently. Long gray hair. A mean look in his eye. Wore a dirty bottle-green velvet jacket every day. And a silver pin in his buttonhole, of the apothecary's oak leaves."

Mrs. Huggins nodded, and the four of them were briefly silent as Lenox noted down these details, impressed that they had been so neatly offered.

"His old shop is no longer a chemist's but a baker's," said Mrs. Huggins, "as you may have noticed when you arrived."

Lenox nodded. "I saw it."

"That is because it was Mr. Martell who was killed here, seven years ago. Just out on the stairwell leading up to the greenhouse on the roof. It was late at night. Someone followed him into the entryway and murdered him for the day's takings—so the police decided."

"Leading up to the roof?" Lenox said. "Not the lower stairs? Are you sure of that?"

"No, the upper stairs—about halfway up," said Ernest. "Ask anyone at the pub. They know every detail of the whole grim damned business."

"Language, Ernest. I knew it had happened when Ernest offered me these apartments," said Mrs. Huggins. "It was not a deterrent. I am not superstitious."

"It's a very eligible set of rooms," said Graham.

"Thank you. Unfortunately, I have not felt so easy in my mind recently. And partly it is plain foolish superstition, I confess, though it is embarrassing for a Christian to say. They never caught the murderer."

"Do you often go to the roof yourself?" asked Lenox.

"Yes, every day. Martell was a chemist, as I mentioned, and he had a hothouse with an herb and physic garden. I keep a garden there, where I spend as much time as I do here indoors.

"But there is something else, too. Twice a week or so, a man has taken to sleeping in the entryway downstairs."

Lenox and Graham exchanged a quick glance. The cigar marks. "For how long?"

"About two months."

"Do you know anything about him?"

"Nothing."

Graham frowned. "Can the police not help? Or your nephew, here?"

"I am frightened to go past him to fetch them when he actually appears," said Mrs. Huggins. "Ernest comes to check most nights, but of course he can't be here all night, every night. He comes after midnight and is gone before six in the morning."

"I am surprised you should have noticed him in that case," said Lenox, who knew there was scarcely a square inch of pavement in London that hadn't been slept on once in a while.

"I rise early, when the first shops open. I almost stumbled over him one morning, and since then I have been watching out for him. You can see the street very well from this front window."

Lenox got up to follow her, and saw that indeed one could see the vestibule clearly from here, since the lower level of the house jutted out.

The detective nodded, frowning. "Certainly we can help. But is there anything to make you think that he is connected to the murderer of this chemist, Martell?" he asked. "Or are the two things separate?"

Mrs. Huggins, returning to the tea table, gave her nephew a pointed look. "Down the pub," said Ernest, as if admitting something a tad embarrassing, "they're saying it's him, back."

"Who?" asked Lenox.

"Why—the murderer. The rumor was always that Martell got it in the neck from a client," said Ernest. "He was a nasty piece of work, you see."

"How so?"

Ernest looked at his aunt, as if he would have had more to say in unmixed company. "He was a greasy, down-at-heel sort of fellow, in the first place. Martell, I mean. Dirty cravat, dirty fingers. Shop dusty and grimy. Dirty long gray hair, like I said.

"And his business was the same. I'm the new fellow in these parts, but the old inhabitants tell me he thought nothing of conning an old woman out of her few pence for some useless physic. He kept the regular chemist's things in stock—liniments and the like, you know—but he was always after selling you one of his own potions, the things he grew up on the rooftop."

Outside, rain had just begun to speckle the windows. It was London weather, gray, mixed, uncertain; the winter coming on and the light glowing white even toward midday. Lenox took a sip of the strong, fortifying tea. He was touched that Mrs. Huggins had remembered all these years later how he took it.

"Was he a criminal?" asked Graham.

"He may have been. No one at the pub sounds quite as sure about that. But you see it was no one's business, like, till he got murdered."

"Mrs. Huggins said it was for the day's takings, but you seem to be implying it was personal," observed Lenox.

"There was a suspect anywise," answered Ernest. "A fellow named Phipps. Jacob Phipps. His wife was ill with a tumor. They were too poor to afford a proper doctor, in a coach and all, and so the wife used some of Martell's physic."

This made sense: for almost every Briton, the chemist was the first port of call in the case of sickness.

"Without improvement, I take it," said Lenox.

Ernest Huggins shook his head gravely. "She died. It was held hard against Martell, from what I hear. Beth Phipps was well-loved in Conduit Street."

"What became of Jacob Phipps?"

"He emigrated to Australia immediately after the murder. Which folk thought was mighty suspicious."

"No children?"

"No, and you never heard of him coming back. But now there is this rumor it's him sleeping in the doorway. No one has been able to say why. But everyone's very eager to tell me it's him, knowing that my aunt lives here. This Phipps would have to be mad to think she were Martell and hurt her, wouldn't he? But then again—people are mad, aren't they!"

Ernest looked worried, in his scowl-faced bearded way, and Lenox found himself liking the beefy publican. "If he meant Mrs. Huggins any harm, he would have had time to act by now."

"I am glad you think so," cried Mrs. Huggins. "See, Ernest? It is he who has been worried. I can wait out a London vagabond."

"You shouldn't have to," said Graham.

"Please, leave it in my hands," said Lenox. He suddenly felt tired, saying these familiar words, which he had uttered so often before—unequal to their promise. But then, this was Mrs. Huggins. He knew he must try. "I shall look into it directly."

"Are you sure?" asked Ernest doubtfully.

"I am quite sure," the detective replied briskly. "Are there any other details you can tell me about the Martell case?"

"No—only rumors, very few facts," said Ernest.

"I see. Perhaps I might inspect the rest of the building, then."

"Of course."

"But you think the murder and the new visitor are unrelated, don't you?" asked Ernest.

"Yes," Lenox replied. "But one must remain open to every possibility. And after all, perhaps the gentlemen in your pub know something we don't. Pubs are often wrong, yet rarely wholly wrong, in my experience."

Mrs. Huggins had stood up and was bundling herself in a wool cardigan. When she was ready their small party proceeded up toward the greenhouse on the rooftop. The rain was falling more steadily, from the silvery cold sky. Lenox wondered how his new charges were faring, Angela and Sari, and hoped they were having a peaceful day after their arduous travels. It was Ernest who led them into the greenhouse itself.

CHAPTER EIGHT

Inside the small glass rooftop structure it was homelike, with the rich loamy smell of summer. Young fruit trees lined half of the hexagonal space. Lenox looked about the place as he would have a crime scene, and only when he glanced up saw that Graham had gone to look at the flowers instead of immediately searching for the murderer. That was probably better manners.

"I must compliment you, as a gardener myself!" Graham said, kneeling down to eye level with a cluster of closed white rosebuds.

"Why, I never knew you gardened, Mr. Graham," said Mrs. Huggins.

"When I was a boy. But very passionately. I have long thought that in my retirement someday I shall take it up again. I miss the dirt in my hands. And the fresh air."

As they began to discuss cuttings, Lenox drifted away toward what looked like a small well at the back of the room, away from all the plants. It smelled strongly of ammonia. He couldn't pry up the board that covered it.

"That leads down to a chimney," said Ernest, who was standing in the door. "We nailed it shut. Daft idea."

Lenox nodded. "I see."

He checked the locks on the glass doors to the greenhouse, then opened one and stepped onto a tiny turret. It offered a pretty view of a London lane, with people passing back and forth below, a few umbrellas up. He didn't blame Mrs. Huggins for spending so much time in this aerie, which, though it was no bigger than ten feet by twelve feet, seemed as warm and green as the countryside, in the cool gray of winter London.

Looking around at the prosperous working-class street, it was hard to imagine it much plagued by crime. On the corner, the Coach and Horses, Ernest's pub, was already bustling with clerks and tradesmen seeking refuge from the rain. All the shops were bright and full. None matched the grimy description Ernest had given of Martell's apothecary, and Lenox guessed that this was what the newspapers liked to call an "improving area." If so, it might well just be standard local gossip making a fearful creature out of the sleeper in the portico—linking it to another dramatic story in the vicinity, Martell's murder.

After twenty minutes or so they went downstairs, where Lenox made a closer inspection of the front door. Here he saw something that gave him a fresh apprehension.

"There are new scratches around this keyhole," he said. "They aren't yours, Mrs. Huggins?"

"By gum, there are!" said Ernest, bending down to the doorknob, an effort that cost him a grunt of effort.

"I doubt they are from my key," said Mrs. Huggins.

"They look as if they were made with a knife to me," Ernest said. He stood up straight again. "Thank heavens I installed good sturdy locks, Aunt Elizabeth."

"I don't think we can assume they were made by a knife," Lenox said.

But he was perhaps a little more determined than before, and carefully inspected the area again—for he was not at all sure that Ernest was wrong, either.

He stooped to look carefully at the cigar marks he had spotted with Graham, gently rubbing them away at the edges to confirm they were new—yes, no doubt of it. He also saw a small symbol scored low down into the dark polished wood of the vestibule, at about where eye level might have been for a person sleeping there.

$$\mathcal{K}$$

It looked too old and weathered to have been made by the person presently disturbing 12 Conduit Street, but he copied it into his notebook.

When he had finished this closer inspection, he asked Ernest Huggins what time the Coach and Horses got busy.

"I should say around five" answered the barkeep.

"I see. Then I shall just examine the storefront that Martell had—this bakery—and take my leave. But I mean to return this evening. Let us see you back upstairs, first, if you please, Mrs. Huggins."

Upstairs they stood for some time discussing the case with Mrs. Huggins, who at last permitted each of them to leave with a small cloth parcel holding a few sugar cookies. Lenox put his in his coat pocket.

"What do you think, Graham?" asked Lenox, as they walked slowly up Conduit Street.

Graham's hands were in his pockets, and he studied the ground, thinking, in his familiar way. "I hardly think the new problem can be related to the murder."

"Nor I. But I don't like those scratches at the keyhole."

"Perhaps this vagrant saw an old woman on her own and figured her for an easy target."

"Yes," said Lenox. "Anyhow we must attempt to run him off one way or another. The first thing I shall do is have a word with the constable I saw at the end of the road."

They stood out of the rain and discussed the case for a few minutes longer, before Graham had to hail a cab; he was due back in Parliament for a meeting, one of the endless meetings that Lenox recalled with a small shudder nowadays. He had always preferred the freedom of this job to the grandeurs of that one.

"What do you think, Graham, can you make it back here at six o'clock? I will be at the Coach and Horses."

Graham shook his head. "Alas, there is a vote." Parliament's most important meetings took place in the evenings. "But I would be grateful if you kept me apprised of what you find."

Lenox smiled. He was happy to be on a case with his old friend. "Of course."

Graham turned and scanned the street for a hansom. Hailing the first one to turn onto Conduit Street, he offered Lenox a ride home.

Lenox shook his head. "No, no, you go. I sent my own carriage on—I shall speak to the constable and then walk home. It helps my wound."

"I'm glad," said Graham—who had been there that spring. "I have been hoping that you are on the mend still."

"Very much so," said Lenox, smiling more confidently than he felt.

Just after Graham had driven off, the detective heard a voice behind him—the voice of Ernest Huggins, emerging from the small building where his aunt lived. "Where's he rushing off to then, your quiet friend?"

"He has had to go to Parliament."

Ernest frowned. "A fellow might wonder whether the people helping his aunt really have her at the top of their thoughts, what with running to Parliament."

"You needn't worry about that. I shall be at the pub tonight," said Lenox, his voice tired even to his own ears.

"Plenty of people will promise to come to a pub—"

"Is anyone else offering to help your aunt?" Lenox said sharply. "Scotland Yard? For I have heard they will not take the matter on. Other members of my profession? Or do you think perhaps you could try to rely on my expertise, combined with my affection for Mrs. Huggins?"

Ernest Huggins stared at him for a moment. Then he touched his cap deferentially. "My apologies. I hope to see you this evening then."

Lenox already regretted his sharp words. "Until this evening," he said, touching his own hat, and strode off to find the constable he had spotted earlier.

CHAPTER NINE

When he finally began the walk home, Lenox went slowly, almost stopping once or twice along the busy route to rest. But he went on, forcing himself to get his blood moving.

Back at Hampden Lane at last, it was as if all the weariness he had paused to attend to Mrs. Huggins caught up with him at once. He used his last strength to nod to a footman in the hallway and then turned right into his study, where he slumped into a soft brown leather chair, closing his eyes. The stitch in his right ribs was throbbing with its own malign heartbeat. He could barely keep himself from falling straight to sleep.

After a few minutes there was a tap at the door, and Lady Jane appeared, holding a glass of water. "Hello, darling," she said. "I thought you could use this."

He rose, summoning a tired smile. "Thank you. How are the arrivals?"

"Both back to their bedrooms, sleeping, I believe," she said. "And I hope they may sleep away the day. They are so dear with the girls. Angela has barely said a word to me, but she read Sophia four books already this morning. As for Sari, she is charming. And they cannot have had an easy time. She let slip after you left this morning that by the end there was barely money enough for food. Certainly they have been in the practice of making their own dresses, at least the ones I have seen."

"She looks like Jasper, Angela," Lenox said.

He rested all afternoon, and as the light dimmed shifted himself to his desk to answer a few more pressing letters. Feeling a little stronger, he departed Hampden Lane again at around a quarter past five, and arrived back at the Coach and Horses punctually at six.

The pub was a large, well-lit, comfortable space. It had a copper-topped bar with a row of pewter flagons hanging above it, and lining the side were small nooks in which people had gathered, while on the walls, there was a clutter of pennants and posters: the flag for a Holborn cricket side, jolly beer advertisements, picture postcards from Brighton and New South Wales.

"Why good *evening*, Mr. Lenox!" said Ernest Huggins, beaming at him with what could only be described as joy.

"Ernest?" said Lenox doubtfully.

"What can I pour you this fine London dusk? And where would you sit? Papers are on this shelf—oh, and if it isn't a good night to come in out of the cold and have a pint of ale, if I say so myself!"

"It's—Yes," said Lenox, nonplussed.

"We have a full roast beef supper this evening, sir. Or toasted cheese if you prefer a snack."

"I'll just sit at this table, thank you. A half-pint of mild, please, and yes, toasted cheese, certainly."

"Take this elbow chair, please, sir. Welcome to the Coach and Horses."

It was raining steadily outside again, and lights were coming on rapidly as darkness fell. Their brilliant yellows and oranges blurred together, as Lenox watched carriages and phaetons and mules and carts and every other sort of passerby you could imagine; keeping an eye on Mrs. Huggins's doorway, he listened in as Huggins greeted the next guest and the one just after with the same singular enthusiasm. Apparently within these walls, Ernest was as welcoming as the little pub itself.

Slowly sipping his drink, Lenox scanned the room, looking for a resident character who could tell him about Jacob Phipps.

The most likely looking group were arranged in a half circle around the stone fireplace, clearly their accustomed place—regulars. Their leader was an owlish, beery fellow in a tweed suit, whose sotto voce comments drew much laughter.

After a few minutes of observation, Lenox sidled up to him. "Good evening," he said when the rest of the group was distracted. "My name is—"

"Charles Lenox! Welcome." The fellow turned and stuck his hand out. "As if I didn't read every bleeding word of the reports about that poor girl in the States! Connecticut, was it? Girls falling from cliffs left and right. A damn shame."

"Tell him, Passenger!" a voice called from a few bodies back in the group, and there was a general laugh.

"Ignore them, ignore them, the swine. Proud to have you at the C and H, Mr. Lenox. Allow me to stand you a pint. Huggins said you might be coming in. We can certainly tell you all about Jacob Phipps, the devil."

Whatever hopes he might have had of the concealment of his identity thus dashed, Lenox thanked the group, all staring at him now, and accepted the offer of the drink.

As soon became clear, the habitués of the Coach and Horses were only too eager to speak to the detective. Phipps? They were sure it was him they'd seen—why, Miles (here a reedy large-eared man in a snuff-colored jacket raised a modest hand) had seen him up close one evening, the same exact thinning black hair, the same deep-set eyes, the same stocky worker's build.

The rest of them thought they had caught glimpses of Phipps, too, and all half dozen were ready to swear on stacks of Bibles that it was him, so long as it put the fellow in Newgate—shame on him, hounding Mrs. Huggins!

Lenox couldn't afford to treat the matter so summarily.

"Have any of you spoken to the man?" he asked.

A great deal of chatter eventually produced the answer that none of them had.

"Have any of you come across him on a recent night?"

No, none, or they would certainly have rousted him out, they agreed; he arrived well after eleven o'clock, when the pub closed. Lenox wondered how this bravado might survive an actual encounter with the stranger in the vestibule, but said nothing.

He suspected that this phantom of Phipps was a product of their collective imagination. Still, they seemed very, very sure, which in itself was somewhat persuasive. The fellow they called the Passenger—James Compton at home, he confided to Lenox, during daylight hours the driver of an omnibus route between here and Hammersmith—was the most convinced of all.

"He was a bad egg from the start, Jacob Phipps. Strong as an ox. Never got higher than about five foot five, but didn't need to be—he was a winning boxer, then worked down the docks, and always made a fair wage."

A boxer: Lenox thought of his friend Skaggs, and that whole underground world. "If he made a good wage why didn't he take his wife to the doctor?"

"Aye!" said the Passenger significantly. "You'd wonder, wouldn't you? Because he and Martell were thick as thieves, so as he went to him for the mummia, and that's for why and wherefore both."

Miles, who had seen Phipps, piped up. "In business together!"

Passenger shook his head. "If you can call their sort of low skullduggery by so proper a name as business."

This was the first Lenox had heard that Martell and Phipps had worked together. "I was told it was a financial decision."

"Of course that's what he said after Beth Phipps died."

"Was she local as well?"

The Passenger nodded his head sadly. "Yes. Never caught a break in this life, that child. A mite of a thing without a parent to be seen when she was small, selling what she could find and sleeping where she fell at night. It was a miracle she got far enough in life to be married. Much good it did her."

There were sympathetic murmurs around the fire. "What do you remember of the chemist himself, Martell?" asked Lenox.

This question elicited a number of overlapping replies, which confirmed all that Mrs. Huggins and her nephew (polishing the bar nearby and listening closely) had indicated: that Martell was a sordid character, dishonest and grasping. They all remembered his gaunt bony frame and his height, as well as his closeness with money.

As for the murder of the chemist, not one of them had a doubt that it had been Phipps, whose departure to the colonies so soon afterward only confirmed it in their view. Several men reiterated that Martell and Phipps had been up to no good—together. Though when Lenox tried to discover more specifically what nefarious business they had been conducting, the answers were vague.

CHAPTER TEN

A fresh half-pint of the crisp golden ale arrived for the detective. "Then why do you think Jacob Phipps has returned?" Lenox asked, after he had thanked Huggins. "Why would he be sleeping in Mrs. Huggins's doorway?"

The one called Miles said, "No doubt he's one of these violent types. He'll do Mrs. Huggins 'arm, see if he don't—'pologies, Ernest, but it's true by jove. That's how these mad blokes are. It's in the papers every day."

There were nods of agreement. "Do you all think Phipps is mad?" the detective asked.

To a man, they did—too many blows to the head in the boxing ring, the loss of his wife . . . the amount of tattle and aggrandizement interspersed in the group's remarks would have brought pride to a sewing circle, but the information was useful. Yet Lenox had learned to be suspicious of madness as an explanation, when in his experience love, money, and revenge had proved so much more common.

By the time he had fully canvassed the opinions of the regulars, his new drink was empty, his toasted cheese a distant memory. He stood and thanked the group. It was hard to extricate himself, but when he said he wanted to watch the house they understood, and let him loose to cross to his seat at the other side of the pub, near the window.

He sat and contemplated the case. It was ten to one odds against it that the person was any kind of threat to Mrs. Huggins and a thousand to one that he was involved with the Martell business. Still, the absolute conviction the men had that it was Phipps set him on edge. Perhaps when they found the fellow he would resemble Phipps. Or perhaps it really was the mysterious émigré.

Nor did Lenox like the scratches around the lock; and then, with so many places to sleep nearby, parks, quiet ditches, back alleys, why choose this hard stone bed?

"Ernest," he said quietly, when the barman circled by again, "is it just here in the pub that people suspect Phipps? Have you spoken with anyone else about it?"

"Why, the street's not talking of much else. Every shop owner is sure it's Phipps. Miles works at the post office, a reliable fellow, and saw him dead-on, with his own two eyes."

Lenox left to the side the question of how reliable anyone who spent each night drinking at the Coach and Horses could be. "Have you inquired with Phipps's family?"

"He doesn't have any left here, sir, nor any friends who will own him. His parents died some ways back. He might have a stray cousin or two I suppose."

"Could you find out?"

"I can try."

At around eight o'clock Mrs. Huggins came walking down the street toward home, raising a great deal of commentary in the Coach and Horses. ("She was out to dinner with the Forsythes—pheasant, they had," Ernest reported to his patrons significantly. "I only hope she's double locked her doors," one of the regulars replied in an ominous tone, to a murmur of agreement.) She waved at Lenox through the window, demolishing the last pretense of his anonymity.

He stood up, touched his hat to Ernest Huggins and the gentlemen around the Passenger, and crossed the street. In the vestibule, he sprinkled a little oil of anise upon the inner perimeter of the small shelter. He paused and studied the runic little carving in the wood. Then at last he waved goodbye once more to the men in the pub, their faces pressed against the window watching him, and set off for home, smiling to himself at the odd little crowd.

The rain had subsided and the air was clear and cool. Everyone had retired in Hampden Lane except for Jane, who was in bed, reading a novel by Miss Gaskell. Lenox said hello to her and then went to his study, where he kindled the fire, poured himself a whisky soda, and sat at his desk.

There he found his post—including the agency's findings on Martell's death, which had been delivered since he left. Bless Polly. There was a note on top of it from one of the agency's young detectives, whom Lenox barely knew, because he had been hired just this year.

> Sir,
> My acquaintance at the Yard would not release the file to me, but gave me a description of the contents. Signs pointed to a violent argument between Jacob Phipps and the victim (Martell) three days before Martell's death.
> Lead was pursued, however, and Phipps had an unambiguous alibi (passed the night in a crowded gin mill in Duck Lane, dozens of witnesses). That fact verified many times over by the Yard. The case thus remains unsolved. As far as I can gather there are no other leads and the matter remains open. Clarence Adamson was the inspector assigned to it seven years ago; he is still at the Yard.

```
My more detailed findings are enclosed
along with a photograph from the
contemporary newspapers of Martell.

Most faithfully yours,
Montague
```

So Phipps was not the killer.

In his photograph, the chemist had a cruel face, with sullen, untrusting eyes. Lenox studied him, trying to circle closer in to who had killed him and why. Sometimes you could almost tell from a picture, and as he gazed at the face of the murdered man, the answer seemed just there at the edges of his mind, liable to disappear if he looked directly at it.

CHAPTER ELEVEN

The man sleeping in Mrs. Huggins's entryway didn't return on any of the next three nights. Lenox began to suspect he had drifted on—perhaps sensing the opprobrium of the street, unfortunate soul.

In the meanwhile, shy as she might be, his niece could hardly hold out from the general conversation at mealtimes, and Lenox grew to know her better.

"What are your impressions of London?" Lenox asked one night over the soup course. "The weather is just a touch warmer in India, I'm afraid."

It had been particularly cold and wet, and a smile cracked the girl's serious face. "No."

"Sari, do you mind the weather terribly?" said Lady Jane.

"No, I love the weather. And I like that you have cheese with every meal," said Sari.

Angela nodded. "At home we ate very simply, mostly in the Indian way. Rice and vegetables in curry. Once in a while we did go to the officers' club and have a Sunday roast. My father missed that about England."

"Did he talk much of home, Jasper?"

"Of certain things. His old horses, he would talk about them for ages. School, now and then."

"Cricket," Sari added.

Lenox smiled. "What a sportsman he was. And what a wonderful fellow, too. Never mean about sharing his pocket money, kind to everyone. But as you say, better still with horses. The summer I turned twelve we had a cranky five-year-old," he went on, setting down his spoon to reminisce, leaning back. "A white mare with a black blaze, and so of course named Blaze, since the fellows in the barn were not overly creative. Well, the groom could ride her, perhaps, but maybe not even him, and none of us children. Certainly not I. But Jasper stayed in her stall for a month, feeding her apples, day after day, whispering to her, until at last she loved him. And then he rode her for years afterward. It was such a lot of patience for someone our age. That is how I think of him now."

There was a brief, sad pause.

"Did you wish to be a detective even then, Cousin?" asked Angela.

"I don't think I knew such a creature existed."

"You always asked a lot of questions, however," said Lady Jane.

Lenox smiled. "That's true. And when I was a schoolboy, I was a great reader of adventure stories. Penny novels about the highwaymen of the old days—"

"Highwaymen?" said Sari.

"It's only another word for a thief," said Lady Jane.

"But a thief by horse, crucially," Lenox amended. "A thief by foot was known as a footpad. Most highwaymen were Royalists who had been stripped of their estates and kept only their horses. Many of them were high born. Indeed there were one or two women among them. For instance Katherine Ferrers, the infamous Wicked Lady, spent years robbing travelers all over Hertfordshire."

"How thrilling!" said Sari.

Lenox nodded. "Yet I remember being impressed by their adversaries. Their virtuous adversaries. They were usually the stewards of a local family—doughty, chivalrous, courageous characters, in the stories at least. Our own family steward was a miserly old chap who fretted over property lines all day."

"So it was they who inspired you," Sari said.

"I suppose. At Oxford I started to read *The Times*, and the crime reports astounded me. Edmund and Jasper and I were all country boys, after all—even if we did visit London now and then. Something about the very dry, undramatic headlines in the paper made it awfully tantalizing."

"Perhaps we should become highwaywomen," said Sari to Angela.

"These days the equivalent would be train robbers," Lenox said. "If you're feeling ambitious, I mean. Though they do better in the States."

After supper they sat in the drawing room, Lenox reading the newspaper, Jane and the girls playing a complicated rummy-like card game called monopoly deal that Angela and Sari had brought with them from India. They discussed the dinner party that Saturday as they played, what they would wear and whom they would meet.

"Hearts!" cried Angela at a winning turn, and as her face flushed with happiness Lenox once more saw her gangly father as a young adult, and smiled.

The subject of what Angela and Sari would do was one that lurked behind all such exchanges. Would Angela marry? Sari spoke of being a governess. Lenox didn't have the heart to disabuse her of the ambition, but he did not think it likely a young woman with her skin color would be considered for such a post. A real shame, given her natural way with the girls. It was just possible that she could accompany a family out to India as a governess.

Lady Jane was the most confident of the four; she was going to bring Angela into society and find her a husband, if Angela would accede to it. So she had said to Lenox.

It was the next morning when Lenox and his young cousin had a conversation that he had been waiting for since she arrived. It was ten o'clock, and Angela was sewing in the morning room, at work on a delicate brocade. Lenox had come in to look for a journal.

"Good morning," he said. "I heard you had breakfast with Sophia and Clara."

"They're lovely, Cousin, I hope you are very proud."

"Indeed I am. Probably too proud." Lenox's daughters were enthralled by the new arrivals, Angela just as much as Sari since she had proved such a willing reader to them. "I shall leave you to your work—unless, could I ask you a question, Angela?"

"Of course," she said, bowing her head slightly and setting down her lace. "I owe you any answer it is in my power to give."

Yet she sounded as if she were going to the gallows, and he wondered if he ought simply to leave her alone. He sat down. It was finally clear out, the weak sunlight falling shyly over the streets. A last few leaves clung to the branches of the trees.

"I was wondering—how can I—I was hoping you could tell me more about Sari."

"More?"

"Clearly my cousin took a very close interest in her fate," said Lenox in as gentle a tone as he could. "And I know that you and she are inseparable. I was only curious about the origins of that. How you came to be so close."

"I think I know what you are asking. She is not my sister. If that is what you mean."

In fact that was exactly what Lenox had wanted to ask, without knowing how. "Is she not? Though I saw no resemblance to Jasper, the idea crossed my mind."

"When my father was very young, before he had me," said Angela, "indeed when he was still new in India, he fell in love with a local girl. Truly in love, you must understand—not like an English marriage, but a match of two souls, two hearts."

"They are not unknown here," Lenox said softly.

"She was the daughter of a merchant. They met in a shop, quite by chance. After that they started to meet in secret for tea each afternoon, until one evening—my father told me this story many times—they stood by the river, held hands, and vowed to be true to each other for eternity. He was nineteen, she a year younger."

"I had no idea!"

"But he made the mistake of writing to tell his family the news. Once the news arrived in England, it set off a chain of responses. You know that my father's family was all in the army."

"They are my family, too."

"Their reaction was furious. All of my father's superior officers, all of his messmates, everyone set their face against the marriage. In the end, as he told it, he didn't have the courage to defy them all. In a way I think it was this that broke him, this failure of courage, which he could never forget. He was used to taking orders, you see—or so he once put it to me. They sent him to northern India. By the time he was back, the girl had been married off to a much older man.

"Her marriage was short and unhappy—both she and her husband died of a fever after just a few years. But it was long enough that they had a daughter."

"Sari."

"Yes. Her parents died when she was two, and that was when my father took her in. He had lost her mother, but could care for the child, he told me. I was an infant myself. He had married my own mother by then—and lost her, too."

Angela's mother had died in childbirth, the highly suitable second daughter of a colonel. "Hadn't Sari any of her own family?"

"They didn't want her."

"I see." Lenox paused. "How good of Jasper."

"I think it's the best decision he ever made," said Angela quietly.

CHAPTER TWELVE

"Do you remember a time when he was different?" asked Lenox at length. "Perhaps even when he was happy?"

"Happy? Not exactly," said Angela. "But he was always full of love. He could be so funny. Nobody made me laugh like him. And he was good. He was so terribly good. I think some people don't find it easy to be happy. He held it against himself about Sari's mother. Diya. He held himself responsible for her unhappy marriage and even her death, and he felt guilt over marrying my mother when he didn't love her. And she died, too."

"Do you miss home?" he asked.

She glanced up at him from her lap. "Yes." She paused a moment. "Cousin, though I am dreading it, I must tell you something," she went on, bringing her sewing up to her chest with both hands, anxiety in her face. "I know it would be convenient if I married quickly—but it is important that you know I shall never marry. Never."

Lenox was surprised. "May I ask why not?"

"It is not for me," said Angela. "Besides—who could want me! Yet even if someone did . . . I am not fit for it, you see. I hope you are not disappointed."

"Never," said Lenox gently. "More importantly we needn't decide anything right away. You have barely arrived!"

"Yes," said Angela, meeting his eyes. "But I mean what I say."

He checked his watch. "I must go out, I fear. But I understand."

"Of course." Her politeness returned, her reserve, and he saw that their window of intimacy had closed. "Where are you going?"

Lenox smiled ruefully. "The gymnasium."

In every respect, Lady Jane was the fashionable partner in their marriage, as Lenox would gladly concede. Yet that morning, he could briefly and truthfully have said that he was the one who held the honor—for every gentleman in London, that autumn and winter of 1879, was desperately angling for what he had: a standing weekly appointment at the gymnastiksaal.

As he was approaching its doorway, a mile or so north of Hampden Lane, he heard a voice. "Mr. Charles!"

This bright greeting was issued by an impossibly fit young Swede, dressed in a stretchy blue woolen singlet and a watchman's cap, in the chilly Martinmas air. He had stiff blond hair, an angular face bearing a perpetual smile, and muscles as firm as packed snow.

"Hello, Sven," said Lenox glumly.

Sven stopped, shook hands, and looked at him gravely, holding the grip. "Are you ready for a morning of attuning your body to its highest strengths?"

"No," said Lenox.

Sven was not a listener. He beamed in reply. "Wonderful!"

Lenox had started coming to the Swedish gymnasium upon the advice of his physician. His injury from the American case had persisted over the summer months, and Dr. Bock had insisted that for Lenox, movement must be the cure; otherwise his muscles would knit around the wound, and its ill effects become permanent.

This had been the prescription. The gymnasium was located in an airy set of rooms overlooking the beautiful green medallion of Regent's Park. It advertised itself as the most modern and comfortable such establishment in the world—presumably including even the ones in Sweden upon which it was based.

To be sure, it had an accommodating atmosphere. Lenox and Sven made their way up the wide staircase to a lounge paneled in dark wood, with chairs, sofas, newspapers, and an enormous punch bowl of water with slices of orange and lemon in it. Some people swore that this water alone had cured their digestive problems—though this seemed fanciful.

On the far side of this room were two broad doors leading into the main hall, where the dread exercise equipment lay in wait. It was a high-ceilinged room, with springy wood floors and a bank of huge windows running along one wall. Two young lords were fencing furiously along a piste; an aging minor member of the royal family was boxing against another young Swede; and at each piece of equipment, some gentleman of perfect suavity in his regular life was laboring, red and drenched, to grow fitter.

"What about the pommel horse first?" asked Sven brightly.

"No, thank you."

"Excellent!"

In fact Lenox felt fairly well that morning. He and Sven began at the pommel horse, and spent the next hour proceeding from station to station. For all his flaws, the young man was a patient and gentle teacher, guiding his pupil through the motions of the box horse, the wall bars, the hanging rings.

Just when Lenox was feeling a little more chipper, though, he raised his right arm—innocuously, he would have said—and felt a slash of fire across his ribs.

In moments like this his arm flew in a curled tense motion to uselessly protect his side, and he hunched, as if against a blow. His breath sped up.

"All is well, Mr. Charles?"

This means of address was Lenox's foremost quarrel with Sven—a wise old soul of about fifteen, it seemed to Lenox: nothing on earth could induce Sven to call him either Charles (which would have been bad enough) or Mr. Lenox.

"Lenox," panted the detective.

"Mr. Charles Lenox," agreed Sven.

"Just a moment, please, just a moment."

The pain subsided in waves, and soon they resumed their task. Lenox touched his toes, stretched his sides, ran in place. After a while he felt an obscure and slight release of tension where his wound had been—and as usual, it was at this moment he remembered why he returned here each Tuesday and Friday. The blood began to circulate, the smallest muscles to awaken.

Sven, it had to be owned, was masterful in his understanding of how far Lenox could be pushed—when he had another inch of stretch to give or burst of energy to exert; he never, so far, had called upon Lenox to add "One more repetition!" or to "Push a little more harder!" and come up empty.

At the end of their ninety minutes together, out of breath, Lenox thanked his young teacher. He took a towel from the fresh white pile of them near the door and returned alone to the lounge, where he poured himself an enormous glass of chilled water, took an armchair, and closed his eyes, utterly and gratefully spent.

After a few minutes he summoned the energy to run his fingertips over his ribs. Still tender. What a sickening feeling it was, he thought, not to trust one's own body; for of course one was one's body.

He picked up a copy of *The Times* and scanned its headlines. He nodded to one or two acquaintances, and eventually a slender young baronet named Sir Francis Kimbrough, whom he knew only by reputation, came up to him.

"I am entirely in accord with your wife's position on the matter of suffrage," he said, bowed, and withdrew without waiting for a response.

You could have knocked Lenox over with a feather—Jane once every month or two attended a meeting about the women's vote in

North London, but how news of that would have made its way to a fashionable young aristocrat he didn't know.

Nor did he have time to consider it, because a voice said from behind him, "Hullo, Lenox."

The detective twisted in his chair; but saw it was only Wickham Murdock, a pompous, dark, floppy-haired fellow with small eyes and a wildly successful collection of gutter newspapers. He had just stood for Parliament and won. "Hello, Wickham. About to start?"

Murdock was as red as jam, clearly having already been through his paces, and snorted an indignant denial. "Just finished a ripping two hours."

"Oh, excellent."

Murdock looked put out. "Fancy a round or two of boxing?"

"Not just at the moment."

He shrugged. "Perhaps Lord Crabbe will do me the honor. Good day."

Lenox stared behind Murdock, wondering why he was being picked on—before realizing that it was likely because Murdock wanted an invitation to Lady Jane's supper for Angela and Sari that Saturday. Perhaps that accounted for Kimbrough approaching him, too. Princess Alexandra had just responded that she would be coming. Word was getting round.

After he washed and changed, Lenox went into the massage room. Here Sven met him again—and the true joy of the gymnastiksaal began.

Sven's only intelligible conversation was about the Växjö gymnasium, which Lenox had slowly pieced together was the site of his training in Sweden. (There was no detail about the Växjö he deemed too uninteresting for Lenox's eager consumption: At the Växjö they discouraged walnuts, at the Växjö massages were given *before* the exercise and aquavit after.) But he delivered this conversation as he massaged Lenox's shoulders and back, and the release in his muscles was so profound that the conversation was at most a minor irritant; so that by the time Lenox had reached the London street again, two and a half hours after entering the premises, he was happy he had gone.

As he walked home, he took out his notebook and looked over everything he had written down about the Huggins case. He ran his finger over the small symbol that had been carved into the wood of the vestibule of the building.

$$\mathcal{K}\mathrm{F}$$

It said nothing particular to him. It was old enough that it might well have been from Martell's time—perhaps a seal of the chemist's art.

It occurred to him that he might learn more about Martell from his profession. They also ought to add a new lock to that front door.

He put his notebook away then, only a block or so from home now. Kirk was in the front hall when he arrived. "Telegram, sir," said the butler.

"Thank you," Lenox said, taking the folded paper.

He was here last night STOP Left five in morning STOP Attempted force lock but Aunt Eliz scared him away STOP please advise STOP E Huggins

The detective read this, then dashed upstairs to change clothes, reappeared asking for his carriage, and in only a few minutes set out—not for Conduit Street, just yet, but in the direction of his detective agency. He had a plan.

CHAPTER THIRTEEN

The agency stood in a handsome brick building near the Strand. Going there would mean seeing his partners, to whom he owed some work. It couldn't be helped.

There were two of these partners. Lord John Dallington had once been Lenox's protégé, and was now an excellent detective in his own right. The fourth son of a duke, slight, handsome, and feckless, he had famously been a lost cause in his early adulthood, a drinker and a rake. His career had reformed him. The second partner was Polly Buchanan—as she was still known professionally. She was the detective with the largest female custom in London. She had discovered this gap in the market, and her cases were mostly drawn from it: stolen jewelry, straying beaux.

In retrospect perhaps it had been inevitable that Polly and Dallington, brought together by Lenox and the new agency the three of them had founded, would fall in love; or at least, that Dallington would fall in love with Polly.

Her conversion had taken longer. But at last they had married, and now Polly was with child for the first time.

It hadn't kept her from her desk. "Charles!" she said, when he arrived at the office. She happened to be out among the clerks and junior detectives at their slanted desks, in the big airy room they inhabited.

"Hello," he said. "Are you feeling well?"

She was in a conservative gray and blue dress that showed the slight curve of her stomach. "Thriving. How are you?"

"Splendid, thank you," said Lenox.

She gave him a shrewd look. Fortunately at that moment Dallington's office door opened, and the young lord poked his head out. He was, as always, in a black suit with a carnation in the buttonhole.

"Charles!" he said. "I thought I heard your voice."

"I'm only here to get Freddie."

"I'll come with you."

"So shall I," said Polly.

As they descended the stairs to the building's ground floor stables, he asked after Polly's blackmail case—a highborn young woman, Lady Julia Lundeen, had, when she was not yet seventeen years of age, sent a series of indiscreet letters to an Italian polo player, and now someone, perhaps the Italian himself, was trying to extract money from her father.

As they entered the stables, its familiar dusty-sweet tang, hay, horses, and tack, reminded him briefly of his boyhood.

"Her family won't hear of prosecuting him," said Polly with dissatisfaction. "Apparently he played polo with the Prime Minister's son last week, the bounder. They don't want to lose the acquaintance."

"Why do you need Freddie?" asked Dallington.

"A curious little case," said Lenox—but was brought short before he could go on, because they had found their quarry.

Freddie was a squat, scarred basset hound, probably part mutt. He could not move quickly and his ears touched the ground even when he stood at his full height; and his fiercest admirer could not have defended his breath. But he was one of the best scenting dogs in London.

The groom, old Ollie Watkins, put the dog in a leather leash, and

Polly and Dallington walked Freddie out to the busy street with him. As he bid them farewell, he saw in their faces that they—well, missed him, he supposed.

He found that he missed them, too.

"As soon as this case is over I shall be back in more regularly," he said, climbing into his carriage. "It's an old friend's problem."

"Anyone I know?" asked Dallington.

"She was before even your time," replied Lenox with a smile. "But listen—are you two coming to the dinner for my cousin on Saturday? If so, we shall discuss your cases then. I promise you I have been reading the notes. Come early, if you like."

"Perhaps we will, too," said Polly seriously. Polly did more than either of them administratively, as well as managing her cases. He knew she needed more help, though they had recently hired an extra junior detective in his absence, a young woman rejected by Scotland Yard. She helped Polly with the household thefts—a large business—and the other detectives had taken on Lenox's cases.

"By the way, Montague did a good job finding information for me about this murder I'm looking into. Give him my thanks. Do you rate him?" asked Lenox.

"Monty? Very highly," said Polly.

Lenox's coachman was easing the horse into traffic even as the detective attained the first step of the stairs into the carriage. Dallington stepped back to the curb—but before the vehicle itself moved, Polly put her hand on Lenox's forearm, on the windowsill of the carriage, and looked into his eyes.

"Take care of yourself, please," she said seriously.

He knew that she saw more deeply into him than her husband—more than nearly anyone. "I will," he promised.

The carriage lurched out into a gap in the traffic, and as they departed, Freddie happily patrolled the floor of the compartment, sniffing its corners. Lenox absentmindedly scratched the beast's ear.

It was a good thirty minutes of London traffic later (and an overturned omnibus bypassed) when Lenox arrived at Mrs. Huggins's building. He rang the bell and Mrs. Huggins appeared after a moment, in a mauve dress and a gray bonnet.

"Thank you for coming," she said, opening the door and glancing down at the dog. "As you can see, the lock is broken."

"I'm so sorry you've had a bad night."

"Would you like to come upstairs?"

He shook his head. "Not yet, thank you. Can you tell me what happened?"

She nodded soberly. "It was at about four in the morning. I am a light sleeper anyhow, and I have been a little on edge"—she smiled—"just a little, you know. When I woke up, I felt something was wrong. It must have been a sound that woke me. I opened my door and could see down the stairwell that someone was outside."

"You must have been frightened."

"Only a little. I have a whistle and a pistol by the door—both new, given to me by my friend Esme Forsythe, whom I confided my troubles to. I used the whistle first," said Mrs. Huggins.

"A pistol, Mrs. Huggins!"

The old domestic nodded. She was recounting the story bravely, but she was shaken, visage pale. "I blew the whistle long and loud first. It startled him right away."

"Did you see his face?"

"No. He wore a low dark hat. A heavy dark cloak."

"Were the clothes of good quality or bad?" Lenox asked.

"About average, I should have said."

Lenox looked down at the woodwork. He saw only one or two cigar marks this time; their visitor had stayed a shorter time. "The whistle scared him away?"

"Not immediately. He only looked up. Then I fired the pistol into the stairwell."

"Mrs. Huggins!"

"Yes, I know."

"Well done, I suppose." Lenox glanced around the street. After a moment, he asked, "Does Ernest have a spare room in Belsize Park?"

"Yes, he has a mews house to himself."

Lenox nodded. "Then you must pack a carryall and go stay with him for a night or two, if he is amenable to it. If not, you must come and stay with me in Hampden Lane."

A look of powerful relief passed over Mrs. Huggins's face at this suggestion. All she said, though, was, "Oh, do you think so? No—Ernest will have me."

"I do think so. And if you wouldn't mind, I would like to have a key to your rooms until this is over."

She took a small leather bag from the fold of her dress at her waist, and opened it to fetch her keys. "Here you are," she said. She looked down at the dog. "Do you think it is this Mr. Phipps everyone is mentioning?"

He shook his head slightly. "It isn't impossible," he said. "But it isn't my first guess either. Go and pack. I shall stop back in at the Coach and Horses later this afternoon—leave word with Ernest that you are safely removed to his house, if you don't mind."

She nodded, looking a little stronger again. "I will. Thank you, Mr. Lenox."

"Don't thank me until I've solved it. My carriage will take you to your nephew's." He signaled up to his coachman to take her.

"Don't you need it?"

"No, now I must let Freddie do his work."

Indeed, the little hound was tugging at the leash as they stood out on the pavement, occasionally emitting a low whine.

Like all dogs he was almost insensibly attracted to the smell of anise, one of the ingredients in licorice. He would follow it to the ends of the earth. Lenox let him off the leash and the animal dashed into the vestibule, snuffing it frantically up.

After fifteen or twenty seconds he turned, stood stock-still for a moment, and then raced out into Conduit Street so quickly that the detective had to run to get the leash back on him.

"Thank you!" called Mrs. Huggins behind them.

"Goodbye!" Lenox called over his shoulder, and held on as the dog tugged him forward, pursuing the scent of the oil that had clung to Mrs. Huggins's intruder.

CHAPTER FOURTEEN

The central facts of the case had changed, and as they ran along Lenox's mind was calculating precisely how drastically: before, his best guess had been that someone had simply been sleeping in the entryway to the little building on Conduit Street. Now he knew that someone was trying to break in.

That changed the case into something graver than it had seemed. He felt the urgency.

As Freddie settled into a steady pace, ticking off the quarter miles, nose to the ground, tail occasionally twitching with excitement, the detective let his mind revolve around the facts he knew, seeking that crucial point of entry that would give him a lead. They were bound roughly southeast, through Covent Garden and toward the river. Because it was London they only got a few second glances, though nobody looking closely could have mistaken that they were on the trail of something, or someone.

The essential fact to consider, he reflected, was that Mrs. Huggins herself didn't have anything this intruder wanted. Lenox had been in her house, seen the modest china ewer that stood in a place of pride on the mantel, the plain silver cross she wore around her neck. Probably the most valuable portable property in the rooms was a trunk filled with yarn.

Nothing there to entice a simple thief.

But could Martell have left or concealed something in the rooms? Would it still be there, seven years on? And was it worth risking prison for?

Freddie started to whine and pull more insistently on the leash. They were by Waterloo Bridge, and Lenox realized that the dog, superb animal, was leading him directly toward a long peeling sunburnt dock just beneath the bridge.

Dozens of small craft bobbed on the silvery river, barges carrying coal and hay, six-oared cutters, lighters transporting goods. "Fair lemons and oranges!" sang a peddler. "Sweet violets a penny a bunch!" They were always plentiful here where the Thames did its trade. A large stenciled sign read BLANK QUAY.

Their progress was arrested not because Freddie lost the scent, but because a porter stopped Lenox at the head of the dock. He was a smallish fellow in a brown work shirt.

"What are you doing here?" he asked suspiciously.

"I'm searching for a man who is wanted in questioning for a crime. This dog has his trail. His name is Jacob Phipps."

The porter studied Lenox. "Are you with the Metropolitan?" he asked, then volunteered, "My brother is a constable on Carnaby Street."

"No, a private detective," said Lenox.

There were times when Lenox's birth counted for a great deal, as he was well aware. The porter took in Lenox's dress, accent, and bearing, took in the eager dog pulling and mewling, and evidently made a decision based on this collective evidence. "Jacob Phipps?"

"Yes."

"Wait here."

The porter walked toward the end of the dock, where forty or so men were at work, moving goods on and off a small cluster of riverboats. Lenox lost sight of him amid a group of shoulder-high crates.

He returned a few moments later, shaking his head. "No Jacob Phipps here."

"Unlucky," murmured Lenox. "Do you think I might take the dog down and look for myself?"

"No, 'fraid not. More than my job's worth."

"I understand," Lenox said. "Thank you."

The detective turned away and, after walking ten or fifteen feet, contrived to drop the leash.

The basset hound, who had been coming along very reluctantly, dashed down the dock. "Freddie! No!" Lenox called after him.

He had no time to experience any contrition for this unjust blame. The porter was barreling after the dog already, but the animal had reached the end of the dock in a trice, and now stood with his nose in the wind, motionless, trying to recapture the scent.

Evidently Mrs. Huggins's intruder had departed this dock by boat.

There was a genial crowding around the basset by the men on the dock, who scratched and petted and gently cuffed him, until the porter could take the leather leash and bring him back.

"There you are, sir," he said, trotting back.

"Thank you," said Lenox. "I'm awfully sorry. One last question: May I ask what boats these are?"

"Small goods transport, sir," said the porter.

"No passengers taken?"

"None."

"Is it the same men here every day?"

"There are rotating shifts, starting at three in the morning. But nobody here had heard of Jacob Phipps, not any of the foreman, like."

"How many men would have been here at four or five this morning?"

"Roughly as many as you see now," said the man. "It's the same all clock long."

Lenox thanked the man before he and the dog, occasionally still looking back, took the stairs back up the Embankment to Temple Place. They walked slowly now back in the direction of the agency—Lenox stopping once, to buy two strips of cured bacon from a vendor, which he passed down to Freddie with a pat on the head.

"Good dog," he said.

Freddie gave a low growl of happiness as he accepted the snack, and then walked steadily alongside Lenox the rest of the way back. The scent was gone.

After Lenox had returned the dog to the stables, he went upstairs into the agency's offices. There he found, a pleasant surprise, that Graham was waiting, deep in conversation with Dallington about something.

"I was just filling Lord John in on the case. Any developments?" Graham asked.

"Yes," said Lenox. "If you let me drive you back to Parliament I can tell you about them."

This was what they did, Lenox telling Graham how he had passed the last twenty-four hours. Graham absorbed it quietly; as it had for so long, their detective work together turned him into an audience for Lenox's theories and mistakes, his false starts, his sparks of insight.

"Something stands out to me," said Lenox. "One of the few verifiable facts about Jacob Phipps was that he worked at the docks before his wife died and he went to Australia. If he has returned, it seems only too possible that he should be back in his old trade."

Graham raised his eyebrows. "Yes. Only too likely."

The two men made a plan in consultation; Lenox would begin a watch of the little building that night, armed with a blackjack and a police whistle. (He was not himself an enthusiast of the pistol as a weapon—he had seen too many people, remarkable marksmen among them, shot with their own firearms.)

Meanwhile Graham said that he would press upon Scotland Yard to bring more attention to the case.

It was a melancholy reality to Lenox that this appeal to the Yard was now within Graham's power more than his own; he no longer had much influence there. They had turned hard against private detectives recently, once their numbers started to increase and the newspapers became more fulsome in their praise of the nonprofessional investigators. He still had a few friends left among the police force, but it was Graham who voted on their budget each year.

They reached Parliament and drew to a stop. "You look tired, if you will forgive me for saying so," Lenox told his old friend, extending his hand.

Graham offered a rare smile and took Lenox's hand. "You look tired, too, if you will forgive me for saying so."

They both laughed, and parted, agreeing to be in touch that afternoon.

When he reached Hampden Lane there was a stack of mail for him, and rather than tossing it onto his desk, he sifted through it. He was happy to see that Montague, the junior detective at the agency, had written again in response to Lenox's scrawled request of the night before.

> Sir,
> There is little that I can discover about
> Martell as a chemist. But if you wish
> there are two places I might yet inquire
> about him. One is the Royal Pharmaceutical
> Society, in Bloomsbury Square, the other
> the Worshipful Company of Apothecaries,
> whose Hall in Blackfriars you would no doubt
> recognize on sight. I do not know whether he
> was familiar at either hall but there is a
> chance of it. Please advise.
>
> Yours,
> Montague

Lenox wrote back, inviting Montague to meet at the Apothecaries' Hall at four o'clock that afternoon. He did indeed know the building, had always been curious about it. He needed to recover for an hour, though; the stitch in his side was painful, after that hard chase on the scent of the anise. And then he needed another hour to himself before pursuing Mrs. Huggins's case further—for while its call was strong, the call of friendship was stronger still, and Lenox wanted badly to check in on Thomas McConnell.

CHAPTER FIFTEEN

At the doctor's house in Belgravia, the shades were drawn in the upper stories, and the butler, who knew Lenox well, had informed him that Lady Toto McConnell was in the country.

"And the doctor?"

"Out upon errands, sir."

Not for nothing was Lenox a detective, though. He sensed deception in the butler's manner, and after thanking him and leaving, ambled over to the other side of the street and concealed himself in a doorway there.

Sure enough, a few moments later he had seen a shade on the second floor pulled back, and McConnell's handsome, tired face briefly appear, scanning the street.

With a sigh, Lenox stood watching for a moment, and then walked on, pondering his friend's situation.

But soon enough he had a fresh problem to solve, and Montague to help him do it. The two detectives met at the appointed time that afternoon, in front of the imposing brick-and-stone hall of the Worshipful Company of Apothecaries.

Montague was a young fellow, eager and bright-eyed, so slender that he looked as if he had yet to grow into his ears and nose. He had a bright wave of blond-ginger hair.

"How do you do?" said Lenox. "Thank you for coming. Let us see what we may discover."

There were a hundred-odd livery companies within the City of London—not to be confused with the city of London, the great metropolis, but the neighborhood known as the City, or sometimes the Square Mile, which was the tiny warren of streets that made up the financial heart of the British Empire.

Each of these livery companies had its own hall, its own traditions, its own heritage. For Lenox, who had grown up amidst an aristocracy defined by all sorts of recondite rules and codes, the companies had always been a source of fascination, a working-class analogue to his world. Each of the beautiful buildings was covered in elaborate seals, coats of arms, and Latin tags, as densely allusive as any building at Oxford or Cambridge. The halls elevated a company, the Worshipful Company of Fishmongers, say, or the Worshipful Company of Haberdashers (for whatever ancient reason all the livery companies were Worshipful) into something mysterious and beautiful.

The Apothecaries were fifty-eighth in precedence among the livery companies. (The Mercers were first. There was an unending dispute between the Skinners and the Merchant Taylors about which company was sixth and which was seventh in precedence—in order to solve which, they grudgingly switched off every Easter, a custom that had given birth to the useful phrase "at sixes and sevens.") This put it one spot ahead of the Worshipful Company of Shipwrights and one behind the Worshipful Company of Loriners, who made bits and bridles for horsemen.

But the Apothecaries had a good claim that their hall was the oldest still surviving. It had been built just after the Great Fire of 1666, and as Lenox approached its front gate, he felt a respectful awe: a secret place, with its own rules, upon which he knew one must not trespass.

Coming in from the noisy street, they passed through the black wrought-iron gate and into a hushed inner courtyard. Here there was a porter in a bowler hat, sitting in a small freestanding lodge.

"Good afternoon," said Lenox.

"Business?" said the porter, stepping outside of his tiny abode.

"We wondered if Mr. Beaumont was available."

Beaumont was the master of the company. Lenox had looked him up in the City directory. "Mr. Beaumont lives in Chipping Norton," the porter replied, "besides which he's been convalescing there for the last few months. He was after having the pneumonia."

"Poor fellow. Does he have an associate?"

For the second time that day, Lenox's accent and bearing gave him an advantage with a London's gatekeeper; the heavy-lidded porter, suspicious by the nature of his job, looked him up and down carefully, then said, "I'll check, sir."

Lenox and Montague remained in the courtyard, Lenox pulling up his heavy black cloak around his ears. The light was getting wan in the sky, the brief day nearing its end. The rain had stopped. As they waited, the detectives discussed Montague's work at the agency, the younger man enthusiastic to share his experiences. He was polite about Polly, but it was clear he would have followed Dallington into battle. Lenox wondered how his old protégé had begotten such loyalty in this young fellow.

After about five minutes, the porter reappeared beside a tall man with a beaky good-natured face. "This is Mr. Jerald Dyson, sir, our senior warden," he said. "He can answer your questions."

"Mr. Dyson," said Lenox, shaking his hand. "Thank you for your time."

"Of course. Please, follow me into the hall," he said, and led them in a diagonal across the courtyard. Opening a heavy oak door, he said, "May I ask why you have come?"

"I am a detective, sir. My name is Charles Lenox; this is my second, Mr. Montague. We are looking into the death of a chemist in Mayfair."

Dyson looked surprised. They entered a large shadowy hall lined with vast history paintings. "Which chemist?"

"His name was Austin Martell."

"I don't recognize it. I'm not sure how I can be of any help."

"In two ways," Lenox said. "First, I was hoping to learn something about your profession, and second, to see if Mr. Martell was on your rolls before his death."

Dyson frowned. "Oh, I see. Because he was a chemist. No, I am afraid that unless he was a doctor, it is unlikely. You might have better luck at the Royal Pharmaceutical Society, in Smithfield. Since 1815, you see, our primary responsibility here has been to license medical practitioners across the United Kingdom. It is true that some of our membership are chemists, but not the great majority."

"I see. Forgive my ignorance," said Lenox.

"It is quite understandable." Dyson paused. "If you really wish to learn something of the profession, as you said, we could take a turn of the physic garden. There is half an hour of daylight left. But first let me check our rolls for this man. You said his name was Martell?"

"Yes, Austin Martell."

"Wait here a moment, please."

Montague and Lenox waited in the hall, through which one old fellow or other occasionally shuffled back and forth holding a newspaper. Dyson was gone about three minutes. When he came back it was with the news he had expected: Martell had never been on the books here. Lenox should have known; this place did not match the description of the grimy, unscrupulous man who had once lived in Mrs. Huggins's rooms.

"Thank you," said Lenox. "If you are still willing, we should very much enjoy that tour."

"Of course," said Dyson, brightening. "Let me lock up and I will take you over."

He led them up one alley and down another until they arrived at the gates of the garden. "There is a much larger one in Chelsea. It is closed to the public or I would recommend you go there. This small little patch offers a few of its highlights—a very few."

Yet to Lenox, the tour of the little garden was a revelation. It had a small fountain set in a rockery at the center, and circling it concentrically were rows of plants, each with a notecard under glass indicating what it was and what it treated. He read the names—calendula, passiflora, holy basil, southern ginseng—and Dyson kindly and patiently explained each one, gently touching their leaves now and then as if they were old friends.

"I myself am a true apothecary by trade," he said. "I grew up not far from here, in the City. Beaumont, however, is a medical doctor. Indeed one of our first licentiates was John Keats—when he became a doctor, all while writing his beautiful poems. A shame he died so young."

"'And yet a thing of beauty is a joy forever,'" said Montague, and then blushed to the roots of his hair.

"Yes, indeed," said Dyson, smiling. "Look, these little golden globes are for toothache—acmella oleracea. They work a charm."

"My mother gave us cocaine wool for toothache," said Montague.

"That is quite common. I prefer the herbal solution when it is there. It is sad how little most people understand of physic. Nine-tenths of these cordials and liniments are stuff and nonsense, if you ask me. Perhaps more. You no doubt have seen the advertisements for J. Collis Browne's medicine?"

Both Lenox and Montague assented.

"That is made up of morphine and cannabis. It treats people's maladies, to be sure, but then, it would treat a draft horse to a good night's sleep." Dyson shook his head a little angrily. "Or what about Godfrey's Cordial?"

This was another of the most famous medicaments in England,

advertised on placards all over the city. "I've taken it," Montague admitted.

"Of course, nearly everyone has. Mother's friend, they call it. Well—I should think so! Its ingredients are water, treacle—and pure opium. Mother's friend indeed! Since the Pharmacy Act the opium dens have found greater difficulty obtaining their product—so one reads—and I often think, get a bottle of Godfrey's! But it is not quite as picturesque as smoking from a long pipe. Look, here is borage," he said, before confiding in them, with a slightly comical zeal, "I have not had indigestion in twenty years!"

"Our victim was an average chemist, I believe," said Lenox. "I think he must have traded in just those sorts of sham cordials and liniments."

"One cannot wholly blame him," said Dyson. "The true art is leaving the cities. My mother grew yarrow for cuts, on our window ledge, lavender for headaches . . . but those ways are going. Mostly it's in the country that they still know them. And not so often there."

Some golden world was always just leaving, Lenox knew—yet he could not help but be moved by Dyson's lament, and as the sun finally fell, reminded himself to ask the groundskeeper about any medical plants they had at Lenox House when he was there for Christmas.

Eventually the three men walked slowly back up the alleys leading to the company's hall, discussing Martell, whose greenhouse was of great interest to the apothecary. When they were back at the hall, and the detectives were taking their leave, Montague, who had been very quiet, suddenly said, "I think it is the most beautiful garden in London!"

Dyson smiled. "Thank you. We do, too. I often go and sit there in the mornings."

"'I know a bank where the wild thyme blows,'" said Montague, and then, though once more blushing, went on. "'Where oxlips and the nodding violet grows, quite over-canopied with luscious woodbine, with sweet musk-roses and with eglantine.'"

Dyson beamed, a full smile, without a single reservation, only delight. "'There sleeps Titania sometimes of the night,'" he answered, "'lull'd in these flowers with dances and delight!'"

CHAPTER SIXTEEN

It had always been a hard-and-fast fact of Sir Edmund Lenox's character that he declined all offers of advancement within his party. He had said in his younger brother's hearing more than once that he would rather be hanged than become Prime Minister.

Over time this adamant principle had given him a reputation in Parliament as a fair listener to all, because he was a competitor to none. He had often been a final arbiter of intraparty squabbles for the same reason.

But that had changed—as Angela and Sari, the newest family members, were learning.

The baronet was a visitor at Hampden Lane once more at supper that evening. It was good of him to be so dogged in welcoming his cousin to England; he looked tired, and the younger brother knew for a fact that Edmund would have to return to Parliament for the better part of the night after this, trying to make up for having been absent during even so brief a period.

Meanwhile supper had thrice been interrupted by messages, and outside of the house two carriages stood impatiently, one waiting to retrieve Edmund the moment he could be chivvied into it by his political secretaries, the other full of his junior associates in the party, holding discussions while waiting for him. Lenox could easily guess who it would be: James Faraday, Lord Chelsea, Henry Lamb Hill, young fellows with brilliant minds and impeccable connections, who actually did want to be Prime Minister one distant day, in far off theoretical years like 1898 and 1910.

Edmund still had no official title, because the current Prime Minister was Disraeli, a conservative. But he had consented, after a series of resignations in the party, to be what the press sometimes called the "shadow" Chancellor of the Exchequer. This meant that he was the second man to Gladstone on the front bench in Parliament.

The chamber was the lightest of Edmund's new responsibilities, however; his time now was entirely taken with meetings of strategy and policy, and they were taxing him to the utmost. He had not Gladstone's implacable calm nor Disraeli's ferocious charismatic ambition. It had always been basic to his happiness to oversee the farms at Lenox House, which had in his previous times required a long break in his sessions at Parliament.

At the present moment that was of course out of the question. And the labors told upon his face. He was decidedly thinner. But there was an iron in his gaze that Charles had never seen there, and it fortified the younger brother himself, somehow; tired though he might be, he was going to get to the bottom of this Martell case. Perhaps even tonight.

It was with this borrowed resolve that, at a little before ten o'clock, Lenox carefully opened the front door to 12 Conduit Street, using the key that Mrs. Huggins had given him.

With him was Montague, who had asked to come—and no bad thing, for Lenox's nerves were taut. It was unlikely the intruder would be back that night; he hadn't yet come two nights in a row. Yet perhaps the fact that he had tried to force the door showed he was desperate.

But desperate for what? If he meant Mrs. Huggins harm, there were a thousand moments when he could have visited it upon her.

No—it had to be something in the building. It was their visit to the livery hall of the apothecaries that had finally given Lenox an idea what that might be.

They took the first flight of stairs slowly. Lenox checked the door to Mrs. Huggins's room. It was locked, and the two men proceeded up the second flight of stairs. Lenox was carrying a short black crowbar, not to defend himself, as it happened, though he wasn't sorry to have its weight heavy in his left hand as they reached the greenhouse.

"How did the building come to have a greenhouse on its roof?" asked Montague, as they went through the glass door.

"Martell lived here for some twenty years—the chemist. He built it."

"I suppose these buildings are cheap."

"Oh yes, you can get them for a song," said Lenox. "Everybody is moving to these new suburbs."

They walked through the dim greenhouse, with its pleasant smell of roses and fruiting trees. It was much warmer here, and Lenox took off his coat and laid it next to the doorframe.

"Here's a kerosene lamp," said Montague, looking over a table crowded with shears and the like.

He cut the wick, lit the lamp, and followed Lenox to the center of the little chamber. The older detective had laid the crowbar on the brick rim of the well and was rolling up his shirt sleeves.

"It smells like ammonia."

Lenox smiled. In the carriage ride, he had given Montague a copy of *Fletcher's Scientific Dictionary* from his library. It was flagged to the page for ammonia, and Montague had read the entry out loud.

> *Ammonia.* NH_3. Boiling point-28 F. This simple **hydride** is a powerful fertilizer. Extremely caustic in its concentrated form; should not be handled. In crystal form (*sal ammoniac*) can be used for the prevention of fainting. Naturally occurring in plant and animal waste. Useful in a wide variety of chemical practices as a precipitate. The characteristic scent of **opium.**

Now, as they stood next to the low, sealed chimney in the center of the room, that caustic scent—that characteristic scent—suffused the air.

"The presence of the chimney bothered me from the start," said Lenox, gazing down on the sealed lid. He glanced over toward the working chimney that stood outside the greenhouse. "Why would a building this small have a second chimney? It would only make the space harder to heat."

Lenox bent to the task of pulling up the plywood from the chimney, levering the crowbar upward. It didn't want to give way, rows of nails holding it down. He used all his strength—enough that his side gave a twinge—and just managed to inch the wood up.

"Shall I have a go?" asked Montague.

"It's all right. I think it will be easier now that there is a gap," said Lenox, straining.

With a great shove he prized it open another few inches, and suddenly there was a strong wave of the scent of ammonia in the air.

Lenox paused, his breathing heavy. He hadn't really registered the smell as anything out of the ordinary on his first visit here, because it was so common to notice it near flowerbeds. But now it was overpowering.

"I should have observed," he said, speaking as much to himself as to Montague really, "that it was only strong here, by the chimney—*away* from the plants."

With a last great effort, he pulled up the wood enough that Montague could take a grip of it and help him. In another moment they had it off.

Both men leaned over the open circle, Montague holding the lamp, which cast an uneven light over the space.

"I don't think it's a chimney at all," said Montague.

Indeed, the space was only about six or seven feet deep. Lenox gazed at it. "No."

"And it's empty." This was obviously true—Montague lowered the lamp into the cylindrical space and cast light over every part of it, but it was smooth brick and mortar all the way down. "Perhaps the smell was a trick—some trapped scent, or old fertilizer."

Lenox shook his head. "Lower me in."

"Shan't I go?"

"It's all right," said Lenox.

He went down into the pit, landing on his heels with a soft thud. He couldn't have candidly said he liked it, being down there—and it occurred to him he knew next to nothing about Montague. But a look up at the young man from the pit was enough to reassure him that he was a stolid companion.

"Hand me the lamp, would you please?" Lenox said.

He felt around the edges of the little space brick by brick. None so much as moved. But the smell of ammonia was so strong that he started to feel brick by brick again—and after a moment, he felt something shift minutely under his knee.

Eagerly he put the lamp down.

"There's a false bottom," he said. "Hand me the crowbar."

It took him another minute to pry up two bricks. They began crumbling when he pulled them away, but with five minutes of work he had his reward: a small tin box, about the dimensions of a good-sized church Bible. It was locked, but the smell from it was intense.

"Haul me out, would you?" said Lenox.

He handed the box up and then took Montague's hand and pulled himself out, too. They took the box over to the small table where Mrs. Huggins made cuttings from her flowers. But the box wouldn't open.

"I could break the lock," said Montague.

Lenox inspected the box, which was rusted but sturdy. He held it up to about chest height and then let it fall to the ground.

It thudded, and the top immediately sprang loose. Both men knelt down and looked inside. There they saw two large brick-sized blocks of a sticky-looking black substance wrapped in wax paper. The opium.

But neither lingered on that long—for tucked neatly between

the two was a thick sheaf of banknotes. Lenox riffled through them, counting quickly.

"Almost about a thousand pounds," he said.

"My word," said Montague, awed.

It was an enormous amount of money, more than an excellent and popular London chemist could hope to make from even five years' work.

Lenox inspected the dense, sticky black opium. "And probably double the same amount over again worth of opium, or more. Two thousand pounds, give or take."

"It is a rich prize. Enough to keep returning here for," said Montague, "if that is what our intruder is doing."

"Yes," Lenox said, staring at the rusted little box. "And I should be willing to stake it as well, enough to kill Martell over."

CHAPTER SEVENTEEN

A little while later, Lenox and Montague sat at the Coach and Horses, opposite a tall, angular man with keen eyes and shaggy gray hair.

This was Adamson, the inspector who had originally investigated Martell's death. Each of the three men had a pint of beer, and they had retreated to a corner of the pub for privacy, since the Passenger and all the other regulars were congregated by the big stone hearth, merrily chatting.

Adamson, a quiet sort, was meticulously packing a pipe as Lenox recounted their investigation of the Martell case thus far.

"Do you remember the Pharmacy Act?" Lenox asked.

"I don't think so," said Adamson in a heavy south coast accent, glancing up.

"It passed a decade ago. It made the procurement of opium more difficult for the opium dens."

"Aye, that does ring a bell."

"Seven years ago, when Martell died, the problem would have been at its worst," said Lenox. "So I theorize anyhow. He must have been manu-facturing the opium himself to meet the shortfall. The question we have is whether you had any sense at the time that Martell was doing anything illegal."

"Oh yes," said Adamson. He lit the pipe carefully. "We were sure of it. In fact we even connected him to one of the dens."

"Which one?" said Lenox.

"Lao Chang's, on Martha Street in Bluegate Fields."

Bluegate Fields was perhaps London's worst slum. "How did you track him there?"

"He had a parcel in the back room of the shop that had a receipt of payment from them. It didn't contain opium—there were other medicines, legal as far as we could tell."

"Any criminal associates?"

"Plenty." Adamson glanced around the pub under hooded eyes. "This street has improved a sight in the last seven years, I don't mind telling you. Martell was friends with a thief named Webster, a rotten chap. We looked at him carefully, but like Jacob Phipps he had an alibi. That is my main memory of the case, in fact, alibis in every direction. This was a dank old pub then, the Duke of Gloucester. You didn't want to be in here after dark unless you were pretty handy with your fists."

"So you never established a firm suspect?"

Adamson shook his head. "Never," he admitted. "All of us liked Phipps for it, but . . . and then there was a butcher down the street with whom Martell had had numerous public disputes, a vicious character. I do remember his name—Archie Brodhead. A big fellow, not half intimidating to interview. And I am no retiring daisy."

Lenox did not doubt it—Adamson had come up through the police forces as a city constable. "But you dismissed the butcher, too?"

"Another alibi, rock solid. I can't remember what it was, but I know we confirmed it five times over. And as I told you earlier, nobody saw a thing on the night itself."

"Nobody saw a thing," put in Montague mildly, "or nobody would admit to seeing a thing?"

"I'm inclined to think the former. It was a dark, rainy night, and nobody could remember as much as a shadow moving down the street, leastwise as far as they would tell us."

"Could Phipps have had a partner?" asked Lenox.

"We rejected the idea at the time. You must remember, we interviewed everyone who knew Phipps, from the docks, from his family, even among his enemies, and not one of them said that he had a partner. We would have heard."

"Do you remember which dock Phipps worked on?" asked Lenox.

"In the Surrey Quays half the time, and at Blank Dock the other half."

Lenox and Montague glanced at each other sharply. It was Blank Dock where Freddie had trailed the anise scent the day before.

This was as close to an ironclad clue as they had chanced upon. Could the Passenger and the rest of these Conduit Street regulars be right about Jacob Phipps? It seemed so, astonishingly.

"And then Phipps went off to Australia?"

"Yes. Despite the alibi. He was in no risk of us picking him up."

And yet he must have wanted to clear out of England in a hurry.

Looking around the lively pub, feeling the good solid oak beneath their feet, it was hard to imagine this as a skulking, low place, Lenox thought. A game of darts had commenced nearby. Two ladies sat conversing blithely behind the low door that separated the ladies' parlor from the main bar. In all, a most respectable public house; these days, anyhow.

"What about this?" said Montague suddenly, face fierce with concentration. Lenox liked him for the intensity. "Phipps and an associate are involved with Martell in selling opium. Martell cuts things off with them—perhaps he decides he doesn't need a middleman anymore—so Phipps sends his associate to go and get the opium and cash, but Martell won't give it up. In the struggle, he's killed. Phipps clears off to Australia because he knows if his partner is caught, he'll give Phipps up, and Phipps will hang."

"Mm," said Adamson, taking a long pull from his pipe. "Possible."

"And now Phipps has returned from Australia to get the stuff," said Montague with finality.

Lenox shook his head. "It is a good theory. But it relies upon a completely invisible partner, unknown to his friends and family, never seen with him, for one thing. And then, why would Phipps have waited seven years? Unless perhaps the old partner, the third person, is finally dead, or out of the picture."

"That must be it!" said Montague.

"Maybe. Did you ever get to the bottom of their argument?" Lenox asked Adamson. "Martell and Phipps? Was it about his wife's death—Elizabeth Phipps?"

Adamson shook his head. "That was a rumor. It had no basis in fact that we could discover, and indeed Beth Phipps saw a proper doctor two or three days before she died. But we did learn that the two men had a loud dispute in the street not long before Martell's own death. That is no doubt why Phipps was blamed.

"The truth is that nobody mourned Martell for a Hackney minute," Adamson said, shaking his head. He took a long draught of ale. "We chased leads for a month or two, and then . . . you know how the job is, Mr. Lenox. Another case is always coming down the way."

"Of course."

"Martell was mixed up in nasty things—besides the opium. I've no doubt he was mixing his medicines with cheap liquor. That is how half these chemists wind up killing someone. Was Phipps involved? It is possible. But he wasn't holding the knife."

"No," Lenox murmured, looking away. His mind was calculating likelihoods, angles of approach. "Did Martell ever have a wife, a woman?"

"None. And that was unusual—we asked about it. A lifelong bachelor."

"Could he have been involved with Beth Phipps?"

Adamson shrugged. "Anything is possible, of course, but nothing led us to think so."

Earlier that evening, Lenox had read a good deal about opium. Dyson, the fellow at the Hall of Apothecaries who had so kindly shown them around the physic garden, had been telling the level truth: There was opium in half the medicines, from McMunn's Elixir to Dalby's Carminative, that one saw in every shop. Moreover, any genteel person could go to an apothecary's shop and buy laudanum for a toothache, which was simply a brewed form of opium.

But the two large bricks of opium they had found could only have been meant for the opium dens of East London, those low-lit intricately laid-out establishments into which people sometimes disappeared for years, lost to their families, insensate to the world. They would have to be Lenox's next stop.

The three gentlemen talked in low voices for another half hour or so. Adamson told them as much as he could remember. But it was clear he had no more concrete clue than Lenox did of who had killed the chemist seven years before. The best lead they had was still the man dogging Mrs. Huggins's little building.

Suddenly Lenox had an idea of how they might find him, which didn't involve either him or Montague sleeping in the greenhouse. It would take a little help from an old friend.

CHAPTER EIGHTEEN

The next day was Saturday at last.

That evening thirty-six guests would come to Hampden Lane for supper (the list had ballooned in the past few days, as various unsubtle requests for invitations arrived on Lady Jane's desk), and the house was a whirlwind of preparatory activity, maids cleaning every last corner of every last room for a second time, deliveries arriving by the downstairs entrance on each other's heels, the kitchen fires stoked and pots of food simmering above them.

Lenox, who knew how minimal his own value was on days like this, ate a quick breakfast of porridge with his daughters and then hit the streets, hailing a cab and directing it to an address in South London.

After a meandering southward journey, the cab stopped at a row of white houses on a pleasant, leafy lane, far removed from the clatter of central London. They were the new sort of house popping all over the outskirts of the city in long rows, each standing on a pretty plot of land, most with seven or eight goodly trees around them. They were rather brilliant, Lenox thought, giving people in miniature the estates that for a millennium Britain's working class had gazed enviously upon. The "suburbs," the newspapers called them.

This one was in the vicinity of Camberwell, and like so many places south of the Thames it looked as if it could have been a village from anywhere in England—or at least, it would have, if from certain angles one didn't spy the distant loom of the Tower of London.

There was a setter in the front yard of the house where the cab set him down, and Lenox stooped to pet the animal. "Hello, Seamus," he said softly. "Is your master home?"

He needn't have asked. The front door opened, and one of Lenox's oldest acquaintances in the business appeared.

"Why, good morning, Lenox!"

Lenox smiled broadly back. "Hello, Skaggs. Do you have a few minutes?"

"Of course," said Skaggs, and swept an arm open to invite him inside.

Skaggs had once been a boxer—like Jacob Phipps, which perhaps was why he had come to mind the day before. He was of medium height, sturdy, balding, eagle-eyed. He dressed with pointed respectability, and his home showed the prosperity his labors had won him. He was a first-rate detective. Indeed his knowledge of London was probably greater than Lenox's own, at least when it came to the city's concealed places, its secrets and sins. The converse of this was of course that Lenox could comfortably walk the corridors of power.

Skaggs led Lenox into a sitting room decorated in the dark velvet draperies and massive pieces of mahogany furniture that had last been popular in Lenox's world around the 1860s. So taste descended through the classes over time, he reflected.

"Cup of tea?" said Skaggs.

"If it's no trouble?"

"None at all," said Skaggs, and tugged a little proudly at a red velvet bell pull. A maid appeared in a dress starched to the point of implacability. "Tea please, Sarah."

"Right away, sir," said the girl, and was gone as quickly as if her feet had been winged.

Lenox brought out a piece of paper. On the drive here, he had composed a short description. He placed this in front of Skaggs.

"See what you make of that," he said.

Skaggs read it aloud.

SOUGHT: A man somewhere between 5'4" and 5'9". Dark hair, possibly thinning. 170 pounds, solidly built. Former boxer. Works on Blank Dock and perhaps elsewhere on Thames, including Surrey Quay. Possible former Australian transport. Likely to be a native Londoner. May go by Jacob Phipps. May be dangerous. Five pounds to the man who finds him, five pounds also to whomsoever produces him safely at 144 Curl Street, the Strand.

Skaggs looked up at Lenox and whistled. "Ten pounds. That should fetch him, as I'm sure you intended. A former boxer?"

"One of your own."

"Eh," said Skaggs dismissively. "I don't know the name."

Boxing was one of the most popular sports in the city. Skaggs had been a light heavyweight champion in his youth, and his implication was that if Jacob Phipps had been any kind of serious boxer, Skaggs would have heard of him—which was probably true.

"Still, it will mean he's handy with his fists," said Lenox.

"I shall send it out along the usual channels," he said. "*Do* you think he is dangerous?"

"I suppose we must presume that he is. The good news is that I don't think he suspects that anyone is on his trail."

The maid appeared again, holding a lacquered tray in the Japanese style, laden with forget-me-not-patterned crockery. She set it down and poured two cups of tea; Lenox took his with a thanks and tried a sip of the warm brew, which cut comfortably into the cold of the outdoors, lingering on his skin.

"How sure are you of the name?" Skaggs asked, after the maid had gone.

"It's a coin flip. I'm quite sure of the description, and I'm starting to think the man I'm after is Phipps," Lenox said, "but even so I don't know that you can put much stock in the name. I am fairly sure he has been working at Blank Dock, and nobody I spoke to there had heard it. So he may be using an alias. Wonderful tea, Skaggs."

"Ah, thank you, my own favorite. Comes from Assam. India, you know. Do you want to tell me about the case?"

Lenox did, giving Skaggs a brief sketch of the whole business start to finish, going back to the murder of Martell. The old boxer nodded when Lenox mentioned the Coach and Horses—there was no street in London he didn't know pace by pace—and looked grave when Lenox described the vulnerable older woman who had enlisted his help.

After their business was finished, the two caught each other up with news, the kind of frank professional exchange they had been conducting for decades now.

"We had a doctor out here in Sutton," Skaggs told Lenox as he chose a tea biscuit, "who was murdering his patients."

Sutton was a little farther south. Lenox whistled softly. "Good lord. How did I not hear of it?"

"Hushed up. He swallowed a beaker of poison when we found him. Very respectable fellow. Milliken. Had been at the university in Edinburgh."

"How many?"

Skaggs tapped a pile of papers. "I have found seven, but I think there are more."

"I know I have asked this before, Skaggs, but you would not be interested in coming aboard at the agency, would you? No, I see from your face that the answer is still no—say no more."

Lenox took a last sip of tea and picked up his hat. He and Skaggs shook hands. Skaggs had people all over the metropolis—savvy street children, watchful innkeepers, gin-soaked layabouts—and Lenox knew this network would be their best chance of finding Jacob Phipps, if he was there to be found.

Suddenly a tinkle of piano floated down from an upstairs room. Lenox glanced up and Skaggs, who had stared down the most fearsome men in London, blushed. "My daughter," he said.

"Lovely accomplished playing," said Lenox, as the music continued. "Surely that is Bach?"

Skaggs himself had been born on the wrong side of the sheets, in a dark and rat-infested basement near Walworth, one of seven children raised by an aunt and grandmother. He had come far in the world.

"Perhaps so," said Skaggs. "Right proud we are."

The music continued, a variation on the first notes. "You ought to be," said Lenox. He rose from his chair. "Give her my regards. And please let me know when you hear anything, will you?"

On the drive back into London, Lenox looked idly over the menu for that night's supper. Fried soles in tarragon butter sauce, it said, and saddle of mutton with a spicy jam, and a dozen dishes besides. Dessert was to be sponge cake in rum sauce, but Jane had crossed this out, so perhaps it would be a surprise. Then stilton with celery and milk-bread.

A far cry from what Angela and Sari had eaten in India. He sat back and watched the suburbs give way again to busier streets. He loved crossing the river from the south, back into his part of London. Long ago this city only had four parts on maps: this one, then known as Southwark, the City, Westminster (which was the West End, where Lenox lived) and "That Part Beyond the Tower." But modernity was on its quest to name everything for them, these days.

There was a commotion around the bridge—a florist's cart had overturned—and Lenox, his cab paused, examined the city, its inhabitants so wildly occupied, so fully alive, millions of them in their own absorbing stories—from fried soles in tarragon butter sauce to Bach in South London to the lilies strewn over the cobblestones, which would never arrive at their destinations now—and he, quiet at the center of it all, watching.

CHAPTER NINETEEN

The bright day turned into a sparkling London early evening, shafts of pink light brilliantly flaring into gold along the streets, the air cold but clear, the whole city avid with Saturday activity.

Lenox, still attempting to stay out from underfoot, forced himself to address the tottering pile of letters on his desk; he had a supply of stationery in his right-hand drawer and took out a stack. He filled these very swiftly, answering each letter as he opened it. Many of the requests were rather exotic (no, he wrote, he could not travel to Caracas to solve a murder there, but thanked the government for the request) which was a development he attributed to the American case.

But when he heard the first carriage roll up outside, he set down his fountain pen and went into the front hall, knowing that at last he could be of use.

It was not often that Charles and Jane opened their doors to people in any great numbers, and there was tangible excitement in the household. Extra servants had been hired at double pay, the Saturday night rate, most of them from Edmund's house a few streets over. They wore the familiar dark green Lenox livery.

Eight footmen stood outside on the steps in serried order, waiting to assist. Lenox and Lady Jane stepped outside to the top of the steps, where they, too, awaited their first guest, both smiling. His heartbeat was steady; but he remembered the immense stakes of society when he was younger, and thought of Angela and Sari upstairs, donning their new dresses, choosing bracelets and earrings, wondering whom they might meet.

"Only family would arrive exactly on time," Lady Jane murmured, linking her arm in Charles's.

It was true: a small older woman was descending from a tiny white carriage, his elderly cousin, known throughout the family as Aunt Matilda, who had been born Matilda Grace Lenox ninety years and three months before; but was still perfectly sharp.

"Matilda!" said Jane glowingly.

"I'm not deaf," said Matilda, climbing the stairs on the arm of the stoutest of the footmen. "How do you do, how do you— Jane, you do look lovely, that shade of blue suits you perfectly."

Matilda had come in from Shropshire, where she lived, solely to set eyes on the freshly arrived cousin. She would turn back around the next morning and go home, with a prized new correspondent—for Matilda was a voluminous and treasured letter-writer, who still wrote to Charles and Edmund each once a week, as she had ever since they learned to read. She always wrote in the same vivid three-paragraph format: personal status, comment upon some matter of art or politics, and finally what the brothers called "item of family news." This last was often violently exciting, since she knew every bit of gossip from the south coast to Hadrian's Wall.

"Hello, Charlie," she said, accepting a kiss on the cheek. "Will you show me a chair somewhere quiet where I can spend the party? Not in a corner."

He offered his arm, which she took. "We have chosen one already."

"Have you been stabbed again?" she asked as they went inside the house.

"Not in the last fortnight."

"That's something."

He accompanied Matilda to the large sitting room, which was staged for the immense party—but eerily empty now. He fetched her a hot rum with water and brown sugar, the drink he had been making her at family gatherings since he was ten.

"And where is this young Angela?" she asked. "Oh, poor Jasper—he never would write me back."

"Did he not? Not ever?"

"Not since, oh, '65 or so. Though I kept on sending letters." Matilda took a small sip of the drink and smiled. "Ah, that puts the warmth back into me." She focused on Lenox, homing in on him with her clever long-lived gaze. "Tell me, did she say anything of Jasper's life out there?"

Lenox heard a rattle on the cobblestones outside. "I'm awfully sorry, Aunt Matilda," he said, "but I must leave you for a moment. You will have to ask her yourself—she will be down before long."

This second guest was another relative, Jane's tall, young, amiable cousin, Lord Carbury, twenty years old and rather handsome. Also the most dramatically ill-informed person Lenox knew. Jane still called him Georgie in private—often sternly, in recent times, for the reason that he was an extremely eligible bachelor and had used that fact to "tantalize" (Jane's word) dozens of young women across London, in what she considered a most ungentlemanly way. For his part, he told her, he liked every single one of the girls, and what's more couldn't see the point of meeting *fewer* people in the search for the one he would take as his wife before God.

Now he was second at the party, no doubt, Lenox thought, to torment whatever young ladies would be there.

Suddenly it occurred to him that the young lady he wished to glimpse might be Angela, of all people, and for a moment he felt positively angry at the young man.

"Well, Carbury?" he said briskly, taking over for Lady Jane, who was already halfway back to the street to meet the next carriages. It was vital she be there when the Princess arrived. "Overturned any horses today?"

The young lord reddened. "I say, sir, that was when I was only sixteen, you know. A fellow puts one foot wrong and hears about it for the rest of his life!"

Lenox guided him up the stairs. "What will I fix you to drink?"

"Oh, a brandy sir, if you please," said Carbury, who wore a pristine black tailcoat, with a white silk tie so carelessly beautiful that angels might have sewn it. "It would take the edge ever so off. As if I needed to tell you. Goodness. Thank you. And how is my cousin?"

This Carbury said bravely, knowing that he was held in poor regard by Lady Jane just at that moment. "Jane? She is— But there is the door, Carbury, here is your drink, and please excuse me, I shall be back with whoever it is in a moment. Leave the maids alone. Talk to Matilda."

Carbury looked at him wide-eyed, and then glanced over at Matilda on the opposite side of the room. "Oh I say, the maids! Sir, really! I would never—"

"Yes, yes," said Lenox testily.

Soon the carriages multiplied. The footmen were flying up and down the stairs. As for Lenox and Lady Jane, they were constantly shuttling between the sitting room and the street, and always behind in every conversation, as they tried desperately to greet everyone with the same warmth—for it was a parade of their friends, and the women all looked beautiful, carefully brocaded and patterned into their dresses, the cold of the air putting red in their cheeks, while beside them the gentlemen wore cheerful night-out smiles.

There was a brief moment of respite at about ten to eight, and Lenox stood at the top of their steps, breathless, watching the light dazzle and wane in the west, falling through the bare branches of the trees. He had ended up with a whisky and soda, and took a sip. He felt the pleasant stiffness of his shirt at the wrists and collar—a formal feeling.

Just then Toto McConnell came up and surprised him, giving him a squeeze on the forearm. "Hello," she said.

"Oh, hello, Toto!," he said. "I didn't see you arrive. Why have you come back out into the cold?"

Her eyes scanned the street. "Thomas mentioned that he might drop in. I thought I would come and see if he had arrived."

"Not yet."

"No," she said quietly.

There was a pause. At last, Lenox said, "I thought I had grown old enough to witness the changes of young people dispassionately—but I find it jarring that you young women wear jackets now."

She laughed. "It is very good of you to include me among their number, Charles, as I scurry toward forty. I like my jacket, you know."

He shook his head ruefully. "Yes, of course." It was a snug white garment of silk and fur. "Yet you will admit it is awfully modern. I can remember the vast shawls and capes my mother wore to visit in Sussex . . . of course, a winter ball was treacherous in those days, you might have gotten stuck somewhere."

"And it was the country," Toto pointed out.

"Yes, very true. Undeniable." He spotted a new carriage turning up Hampden Lane. "Look, there is my brother."

"Could I have a sip of your drink? I feel I need it if I am to speak with the Prime Minister."

Lenox frowned. "The Prime Minister?"

"Look."

And there, indeed, was the seal of the office, whipping raggedly in the wind. It had to travel along in any conveyance a Prime Minister took, from ships of state down to Edmund's carriage.

Toto rarely drank much, but she took a good swig of his whisky and soda. "Your cousins shall have something to write back to India about their first party, anyhow. Perhaps Gladstone will lecture at them about the constitution and all that dry old— Hello, Prime Minister!"

CHAPTER TWENTY

Lenox, too, greeted the former Prime Minister and Edmund, and with a smile on his face—for he was genuinely happy to see his brother.

The pair politely and formally said hello, Gladstone sociable in his usual severe way. Edmund distractedly said they would be a few minutes while they discussed something.

"Would you like to use my study?" Lenox asked.

The wind was whipping along into them, and Gladstone already had his coat pulled tight with his gloved hands. "A highly eligible idea," he said. "Much obliged, Lenox minor."

After seeing them into his study, Lenox went back to the party, which was growing into its shape. The tenor of the room rose a notch when Edmund arrived in the sitting room with Gladstone fifteen minutes later—still, familiar as he was to many of them, the Prime Minister himself, after all—and then inflected further still when Princess Alexandra arrived.

Lenox saw her coming from the tall half-circle windows that overlooked Hampden Lane from the second floor. She leapt nimbly from her carriage, and was up the stairs before poor Jane even had a chance to realize she was there.

This was her style—spontaneous, buccaneering. She came in with Jane, dressed both expensively and nakedly, as Jane Austen had put it, in a pink and blue dress cut in at the waist, calculated to look a bit outrageous. She accepted Charles's hand with a curtsy and received the bow of the former Prime Minster with equal brevity, and then of all thirty or so other people in the room gladly and intimately, with a small laugh, before retiring as quickly as possible to a corner where she could be with her particular friends.

Angela and Sari came down at the appointed hour, seven o'clock. There was an instant of hush at their appearance, too, and then a sudden renewal of every conversation at a louder pitch, out of courtesy.

Charles studied them for a moment. Of the two, Sari was infinitely easier to speak with; Angela was at times almost obstinately unwilling to converse. Her long blond hair concealed her face when she wished. Privately, Lady Jane had expressed some worry about the girl, who was perhaps not beautiful enough to be plucked immediately from the harrowing battlefield of the ballroom, nor social enough to conquer the mothers and aunts sitting on the sidelines at such gatherings. What would become of her?

Lenox had not yet told Jane of the additional difficulty: that Angela wasn't interested in marriage to begin with.

"You both look wonderful," Lenox said to them in a quiet voice, guiding them into the room. "Don't be nervous—only friends here, and to begin with you must come and meet Aunt Matilda, who has traveled expressly to meet you. She loved Jasper."

Sari's eyes widened. She put a gloved hand on Angela's forearm. "Not Aunt Matilda? We have read her letters for a decade!"

Angela looked too intimidated to speak, but nodded happily. She had a pink streak in each cheek, a look of curiosity. She was dressed in black, of course, while Sari wore a demure pearl-white bombazine gown, woven with a gray mourning ribbon.

Matilda's celebrity with the girls—Jasper had forbidden them to write back, Sari said, or they would have answered every letter!—

smoothed the way into their conversation. Another cousin approached them, and Dallington, who happened to be entering the room where they stood near the door, met them, too, so that soon four or five people were standing there, one of the many small groups in the room.

It was Dallington, with his impeccable manners, who addressed Sari directly for the first time.

"How was the passage from India?" he asked.

Sari glanced at her friend. "The seasickness wasn't bad after the first six weeks," she said, and smiled at Angela, shrugging.

Angela broke into her shy smile, and a little laugh rippled across the group, even to Aunt Matilda, whom Lenox had watched teeter on the edge of disapproval. It was by no means certain that a woman with brown skin could win her approval.

At about eight o'clock the room attained its fullness, and the door to the small card room was opened. One young couple immediately took themselves to a sofa there, where they could linger with only partial parietal supervision. The princess was surrounded by enough close friends that Lady Jane had been able to return to her duties.

Lenox was downstairs for a goodish period around this time. "No sign of Thomas?" Lady Jane asked him as they passed in the hall.

Lenox's mind was on McConnell, too, even as he returned with two new guests to the party. By now Sari and Matilda were deep in conversation, each of them utterly intent on everything the other said.

As for Angela, she was occupied with young Lord Carbury.

Lenox made a beeline across the room—breaking off a conversation rather shortly, if kindly, with an older gentleman he in fact greatly esteemed, the grave and noted economist Lord Blakely—to where the two youths were speaking.

To his surprise, Angela had a broad smile on her face.

"Hello, George," he said to Carbury. "Angela, how are you?"

She held up a glass goblet of white tiger's milk, Jane's famous punch. Ah—so perhaps that was the source of the gaiety.

"I think this is the nicest thing I ever tasted, Cousin," she said. "Don't you adore coconut? George has kindly offered to get me a second."

Lenox turned a hard look on Carbury. "Has he."

"I said it was good to load one or two in at the front to get rid of your nerves," said Carbury quickly.

At that moment Lady Jane, too, arrived at the scene. She gave her young cousin a withering look, and then took Angela by the hand, saying, "Come along, dear."

Lenox turned his attention back to young Carbury. "She is not available."

"I was only being friendly! You have my word, I am not pursuing her. I should tell you very frankly if I was. London is covered in girls."

Lenox frowned. "I know how you rush at them, George."

Carbury smiled. I cannot apologize for that. Rome was built in a day, as they say."

"Rome was what?"

Carbury tapped his nose to show that it was a bit of wisdom he had picked up. "That's what they say—Rome was built in a day."

Lenox frowned. "It's that Rome *wasn't* built in a day, Georgie. Was *not*."

Carbury looked at him oddly. "Why would they make a saying of that? You could say that of any city."

"Because—"

"Think it through," he said in a sympathetic voice, as you might to an ancient but good-hearted schoolmaster. "London wasn't built in a day. Imagine if that was a saying. Manchester wasn't built in a day."

"It's—"

"Liverpool wasn't built in day. Took years. There's no sense in even mentioning it. Of course it took years. All those cities took years."

Lenox started to answer, then thought better of it. "Whereas Rome was built in a day."

"Yes, by Romulus and Remus. Twins, you know. Dashed efficient ones, from the sound of it."

"Don't bother Angela."

"Oh, I say!"

"George, please tell me you understand."

"Oh, fine. But I say, it is unjust. She is so jolly interesting, and I approached her entirely as a friend, you know. In the warmest and most welcoming spirit I—"

Lenox left to the diminishing sound of the young lord's protestations. The drinking hour reaching its crescendo, he stole into the dining room, which he liked to see standing in uninhabited preparation. The two long tables were covered with a dazzle of silver: berry bowls, butter dishes, salt cellars, spoon holders, decanters, cruets, and of course the neatly laid out triads of forks and knives at each place. Crystal glasses caught the light. And hothouse flowers stood in slender vases, adding a spill of vermillion and orange to the beautiful geometry of the tables.

Lenox heard the door open and saw his brother ease in behind him. "Hullo, Ed."

Edmund looked at the table, frowning. "Why do we have an ice cream fork?"

"I haven't put the whole thing together yet but I suspect we're having ice cream."

Edmund rolled his eyes. "I just meant that Jane never serves it— Ah, but perhaps Angela likes ice cream. Or Sari. Anyhow I came in, Charles, if you must know, to ask you about the extremely delicate questions of precedence involving the PM and Her Highness. It's the kind of innate tact that has vaulted me into the very highest and most trusted circles of—"

"Oh lord."

"Of government and society, and— Oh, there's the bell for dinner. Well, sod it, I suppose. Jane will know what to do."

"That sentiment has carried me through any number of situations."

"Don't I know it."

CHAPTER TWENTY-ONE

Charles and Lady Jane stood at the doorway between the drawing room and the dining room. The Princess entered first, then Gladstone with the Princess's friend and cousin, Lady Emily Roth.

Lenox looked over the drawing room. Angela and Edmund were in conversation. A pair of Honourable Gentlemen in the corner had temporarily suspended a furious argument about taxation to watch the entrance into dinner. And young Carbury had actually stuck by Matilda, Lenox saw with a pang of conscience at his harshness toward the boy, and had to cross the room to find his partner, a pretty and well-born young lady from Hampshire that Jane thought his equal in both eligibility and diffidence.

Lady Jane and Lenox were the last to enter. Soon they were all seated, and the servants began pouring champagne into the flutes at each place.

Lenox was the anchor of one table. Jane was at the other with Princess Alexandra; meanwhile Lenox had Sari to his right and Angela to his left, with Edmund and Gladstone forming a rump state toward the end of the table with a lively young countess who was part of the Princess's chamber.

Sari was more accustomed to the silverware than Angela was, he noticed; or perhaps just more observant of what others were doing.

They fell naturally to talking and she began by telling Lenox more deeply and frankly about their trip from Bombay. He listened with great absorption as the first courses came and went.

"The hardest part . . . it will sound so silly, so girlish, but the cold—I don't think either Angela or I, even with the period at sea, which, as I have explained, passed in sickness and anxiety—I don't think either of us expected a winter like this to greet us. Not that we had not read of snow and bare trees. But you have no conception of what a cold day in India means—how golden warm it would be to the warmest hour I have had since I have been here!"

He saw something crestfallen flash briefly through her.

"But you are young," he said gently. "You will adjust."

"Yes—I feel it already. Or perhaps that is just the joy of being at such a party as this."

"And one day, if you wish to, you shall return to India, whether for a month or a lifetime. This is not forever either."

She glanced at him soberly. "But from what I gather, you, too, have had a painful trip overseas recently."

"Oh, not so bad," he said. He thought to change the subject; but then, suddenly, said to himself that if this girl was to be family to him, why ought he not to repay her candor with his own? And he realized something larger in that moment: how much he liked and trusted this brave young woman, his cousin's bosom friend. "Or, I suppose, fairly bad, in all truth."

"What happened?"

"I went to America last spring. I was thrilled to be going, though I knew how much I would miss Jane and the girls. Still, I had dreamed of visiting since I was a very young boy. But my plans to travel elsewhere among the States were almost instantly derailed by a case in a seaside town called Newport. Perhaps you have heard of it. No? No matter. I was there several weeks. Eventually I was able to solve it, but

I was—hurt, in the process. Stabbed. I have not been quite myself since."

"I credit you for being so considerate of us since our arrival! But how have you not been yourself?" she asked.

Lenox was caught by the question. How!

A hundred thoughts crystallized in his mind instantly. Perhaps it was the slightly surreal event of the party that made it seem like he was considering the question for the first time. The first plates were being taken away, and what in Lenox's boyhood had been called the flying dishes, oysters and red mullet, placed around the table in small silver bowls. He looked down at the piece of bread in his hand, thinking of how to answer the girl.

Even to Jane he had not been able to express it all, no, nor half of it even: the days during this convalescence when even with the best intentions for action he had been unable to rouse himself to aught but lingering in the long armchair in his study, dozing fitfully over some harmless novel. The involuntary idleness had shamed him; the powerlessness had scared him; and above all, the ongoingness of it, day after bright summer day, had wearied his mind, his body—his soul.

He was conscious that Sari had resumed talking, and forced his mind to click back a few moments to collect what she had been saying.

"Is the wound healed—yes, it is much better, thank you. Though if I stay out in the cold it does act tiresome."

At that instant the fowl course came, with lightly cooked asparagus and peas set in Dorsetshire dishes beside them, and the conversation just around Lenox and Sari became general.

He joined in sportingly for his part, yet as the dinner passed, Lenox always felt just slightly separate from it all; the shine of the silver and crystal, the thrum of the voices, the intensity of people's interest in what they were saying and hearing.

It was a feeling adjacent to despair: all the things for which he had once cared so effortlessly—society, friendship, art, crime—seemed pale and inconsequential from behind the veil of ill health, not because he cared so much about himself, or was indifferent to others—but because so little of his mind or energy was left to him these days for more than survival. After all these months of striving simply to stay upright, to march forward, to keep up his good cheer for his girls, as his eyes tugged down in tiredness, as hot icicles darted in and out of the muscles near his ribs—as sleep beckoned him always, the one sure retreat from sorrow.

Only the walking had really strengthened his body. When he was pushed to the brink of sanity by another sleepless night, a long walk could subdue that devil. The walking, and yes, perhaps Sven and his regime. Even still, he lagged his old self. He looked at Dallington halfway down the table and felt a pang of guilt.

He shook his head sharply and forced himself into the present moment. The dinner was an obvious success. No patches of slow conversation at either of the tables, no blazing arguments, and spirits were high. A royal did that. Even the most battered and immune old social warrior liked to say they had dined with a Princess—and if Lenox didn't quite approve of such snobbery, in the final analysis it was of course none of his business. He was only the host of the party.

As subtly as he could, he took a deep, steadying breath, then set about making himself pleasant to old Gladstone, who was slowly chewing his food, and occasionally shedding upon the conversation the powerful lamplight of some brilliant insight.

The Princess was famous for taking it upon herself to switch seats at least once during a supper out, and when dessert was served about an hour later she did this, wordlessly and elegantly indicating to Gladstone to swap with her. He obliged, delighting the table that had missed out on his company thus far, and the dinner crested to a triumphant roar with the arrival of huge mounds of vanilla-flecked ice cream on Jane's old family salvers, from which everyone dug away an iceberg for themselves.

As they ate, Jane raised her glass and offered a short welcoming address to Sari and Angela, who had specifically mentioned that they were curious to try ice cream, as she wittily recounted; then Edmund rose and proposed a toast to the health of the Queen; and some time later, at last, perhaps two and a half hours after they had sat down to eat, they all went through to the hallway. The gentlemen stood talking amiably and watched the ladies' skirts disappear upstairs, before proceeding to the smoking room.

The traditional break between the sexes would on this evening last only thirty minutes, as was Jane's rather liberal policy. But it was incumbent upon the men to join the ladies, and as Lenox saw his male guests pouring brandies and lighting cigars, he knew from long London experience that at least half the gentlemen here would not move from their seats again until they were rumbled into their carriages by their coachmen.

He was finally able to catch a word with Dallington, with whom he had been hoping to speak all evening.

"There you are, John," he said. "Tell me, before someone interrupts us, are you familiar with those opium dens over by Bluegate Fields? In and around the Duke of Albany pub."

"Yes indeed," said the young lord. "I had to chase Charity Mandel-Joselow down there, if you remember that case. She was half gone on the stuff. Guilt over murdering her brother."

"That would do it," said Lenox. "As irritating as Edmund can be. Listen—do you want to come there with me tomorrow? It has been years since I ventured into those streets, and I should be glad of a companion. Though I can ask Montague if you prefer."

But Dallington had always been physically brave. "What! It is no place to be wandering about alone—no, of course I shall come. What time?"

"That sets my mind at ease. About noon? By the way, I like young Montague, a promising specimen. In fact, he is over on Conduit Street for me even as we speak."

"I like him, too. By the way, between us I looked over at her during supper and wondered if your cousin were perhaps a bit overawed. I may be mistaken. Her friend is thriving."

"Sari, yes," said Lenox. "But I hope Angela is, too?"

"I'm sure she is," said Dallington. "I only wonder how she is acclimating—to come here after a life in India and immediately be thrust like Cinderella into a party for princesses and prime ministers . . . I shouldn't know what to think. But all you Lenoxes are so strong."

CHAPTER TWENTY-TWO

The first person to leave the party was Gladstone. When he was gone Kirk informed Lenox that his three personal guards had eaten twelve chops and drunk thirty glasses of ale in the basement. Well, he and Jane could do their bit for the nation.

Upstairs, everyone looked as if they were settling in for a merry evening except Aunt Matilda, who was departing early, the privilege of age.

"It was a splendid supper," Matilda told him, fastening the delicate pearl buttons of her ancient black cloak. "Except for it being such a gathering of the Whigs."

"Matilda," he said reproachfully.

She was herself a dyed-in-the-wool Tory—that is, she was what once had been called a Tory, until the '30s, when the parties had still been the Whigs and the Tories, now, respectively, the liberals and the conservatives. Her actual political views were few, but she associated her party with the red-cheeked, roast beef, sporting Englishman her father had been—never mind that he had been into the wine, Lenox could recall his own father saying, the moment the last spoon at breakfast had been set down. To her, Gladstone, with his head for numbers and coolly deliberative manner, was an example of everything wrong with the other side. It mattered nothing to her that Charles and Edmund were of his party—nor that, as Charles had often told her, he had rarely seen a more complete gathering of nincompoops than the Tories currently in Parliament, not above one or two of whom fulfilled Matilda's chivalrous notion of the type.

Not that the liberals were much better on the whole! Neither was a collection of men to be idealized, he reflected, helping his aged relative downstairs—sadly, for the nation. The best defense of them all was perhaps that the general standard of intelligence and manners in the House of Lords was lower still.

"What do you make of Jasper's daughter?" he asked Matilda as he guided her down the hallway toward the front door.

"It doesn't matter in the slightest what I *think* of her, as you put it," said Matilda. "She is our cousin. But I will tell you that her little friend is a gem. Here we are—let us brave the cold! You are young, it needn't bother you."

Lenox, grateful that someone still considered him young, deposited his cousin with a kiss into her tiny carriage, with the fur blanket on its bench; and promised to look out for her letter by the next day's first post.

He was returning to the party when he heard, in the general conversation, his cousin Angela, more animated than he had ever known her yet.

He turned to see who had elicited this note of freedom and happiness in her voice, which he himself had been trying to coax out since that day on the dock, and saw that it was Edmund, of all people. Lenox frowned—what could Edmund have said that was so entertaining? He glanced between them, and looking at Angela, for just a second, by the timeless light of the candles and the fireplace, he saw Jasper complete: above all else, the large, wide-set, luminous eyes, full of innocence.

Lenox crossed to the pair, who were by the fireplace. Sir Edmund was jotting down something on a piece of paper on the mantel.

"What has left you two so mirthful?" the younger brother asked.

"We were going over sums," said Edmund.

"Sums?" said Charles.

"Yes. These are the total herring catch by coastal county."

"Is this subject of interest to you?" Lenox asked Angela, eyes wide with surprise.

"A great deal! Indeed, Edmund has said I may visit him in Parliament on Monday and look through all the books myself."

"She has a remarkable head for numbers," said Edmund, beaming.

Lenox did not find another moment to breathe until nearly eleven o'clock, when finally the high hum of the party diminished into the noise of several softer, longer conversations, and a few more bodies began to leave. Crossing the hall back to the sitting room after seeing one of Jane's nieces off, he heard, "Sir, sir!" behind him.

He turned and saw one of the footmen. "Yes?"

"Note for you, sir. Left by the door."

Lenox glanced over at the clock on the wall. It was long since the last post. He took the envelope with a thanks and tore it open, hoping it was from Montague; throughout the evening, some part of his mind had remained over at the greenhouse.

But the note was not from Montague. It was unsigned, and bore only four words, written in a crude scrawl.

Your Jane better stop

He felt his heart begin to thump in his neck. He felt the paper crumple in his fist without realizing that he had been clenching it.

Stop? Stop what?

"James!" he called sharply behind the retreating footman.

James turned back, and hearing Lenox's thunderous tone tried to conceal his high spirits—it had been a thrilling workday, after all—beneath a serious face.

"Sir?"

"Who gave you that note?"

"Oh, sir—the bell was rung and it was there on the ledge with no one about, sir," cried the young man quickly. "By the time I got there at least, sir."

"Thank you."

Lenox stood alone in the hall for a few moments, methodically working through the possible authors of the note. It was addressed to him, he observed in the coolly mechanical part of his mind, not to Jane.

His mind traveled down several paths but he could not find a way to make Jacob Phipps the sender of the note. Someone from the opium dens? That would have been frightening, except he was nearly certain he recognized the rude scrawl of a London grammar school Englishman, or was all but sure he did, after two decades of studying his countrymen's writing.

He went down to the street. He had fetched their police whistle from inside and blew it three times.

It was only a moment or two before Watson, their local constable, appeared. He was a stout, light-mustached person of twenty-five or so. He looked just like a fellow named Exeter that Lenox had once known.

"Mr. Lenox?" he called when he was still some twenty yards off. "All well at the party?"

Lenox lifted a hand to him and waited. A few flurries had begun to fall from the sky. "Hello, Watson—could you please take this over to the Square and give it to the fellow in charge."

Watson read the note, as Lenox had indicated he should, and his eyes widened. "Straightaway, sir."

There was a police stand on Grosvenor Square, where several officers were always stationed. "I would be happier if someone looked down the street regularly tonight. I shall tell the staff to set double locks and extra lights outside."

"No one will get in, sir," said Watson, nodding. "Let me run back to the Square." He paused. "Sir, is it true Princess Alexandra was here tonight?"

"Yes, but I don't think this involves her."

Lenox hadn't needed to clarify that the Princess was safe, though, he saw after answering—it was the celebrity of the thing that interested Watson. "Very good, sir. Someone will be back shortly. Should have been here anyway." He glanced at the carriages.

"You can report back downstairs. Speak with Kirk—he will tell me the news. I have these guests to see to. Thank you, Watson, thank you very much."

Lenox went through the next hour on reflexes, his mind only on the note; he embarked upon no new conversations, only rounding off old ones with goodbyes.

Two of the very last people at the party were Sir Edmund Lenox and young Angela. They were just by the mantel where Lenox had left them counting herring earlier. Carbury was lingering nearby, laughing along with them when he understood what they were saying—three sheets to the wind.

"Hullo, Charles!" said Edmund, who his brother knew from his voluble cheerfulness had also drunk a bit too much wine. "I am due back in Parliament, damn the place. But sometimes the call to conversation of a relative requires—no, commands"—he hiccupped twice, behind his short brown beard—"the delay of other plans, however crucial they may—"

"You are tipsy, brother," said Lenox, smiling.

"I resemble that!" said Edmund, and his eyes narrowed as he laughed at his own wit, banging the mantel lightly with a fist.

Angela was looking at them both with curiosity, a little stupefied by drink herself. Lady Jane had come from across the room.

"Where has Sari gone?" Angela asked her.

"Sari went to bed an hour ago, dear," she said. "And so should you do. Here is the maid to take you upstairs—thank you, Ginny—Charles, get your brother a glass of cold water. Edmund, one of your young men is down in the billiards room. He will take your legless inebriate self to a carriage—"

"Oh, Jane! The unfairness of that!" cried Edmund.

Jane was giving Angela a squeeze as she guided her and the maid toward the door. "And, Charles, I would like to speak to you," she said over her shoulder.

He recognized urgency in her voice, though it remained mild. He wondered why. "Of course," he said.

"It really is unfair," Edmund said, shaking his head and setting down his glass. Gladstone would not lay eyes on him till late morning—that much Charles knew for a fact, having been his brother all his life. "I had just been thinking what a jolly party it was, too."

CHAPTER TWENTY-THREE

The hosts of the party met again, alone, in the front hallway, Lenox coming back inside from seeing off his brother's carriage.

"Hello, darling," she said, taking off her gloves. "There is something I must tell you before someone else does."

"Is everything all right?"

She stared at him levelly. Her pink and lavender dress showed her shoulders to advantage; she looked particularly becoming, he thought.

"Yes, though you won't like it. I went out to protest last Sunday from noon to two, along with three other women—Mary Evans, Rachel McCarthy, and Lady Tifton. I intend to do the same again tomorrow."

"To protest."

"We sat by Westminster Abbey and held up our signs for about ninety minutes, from half twelve until two o'clock. Then we left."

He didn't say anything; they held each other's eyes.

"I didn't think I would be recognized," she admitted. "I dressed inconspicuously and wore my low black hat."

"But?"

Lady Jane's gloves were off and she held the pair in her right hand, loose at her side. She looked away. "Now I know I was. Toto told me tonight that she heard it from Diana Cullen that I was there."

"Oh, Jane." A penny dropped. "A young man mentioned it to me at the gymnastiksaal yesterday, too—Jane!"

A look of fury passed over her imperturbable face. "Aren't you going to ask what we were protesting, Charles?"

"Jane—"

"Because you know full well, you know very, very well—"

"But, Jane—"

"Jane what!"

They were both shocked by the harshness of her voice, and stood there for a moment. Two maids were coming in from the back hall, carrying pails of ashes from the fireplaces, and their eyes went wide. They turned immediately and left.

Jane, trembling slightly, gave him a look of loathing, then stalked off.

He called after her, but she didn't look back. He stood in the hallway, stunned. Around him various half-familiar servants from Edmund's house and thoroughly familiar ones from his own moved the house back into its customary shape, under Kirk's gaze. At length, he retreated to his study.

The idea of women voting was not new. Indeed, it had been a subject of dining-table discussion for Lenox's entire lifetime. It had even come up for vote in Parliament in 1871, losing by seventy-odd votes—though many of the yeses, it was said, were symbolic, and would have turned to nos if defeat had not been assured.

What was new—what was radical of Lady Jane, in a way that worried Lenox down to his bones, a feeling the anonymous letter seemed to vindicate—was the idea of protest. After the Chartists and the Revolutions of 1848, public protest of all kinds was a subject of terror in England. Especially within their class. It was still less than a century since the beheadings in France, after all.

In 1869 there had been a first protest by women in favor of voting rights—so shocking it made the newspaper headlines for weeks. Since then there had been scattered protests here and there by the tiny group of passionate, ardent—many of Lenox's acquaintances would say *deranged*—women who wrote the pamphlets and petitioned Parliament. They met with almost universal disapproval.

As she would readily admit, Jane had been radicalized by having their daughters. Just the week before she had asked him, "Do you mean to tell me that in your view those boys from number fourteen are smarter than our Clara, or Sophia?"

This was a low blow. The three boys who lived four doors down at 14 Hampden Lane, Otis, Winston, and Gerald, were mean-spirited mean-faced little heirs. Their breathtakingly dissolute father was the holder of the Falmouth lordship, which was attached to a boggy parcel of land in distant Northumberland that no Falmouth had visited for anything other than legal reasons in centuries. The boys were all at Tonbridge. They had vile reputations up and down Hampden Lane.

By contrast, of course, Lenox's daughters were to his eyes like two stars plucked down from the firmament.

"I do not disagree in the slightest that women's education—"

"But not the vote?" Lady Jane had said.

"Yes, the vote, too!" For he had always supported the vote for women, mildly and now more surely. But to protest! Socially it would have consequences for her, a fact he felt some sorrow over, for he knew that despite her imperturbable air, she cared about her friendships.

He took a notebook from his top drawer and fetched his cloak and heavy hat and mittens down from the stand. He looked at the fire and the liquor stand next to them with a little regret. His side twinged, and he felt some longing for that armchair. His ribs hurt. He thought perhaps he just ought to go to bed.

Then he remembered Edmund, up every night till four plotting the future of the nation, and went into the hallway.

"Kirk, what is the weather?" he said.

"Starting to sleet, sir. A constable is stationed outside, sir, I was asked to inform you."

"Yes, I know. Check all the doors and windows again, please." Kirk was used to this injunction from his long service in the house of a detective and inclined his head in a nod. "Did you survive the party? And the staff?"

"It went very well, sir. They are eating family supper now, sir."

"Good. I shall be out. In fact, if Jane asks I shall be out rather late."

Lenox went out into the cold street. He touched his hat to the constable and paused outside his carriage to tell the coachman his destination was the Coach and Horses. There was a hot stone at the foot of the backseat, and Lenox warmed his legs against it.

It already seemed like days and days since he had said goodbye to Aunt Matilda at just this spot. The cold made the lights flicker harder; and as they started along, the noise of the rough cobblestones, bearing him once more into the path of adventure, was like a half-attended conversation with a very old friend. He didn't know what to think about what Jane had told him. He didn't like that it had been a secret. He was hurt. But there was work ahead, and he steadied himself to doing it.

CHAPTER TWENTY-FOUR

*E*ARL'S DAUGHTER GRANDSTANDS FOR LADY VOTE!
That was the headline in one paper the next morning. They looked it over at breakfast, at which Angela did not appear at all, and Sari only briefly, shading her eyes, to fetch two plates of food. Lenox told them the maid might have done it, but Sari wanted to choose for Angela, who she said had what Jasper had used to call "a morning noggin"—and said it so ingenuously, in her British-Indian accent, that Charles could not help but laugh.

Now it was Jane and Lenox alone again, she at her correspondence, he reading the damned article.

"Were you really in rational dress?" Lenox asked.

Lady Jane did not look up from the note she was writing. "Don't be absurd."

Charles read aloud from the article that Lady Jane, as if she were the detective herself, had arranged to be brought to her at its first printing at five that morning.

"*Lady Jane Lenox, wife of former Liberal MP for Stirrington Charles Lenox*—well, they act as if Disraeli himself weren't in favor of the vote—*appeared yesterday in Trafalgar Square in a protest designed to menace public traffic and threaten the safe conduct of people through this busy thoroughfare—"*

"Rank editorializing," said Lady Jane, still without looking up.

She was writing thank-you notes. They would be in the hands of the partygoers that afternoon. By her side were two triangles of toast with marmalade, from which she occasionally took a small bite, and a strong cup of tea.

They had not discussed the protest, but her presence here, when she would normally have written these letters in her morning room, seemed like an offer of truce.

Lenox had only arrived home at daybreak. No one had appeared at Conduit Street. But he had gotten to know Montague better, and they had discussed the case so thoroughly that Lenox now had the encouraging feeling that two minds were master of its details.

"Along with three other women, including Mary, daughter of Sir Lucas Evans. Appearing in rational dress, the highborn women, lending their credibility to the vile rabble-rousing of the spinster aunts of Clapham—"

At last Lady Jane looked up, indignant. "That is an unforgivably rude way to refer to those women."

"I agree."

"I was wearing a coat, anyhow" she went on. Her expression showed frustration, not anger. "I suppose it must have been taken for something else, though they would have had to be nearly blind—"

"I'm sorry," Lenox said gravely, and steadied his tired eyes on her. "I'm sorry that—well, that we argued, I suppose."

She looked at him a little dryly. "Thank you."

He knew how the issue of the vote pressed upon Lady Jane's mind. She read about it tirelessly, and had exchanged letters with two of the women of Seneca Falls; word had been trickling back to England that the new country was well in advance of the old one, a reversal of roles from the issue of slavery—to which Jane's more radical readings, which she often spoke aloud from to Charles, compared the status of women.

He read the end of the article aloud. *"Besides her close connection to Sir Edmund Lenox, Lady Lenox is also an intimate of several of the ladies of Marlborough House; whether they tolerate a socialist Radical in their midst remains, though one would hope not for long, an open question."*

Jane did not bother looking up for that, and Lenox was left to mull over his eggs, setting the paper aside, while the scratch of her pen filled the room. There was a beautiful slant of light through the trees, and for a second he felt still and peaceful, and remembered that none of these little squabbles of the world mattered much. Not so long as they were healthy and safe.

"We had a disturbing letter last night," he said, with a heavy heart.

She looked up at him. "A letter?"

"An unsigned note, telling me to keep you at home. Or else."

He watched her face closely, and saw that the threat affected her; it scared her. "Nonsense, I'm sure. You have had fifty notes like that one."

"Maybe not fifty," he said. He reached out for her forearm and held it. "I do wonder who recognized you."

She stood up, taking a bunch of letters in her hand. "It shall not deter the four of us from going out again, that is certain."

"I wonder," Lenox murmured, "if it might have been someone *at* the newspaper. Otherwise how could they have known so early? I can send Montague to—"

"Did you hear me, Charles!"

He looked up. "Yes, I did," he said. "I do not think you should go. I think you shall attract more ridicule for your persons than attention for your ideas—and selfishly, I would not wish you exposed to that."

"You don't understand," she said, and shook free of his hand.

She stood there for a moment, eyes to the side, holding her letters. She wore a high neckline and choker in the style, indeed, of Marlborough House and Princess Alexandra, its royal resident. She looked beautiful, Lenox thought, and perhaps rather modern for his old-fashioned eyes.

"Well, I love you," he said.

She looked at him angrily. "Oh, yes, thank you."

"What else can I say!"

She stared at him for a moment. "How is your wound?" she asked, finally.

"Not so bad." He rose. "I will dine with Montague tonight and decide whether one of us needs to stay at Conduit Street again. Mrs. Huggins is at her nephew's house. Perhaps I may stay. I think the intruder is getting more desperate."

"Did it occur to you the nephew might be involved?" she said to him, still a little crossly. "Ernest, was it?"

He laughed and kissed her cheek. "I considered it, believe it or not," he said. "This is not my first case."

"Will you be home for the girls' bedtime?"

"Maybe so. I will go kiss them in the nursery now in case I am not."

She looked at him searchingly for a moment, then sighed. "I have a thousand things to do—be safe, Charles," she said. "It is London after all."

"I would say the same to you."

CHAPTER TWENTY-FIVE

That night at seven, Lenox dined at the Coach and Horses. The special of the night was eels and duff. Lenox thanked Ernest for the recommendation but ordered roast beef with potatoes and peas instead, and, taking the mustard pot with him to a corner of the bar far from the hearth and the Passenger, spent a happy half hour eating his supper and reading the newspaper. He had made up his mind to stay the night in Conduit Street, in case the intruder returned.

"Dessert?" asked Huggins as he took Lenox's empty plate, its fork and knife neatly lain across it. "There's plum pudding."

"No, thank you," said Lenox.

"Jam roly-poly?"

"No, thank you."

Ernest Huggins looked at him with the most real consternation he had displayed since their first meeting. "Lemon tart in vanilla whipping cream?"

"Just a cup of coffee, please—that is all."

Huggins shook his head, as if to say people still surprised him after all this time, and then, turning his huge frame toward the kitchen, said, "Coming up."

It was a silvery winter night, cold and wolf-black in the shadows.

At eight fifteen Lenox crossed the street from the warm light of the Coach and Horses and remarked how very empty it was, the shops shuttered and anyone with a fire to be by sticking near it.

He found Montague in the entryway. "Anything?"

The young detective shook his head. "No."

"Thank you—go have your night off."

Montague touched his hat. "Thank you, sir. My wife and I have tickets to the theater."

Lenox smiled. "We'll speak in the morning."

Montague had been sitting in a little nook built into the lobby, perhaps for a concierge in some other time. There was a chair with a cushion on it, borrowed from Mrs. Huggins's apartment, and a small kerosene lamp.

Lenox had brought all his notes from the case and spent twenty minutes or so concentrating them into a single document.

Then he fell asleep. He hadn't planned on it, and when he woke it was with a guilty start. He poured himself a cup from the flask of black tea Kirk had packed him, and, circling its warmth with his hand, stepped out into the street.

The cold stung his tired face, not unpleasantly. A few more lights had come on. A brothel, remnant of a less gentrified time in Conduit Street's history, Martell's time, was the busiest place up or down the street, including the pub. Two women stood outside of it in heavy coats with bare legs, smoking and laughing loudly. Otherwise it was quiet. The moon had risen, and stood solitary, two-thirds its whole self, behind branches of thin cloud.

Jane had changed their lives, he thought. And he feared that she did not comprehend it, having never been in the public eye, as he had. Much less in the halls of Parliament and the gentlemen's clubs and the other places where men gathered by themselves, and spoke in a way he was quite, quite sure she could not imagine, however sophisticated she might believe herself. Now some of those words would come for her.

When his tea was gone, he went back inside. He and Montague had decided to remove the light from the entryway, to give the burglar the illusion of a clear field, and it was pitch-dark in the entryway. He turned on the discreet kerosene lamp to have its light once more.

He began reading—and then realized simultaneously in the tiniest fraction of a second that he must have fallen asleep again and that something had just awoken him—but was it someone—where was he?—and then he was fully awake, and understood it all.

There was a scratching noise at the door.

He stayed as still as he could. From the light he guessed it must be past midnight. *King Lear* lay in his lap with his thumb between two pages, and he closed it as quietly as possible and laid it down. He waited for another sound.

After an agonizing moment there was a hard shove on the door. It stood firm. Lenox stood, grasping for his blackjack, a short club of hard metal sheathed in leather, with a loop at the handle for the wrist.

The thief tried the door again. This time the doorknob splintered away, and the fellow's momentum brought him in, a triumphant look gleaming on his face in the kerosene lamplight. He was holding a knife.

He was a stocky, dark-complexioned man, with curls of dark hair emerging from under a navy-colored seaman's cap. Was it Jacob Phipps after all? Same height, same muscular build. Small tattoo on the webbing between his left thumb and forefinger—that was new.

The man saw Lenox, and there was a frozen moment as they stared at each other.

Taking advantage of their positions, Lenox reached out and drew the door inward sharply, which pulled the intruder inside a step more, pulled him off his balance.

"Put down the knife!"

But the fellow was quick on his feet, and leapt back, a snarling look on his face.

The detective's heart raced. They stood two feet apart, Lenox readying himself. "Jacob Phipps?" he said.

The man cocked his head infinitesimally, as if surprised. Then he lunged forward with the knife, and Lenox prepared to meet his end: fighting.

But at that moment, from behind the man, emerged a towering figure—who hooked the thief's arm in his and deftly bludgeoned the knife away, sending it caroming into the street behind them.

It was all very clear and still to Lenox somehow; the rain poured down, and across the street a figure flashed by the building under an umbrella. The streetlights looked unnaturally bright against the dark violet-gray sky, casting everything in sallow London yellow, and Lenox could see the faces of both men.

"Skaggs!"

The thief was fighting like a tiger against Skaggs—but he was a full head shorter, and not much younger, and Skaggs was already subduing him.

Lenox breathed hard, collecting himself. How could it not be Jacob Phipps? The description looked more exact the more Lenox saw of him. Skaggs, who had the man contained in one of his enormous arms, blew sharply on a very loud whistle.

Within a moment a constable had whistled back. At this the thief seemed to give up—he pushed himself back into the entryway, out of the rain, halfway between Skaggs and Lenox, and started fixing his disarrayed clothing.

"All right, sir?" said Skaggs to Lenox.

"Yes, thanks to you."

"I think I've found your man."

They both glanced at the man, and then back at each other, and then both began to laugh. It felt good. The intruder's face went dark with confusion and anger.

"Prompt delivery," said Lenox, and both men laughed again, Skaggs still slightly out of breath from the encounter.

"What is your name, traveler?" said Lenox.

The prisoner wouldn't talk. For an awkward moment it was almost a comedy—the three men standing in the little entrance of the building, at a stalemate.

It was Skaggs who solved the problem. "Listen, chappie, you can talk to us in a police house cold and hungry or you can talk to us in a gin house with a drink in your hand."

"You ain't the police?"

"No," said Lenox. "But we can fetch them."

The young man looked between them. He had a ragged shave. "Very well," he said. "I pick gin."

"And what is your name?" Skaggs asked, pulling him up a little by the collar, though not roughly.

CHAPTER TWENTY-SIX

It was the next night that Lenox had the pleasure of presenting the answer to that question to the men of the Coach and Horses.

"*Ezekiel* Phipps?" said the Passenger with a rare and full-faced expression of real astonishment, the likes of which might not be elicited from such a practiced gossip more than once a year.

Lenox, who had never before managed to perturb the man even slightly, felt a distinct gratification. "I take it you know the name?"

"Ezekiel is Jacob Phipps's younger brother. He was sent to Australia at eighteen, more than a decade ago—and died there a year later, we heard."

"Apparently not. Why was he transported?" asked Lenox.

But it was too late for questions—the men of the Coach and Horses were assembling around the Passenger in their dusty coats and getting the news from him ("*Ezekiel?*" they all said, and one of them immediately added, "He always did look a fair bit like his brother") and it was a long ten minutes before Lenox could command their attention. A crowd of more than a dozen regulars was at the hearth. Moving expertly among them was Ernest Huggins. If he had ever had his doubts about Lenox, they were gone now: the home of his aunt was safe, the villain captured, and the news had produced a most fantastic surge of business.

"Do you need a topping up?" he asked the detective.

Lenox accepted the ale, feeling as if he could do with a topping up, too—he had scarcely slept in two days, between the party and the apprehension of Ezekiel Phipps, a young man who answered, as Skaggs had been the first to observe, exactly to Lenox's circular. The fee had been paid to an enterprising young mudlark from Limehouse way.

Eventually the Passenger worked his way back round to Lenox. "So Miles was right, in the end," he said.

"Is that what you have concluded?"

There were many conversations still going on—but none without an ear trained on the tone of this one. "It was Jacob Phipps's own brother, and the dead spit of him!" the Passenger said indignantly. "Of course Miles was right, anyone with reason could see that!"

"He was not technically right, no."

Now several people were staring, and the Passenger gave him a look as if to say that was pretty boorish. "To spot him in the dark, in the rain and wet, Mr. Lenox, the whipping winds—the famous whipping winds of London—"

He was getting up a head of steam, and Lenox, to head him off, said, "But I—"

The Passenger had not ascended to his position of authority at the Coach and Horses by silence, however, and with great stubborn certainty in his bearing, his stomach and chin jutting comfortably out, went on, "Down the West End they don't get it so windy nor so cold as here in Conduit Street—to spot him from fifty paces dead—"

"Hear him!" said someone squeakily—Lenox suspected Miles himself.

"And more or less be on the way to *solving* the case for you, the great detective—"

"Hello now!" said Ernest Huggins roughly.

The Passenger immediately retracted the statement. "And he *is* a great detective, which is why Miles here—to hand him—"

"Excuse me a moment, gentlemen," Lenox said, for he knew he was not needed here, as the Passenger waved his gin in the air and began to pontificate to Ernest directly.

The truth was that he knew all he needed to of Ezekiel Phipps, after their late night with him.

The young man, still shy of thirty, strongly built and with the darkness of overexercised caution, of lifelong fear in his eyes, had proved a determined drinker—and in the end, a florid talker. Skaggs had sent the constable away and led the three of them to an unmarked red door a street down. It was too late for the pubs, but with two taps on the door, they were admitted into a gaudy, noticeably dirty room where two women were selling gin and lime.

There was a meager fire at one end, radiating a little warmth. The walls and ceiling were black with smoke; some of the men and women were drooped over their gins, others absolutely straight, as if the gin gave their spine shape.

Skaggs had greeted the barmaid. "In the corner, Mary." He turned to Lenox and smiled. "Don't say I never took you anywhere."

Lenox smiled automatically, still shaken. He felt that sharp strange new twinge where his wound had been, and forced himself into a couple of slow breaths, as Sven had taught him.

"Drink that up," said Skaggs, when the gin arrived, "and answer this man's questions with a please and a thank-you. Or it will be Newgate Prison."

The young man obediently followed the first command, watched Skaggs refill his smudged glass, then looked at Lenox expectantly. "I'm ready," he said.

The detective saw a survivor in front of him. "You knew there was opium and cash in the greenhouse at 12 Conduit Street," he said, in a tone that brooked no contradiction. "You tried to break in several times—slept there more than once, though perhaps only twice, from what I have actually been able to verify—and recently, growing more desperate after losing your shift work at the dock, grew more determined. The question that remains is how your brother told you of what was there. By letter?"

Ezekiel Phipps looked at Lenox carefully, hearing this precise account of his activities. He swallowed the second gin, grimaced happily at the fire of it in his gullet, and settled back.

"I saw him on my way back from Oz, guv," he said. "Old Jacob—Jake. I cannot say he was much of a brother to me, but he did me a good turn when I saw him in Bombay, or I would have told you he had, until your man there, his great hulking self, put his hands on me ten minutes ago."

"Please describe what he told you."

"We only had fifteen minutes together, you know, talking over the sides of our two ships. And the first ten minutes we was discussing how I was not dead. Nor him.

"I had to give a rupee to a guard on mine to do it—for I was not free, not till I set foot in India, and bless the day it happened. Jacob told me he was bound for the Gulf of Siam, and they had all watered and provisioned in, so he could not stop with me—and he knew I was England bound.

"It was strange, I tell you, chaps, to grow up in a room with a fellow, then forget he and everyone else you ever knew existed for a decade, out in the desert of Australia, getting as brown as a nut and as hard inside—and then see him for a quarter of an hour, a biscuit's toss from you over the ocean, converse as if it was a Tuesday and pork roll for dinner, lucky us—and then part, knowing we would not see each other again, not ever again. Though who can say, in this world God has made."

There was a pause as Ezekiel Phipps drank off the rest of his gin, contemplating this little bit of philosophy. "What was it he told you about Conduit Street?"

"He said that if I was going back to London, he knew about a treat waiting there. He told me the address and the layout of the place. And what was in there. It was right quick, the whole thing, not forty-five seconds, because he wanted to hear of our sister Jenny, who was sent up Newcastle way before I was born. I said I did see her once, when—"

"Stick to the point," said Skaggs.

"Right. Conduit Street. It took me a night or two to figure out that there was no one living down in the storage rooms, and I nearly scared myself half to death doing that. Then I realized only the old woman was living there, and I decided I would chance it, and break in."

"And crack her over the head if she got in your way," said Skaggs.

"Never!" said Ezekiel Phipps indignantly. "Ah, I've always been too soft for this world, guv, that's the problem. I doubt I would have had it in me to tie her up. Our gran, Jacob's and me, was about the only nice . . . anyhow, I did sleep there three nights, not just two. I was sleeping rough anyhow. There is not much call for an old convict in these parts, one who didn't change his name or stay there. But I wouldn't. London is my home, and Zeke Phipps my name, and I defy any man to besmirch it to my face."

"So you know, the opium and the money are gone," Lenox said.

"I had gathered as much," replied Ezekiel Phipps in a tone of irony.

He was compelling, the young ex-transport—but one of his eyelids was beginning to flutter closed when he talked. "Coffee, please," said Lenox to the woman in the corner.

"Ain't got it."

"What about water?"

She shook her head. "Ain't got it."

"You don't have *water?*" said Lenox, who was exhausted, and suddenly saw every detail he needed was already within his grasp, and all that lay before him was the passive work of hearing Phipps out, and then the heavy decision of how to treat him.

"I'll get it from the pump," said Skaggs neutrally, but quickly bracing Lenox on the shoulder. "Give me a pitcher, Mary. Back in a blink."

CHAPTER TWENTY-SEVEN

The water seemed to refresh Phipps. He splashed a little on his face and wrists.

"That first night, anyhow, " he said, fondling his gin glass, "I wished someone might come out and let me slip in. And I happened to fall asleep, waiting there. Well, I ain't averse to a hard bed. The second time I went back I waited again . . . then sort of got into the habit of checking now and then . . . 'course if I had known I was noticed, I never would have risked it like that. It seemed such a busy street that I thought I could hardly be spotted."

He glanced between them, the tired toff and the steely former boxer, as if to indicate that his present predicament was evidence they could assess for themselves how that had turned out.

"Did he tell you anything about the reason the opium and money were there, Ezekiel?"

"Jacob? No. Oh!"

"What?" asked Lenox.

Phipps looked momentarily guarded, then let his face lapse. "He did rattle me one thing in passing about it."

"What was that?"

"He said he *wished* it was him that killed Martell, and he'd say it to anyone's face. I asked him why, naturally, and he said to me, 'Ezekiel, he killed my poor Bethie as surely as if he had strangled her.' I asked how, and he said—"

"That is Elizabeth, his wife?"

The prisoner nodded. "And I asked what he meant, naturally. And he said to ask our cousin Webster, who knew—may he rest in peace, for he died before I returned, but his common-law wife, or if you like common-law widow, Katty, a retired whore around St. Martin-in-the-Fields—"

"Language, now," said Skaggs.

"She told me that it was Martell who gave Beth opium, which led her back into the low sort of life of and which with what she'd grown up in. But this time 'round she died."

"I thought she had an illness," Lenox said sharply.

"No," said Ezekiel, shaking his head. He looked at the gin glass. "Could I have one more glass?"

"Yes. Go on. Why did Martell give her opium?"

Skaggs poured it from the stone bottle. "He worked with the dens," said Ezekiel Phipps. "But now you know all I know—swear it to God."

"How did your brother know where Martell's cache was?" Lenox asked.

"After Beth died, leastwise according to Katty, Jacob took to following Martell, threatening him. He was spying on him and saw it with his own eyes."

"You brothers can't stay away from that house," said Skaggs.

Phipps laughed bitterly. "We can now, guv."

He drained the new glass of gin. His eyes had started to fall shut more insistently now and after a moment, he began slumping against the wall.

Lenox was about to ask him a question when in the corner a drunk man started to loudly remonstrate with a small woman who had a hard grip on his wrist.

Lenox did a little moral arithmetic in his head, and with a sigh to himself, reached into his pocket for a five-pound note. Polly would call him hideously softhearted. Well, perhaps he was. He had come to terms with it, and knew what a bitter blow it would be not just to lose your vision of a thousand pounds, free and clear, as Ezekiel Phipps had, but then to be thrown in city jail afterward. He was clearly no threat to Mrs. Huggins.

But just at that moment, with Skaggs turned a fraction to watch the drunk argument and Lenox reaching into his pocket, Phipps, quick as a rabbit, jumped out of his slumbering posture and sprinted for the door.

It wasn't even ten steps. He was gone in an instant. Lenox and Skaggs exchanged a look, and dashed out into the street.

A costermonger setting up his stall by lamplight pointed left. "But you'll never catch him."

And indeed, at that moment, Skaggs and Lenox turned to see Phipps sprinting at full pelt east, toward the complicated maze of streets nearby. A beat, two, and then he turned and was out of sight.

Lenox and Skaggs looked at each other—held the stare a moment, still both surprised—and then burst into laughter, both of them some mixture of bewildered, thrilled, and amused, Skaggs's low quiet laughter rolling on and on, Lenox's, too, as the costermonger gazed at them wonderingly.

"Who can want fruit and vegetables at this hour?" Lenox asked, a little giddy, cleansed by the laughter.

"The boys who are up early cooking and selling on carts themselves," the fellow said. "They must be here at two o'clock to be out on the streets by three."

There would never be an end to the secrets of this city, Lenox thought, breathing harder than usual—for even Skaggs did not know all that happened here.

They had conversed for a moment then before separating with a rueful handshake. "Do you want him caught?" Skaggs asked as they parted.

Lenox shook his head. "No," he said. "No harm in him."

"Agreed."

Lenox had returned home, making straight for bed after writing a short note to Mrs. Huggins, letting her know that she could go home upon the morn. But, tired as he was, he found only a fitful sleep, full of confused dreams about the case, the party, the Prime Minister, the two ships in Bombay, with Angela and Sari mixed up in them, and confused images of Ezekiel Phipps, of suddenly needing to attend to something he had forgotten.

He sleepwalked through the following day, to end up at the Coach and Horses that evening—the deliverer of this remarkable news to Conduit Street. For the first time that day, as he sipped his beer and watched the Passenger and his friends rabble among themselves, he felt quite at peace.

Over the next hour and a half he heard various conversations about Ezekiel Phipps, Jacob Phipps, Jenny Phipps—and then Beth, the wife who had died, and her relations and acquaintances.

It was at eight o'clock that Lenox heard a tap-tap on the window next to him, and turned and saw Mrs. Huggins, who was beaming.

He went outside and saluted her with a smile and a wave. "Good evening, Mrs. Huggins!"

"Oh, I could hug you, Mr. Lenox."

"Fire at will, Mrs. Huggins," said Lenox.

She did hug him then, and bestowed a kiss upon his cheek, too. "I am so relieved to be home by my fire, you can't know, Mr. Lenox," she said. "With the cats settled again in their poor minds, too, the dears. My knitting back in my hands. I am in yours and Mr. Graham's debt."

"He scarcely did a thing."

She laughed. "Will you walk me home?"

"Of course," said Lenox gallantly, and offered her his arm.

Colored by the new safety of the little building from intruders, the sitting room looked lovely, with a cat lying on each of the two ornate knitted blankets that lay over the room's pair of armchairs. The scent of chamomile and chimney was in the air, and behind it the clean bracing air from a cracked window in the next room.

"Would you like some tea?" asked Mrs. Huggins.

"Why not?"

She invited him to sit, and poured him a cup—she had grown the herbs herself, she said—with a glob of honey from her cousin in Hampshire. She asked him politely about the case and listened to the story of the last day. When he was quite finished, she reached into a small brown leather bag at the side of her chair. She pulled from it a blue-and-white-striped jersey, beautifully and densely knitted, the kind of good old rugged jersey Lenox remembered from his boyhood, and that were so hard to find nowadays. One of the arms was unfinished.

"I started knitting it after you visited—I said to myself that I would give it to you when you solved the case. But you have been too quick. I will have to drop it by next week."

He was more touched than he knew how to say to Mrs. Huggins, perhaps more susceptible, too, tired and worn-out as he was, as hard a year as it had been. He had a faraway thought of his mother, another of himself at twenty, when he had met Mrs. Huggins. He felt the sting of tears forming in his eyes, but quickly opened them, shooing the feeling away.

"Thank you, Mrs. Huggins," he said. "I shall treasure it."

CHAPTER TWENTY-EIGHT

The next morning, the detective went with sluggish footsteps to the gymnasium, where he moved through his exercises even less enthusiastically than usual.

Sven frowned at him at the end of their appointment. "You are eating pheasants, Charles," he said. "I suspect you of eating pheasants."

"Excuse me!"

"Pheasants and gravy. You Englishmen are digging your graves with your teeth."

"I have not either been eating pheasants," Lenox said with what he hoped was dignity.

"Beefsteaks in ketchup then," said Sven angrily.

"No!"

This took him aback. "Pork pies? With applesauce?"

"No!"

Sven stood there, arms crossed, considering this impasse. "Then you need rest and vegetable broth served boiling hot," he said. He clapped Lenox on the shoulder. "Next week will be better."

No massage that day; Sven had another client. Lenox dragged his aching carcass into the members' room and drank a glass of cool lemon water. His head was pounding. He could scarcely coax himself to get downstairs into the cab, the pressure between his temples became so intense.

Things improved with a lunch and an hour's sleep in an armchair in his study. He felt nearly himself when the bell rang, and there was a knock at the door. It was Dallington, Kirk announced.

"Hullo, old chap," Dallington said to Lenox. "I got your wire. No need to go to the opium dens, you said? Kirk, could I trouble you for a glass of beer? Very well done on the Conduit Street case, Charles."

"I did next to nothing at all, I am sorry to say. Come sit by the fire." Dallington took an armchair. "I have rarely felt more dull-witted after a case. In the end the fellow walked straight into my arms, and might have killed me then and there anyhow, but for the help of Skaggs."

Dallington heard this, and responded with a polite murmur—but Lenox saw he was far away.

"I am sorry, though, John. I suspect something is on your mind."

"Oh!"

The young lord looked embarrassed. Kirk came in, with one of the cut-glass mugs that had belonged to Lenox's father, and which the butler reserved for very special guests.

"Lovely," said Dallington gratefully. He drank beer once or twice a week now. He had once told Lenox he drank up his share of stronger spirits by twenty-three.

Kirk withdrew. "I hope it is not about Polly?" said Lenox with concern.

Dallington's dark eyes met his. "No, nothing like that," he said. "What I have been wondering—how do I say it? What if I am a wretched father, Charles! What if I should blow it all up—what if, oh, I don't know!"

The young man buried his face in his hands, and in that instant Lenox felt heartily sorry. He had paid his friend too little mind.

"John, you must stop that. You are going to be the best of fathers," Lenox said, half-consciously mimicking his grandfather's voice, which had been like the voice of God to him when he was young. He knew now, past fifty, that the young sometimes needed strength from their elders.

Dallington looked at him with despair. "What if I am not?"

"Listen to me, Dallington, I am sorry that I have not talked about it with you before. I have been so caught up in my own weather—Anyhow, be that as it may, I can tell you that I have watched my generation go through youth, university, young adulthood, and fatherhood, a whole lot of men, some good among 'em, many rotten, and the majority somewhere between, and you will be as good a father as any. I know it."

"But I was once—"

"But nothing, John, that was years ago. You are married, the hardest working person in your family, if you will forgive me the indelicacy"—Dallington laughed, and Lenox grinned, for they both knew about the Duke and Duchess of Marchmain's children's idle lives in full detail—"and you must start to think of that as yourself. Not whoever you may have been at twenty."

Dallington stood. He drained his beer and rang the bell. Kirk was there almost instantly, and after taking his glass went to get him a fresh one.

Dallington lingered near the round table upon which Lenox kept the latest monthlies and leafed through one, waiting. It had been an unwonted display of emotion.

Lenox picked up an old copy of *All the Year Round*. They both idled in this fashion until Kirk returned, after which Dallington returned to the armchair, setting his beer down and looking at the fire.

"Sorry, old chap," he said in a clipped voice.

"Never mind. Listen, you and Polly come for supper this week, it has been too long, and we will have it with the girls, too, and you may hear about the great joys of fatherhood. Clara and Sophia will be happy to give you a very clear-eyed accounting of my faults."

Dallington smiled, though his eyes remained on the fire.

"Too strict on sweets, for a start. And Edmund always handing them hard candies behind my back."

Kirk, perhaps sensing with that capacious empathy of the best butlers that there was high emotion in the room, returned with a bowl of salted almonds and some chocolate ship's biscuits. Lenox took one of these, thanking him.

At length, he said, "I fear I've failed you, John. I have taken it so for granted that you will be a wonderful father—a father in a million—that I overlooked the doubts I should have known you must have. But think, John. Would Polly choose the father of her children badly? Polly, the smartest person you know?"

Lenox saw the tense muscles around his eyes give way a millimeter. It was true about Polly. The point had struck home.

They sat in silence for some time, as old friends can. Dallington drank down his cup a third of the way, before standing suddenly. "Goodbye for now, Charles. Yes, we should love to come to dinner."

Lenox stood, too. "I have a misgiving, too, if you will be an audience. I have been awfully worried at leaving you two alone at the agency."

"The *agency*?" said Dallington, as if he had forgotten such a place existed. "Oh, lord no, that ticks over perfectly well, with or without you."

"Thanks."

Dallington laughed. "You know what I mean," he said. "It is so large now, the junior detectives so enterprising . . . put that from your mind." He was putting on his scarf. He seemed lighter. "I'll see myself out. Give my love to Jane. What are you doing this evening?"

Lenox sighed. "I wish I could say I had it in—but it is dinner out, alas. I am beaten half to death. I may leave detection to you younger fellows from now on. I like Montague."

"You know he is a fan of yours?"

Lenox frowned. "Eh?"

"Oh, yes. Knows your cases all backwards and forwards. Asked me a question about one the other day. At any rate, you are still recovering from America—give yourself a spring to get strong!"

CHAPTER TWENTY-NINE

The next morning when he woke up, Lenox's first dim thought was that the case was over. He hadn't looked for it to be finished so soon, and he felt a delightful schooldays sense of openness, as if the summer holidays had unexpectedly started early.

He was a little tired at breakfast, but went out on his usual morning walk to wake himself up. It was cold on the streets, however, and by the time he had returned home, he felt a strange sluggishness in his body under the warmth of the exercise. He ate lunch ravenously, then fell into a heavy nap; woke for dinner, had a brandy and water to try to pep himself up, but felt awful during dinner, could not touch his food. He excused himself and went upstairs to sleep it off.

By midnight he had a fever of 104, and the doctor had arrived at Hampden Lane.

"What year is it?" the doctor asked.

"It's 1879," Lenox murmured, from behind a mouth that he realized after speaking had barely moved.

He was racked with chills, which seized different parts of his body in an erratic sequence. His head felt fuzzy, achy, dim, far away.

"What is your wife's name?"

"Where is Jane?" said Lenox, apparently so quietly that the doctor had to lean forward.

"I'm here, darling," said Jane, and he realized someone was holding his hand.

"Very cold," he managed to murmur to her.

"Chills," he heard the doctor say.

"Could you drink water, Charles?" she asked.

"No."

"Who is prime minister?" the doctor asked.

"Jasper," said Lenox, then felt himself fall almost instantly into sleep.

It was a sleep interrupted by the worst nightmares. He awoke soaked in sweat. He drank a glass of water in two gulps. The room was empty, though he saw a soft light on in the hallway and heard voices there. He momentarily remembered this as being from his boyhood and assumed he was there—the feeling of being sick and in bed, those same voices speaking, that same hallway.

But no, he was delirious. He was in London.

"Charles? Are you awake?" said Lady Jane's anxious voice.

"Yes," he said—but a few seconds behind the darkness of those closed eyes made a liar of him, and he was asleep once again.

When he woke once more it was late afternoon. The pain in his temples was excruciating. His eyes came gently open and he saw, in the unlit room, the busy shadows dancing sadly against the gray wall. A different doctor had shaken him awake, he realized, a young fellow with a round face and equally round glasses.

"Mr. Lenox," he said.

Who else could it be, Lenox wanted to say. More than that, he wanted to sleep.

"Mr. Lenox," he was saying.

"Yes?" said Lenox, coming back to alertness.

"Have you any appetite, sir?"

"No," said Lenox.

"Do you know the year?"

"Yes," said Lenox, and sank back wearily into his pillows, not as tired as the last two times he woke up. "What do I have?"

"About what year is it—"

"Disraeli is Prime Minister," he said angrily. "What have I got?"

It was so rare that Lenox exerted the privilege of class he knew himself that even Jane would have been surprised. "Influenza," said the doctor deferentially. "Your fever is improving."

"What is it?"

"A hundred at the moment."

A terrible thought occurred to him. "Does anyone else have it in the household?" the detective asked.

"No," said the doctor. "You alone. You have pushed yourself too hard. May I raise your shirt?"

Lenox lay back and let the doctor palpate his liver, his stomach, listen to his breath, check his pulse. He let his gaze fall upon the motley beautiful chimneys of London, his home. The familiar view from the third floor here ranged down to miles east of the house. Someday it would all be built up.

He wondered where Jane was.

"I am pleased to say I believe there is no acute danger," said the doctor at last, having written in his notebook for a goodish time, as if to assert his importance. "Could you eat something?"

"No. I don't know. Yes, if they bring it."

Lenox allowed his eyes to close as he said this, and nearly fell asleep again as the young doctor (fit and happy, Lenox observed, as the sick always will of their caregivers, no doubt going to supper that night with his young wife, or playing a hand of cards at his private club) closed his brown leather bag.

Only then did he see McConnell stride forward. The Scotsman looked disheveled by his usual standards, but handsome, as always. He had long golden brown hair, streaked with gray. He shook hands with the doctor, only glancing at the bed. "Halley."

So this must be McConnell's fellow. Lenox could only force his eyes to stay open long enough to see that before he fell asleep again. A housemaid appeared with a plate of apple slices and he ate three before forcing them away and turning his back, into grateful sleep.

Then it was the middle of the night; and Jane was there; and his hand in her hand, the gentle touch of her nails on the inside of his wrist, gave him hope, though he was hot, and chilled, and miserable to the touch.

But at dawn she was gone. He woke with a start from a dream of being back in Newport, and the wound in his side was throbbing as it never yet had, a metallic fire that he had to gasp over—around—and finally he fell back one last time, and slept without interruption for three days.

Three long days. It was Lady Jane who suffered through them. Later he would tell Sophia and Clara that he remembered dreaming of them in his slumber, though it wasn't true. He tried to read their faces for worry after he had woken again. They had spent most of the time with Sari and Angela, Lady Jane told Lenox.

As for him—"You are about as fit as a man of fifty who will insist on drinking several alcoholic beverages a week," McConnell said on the third day, Lenox weak but better. The Scot grinned at the pad and refused to look up, reading on instead, "and only recently took up vigorous exercise, and goes days without sleeping to host fashionable parties, and chase petty criminals through—"

"Enough, Thomas," murmured Lenox from the bed. He was stronger but not strong enough yet.

"I'm sorry." McConnell closed the pad and looked up. "You are fit, and this is a case of nervous exhaustion. You need two weeks of absolute rest. That is the opinion of young Halley, whom they say is about the best doctor we have."

"Two weeks!"

Nearly to Christmas. "From what I can gather, Jane is determined you shall have it."

Lenox took a sip of tea, and he knew from its strong, fortifying flavor that he really was better; that what McConnell had said was true. Yet he felt, still, this throbbing ache in his ribs, even if it was improved.

McConnell tapped on the armchair. "Have you heard," he said candidly, "that Toto and Jane have fallen out?"

"The protest?"

McConnell nodded. Lenox groaned and lay back on his pillow. "Thank you for coming, Thomas. Send Toto my love. And take care of yourself."

McConnell stood. "I shall visit again," he said, though Lenox knew from a certain inflection in his friend's voice that the reliability of this pledge was uncertain.

CHAPTER THIRTY

Deep winter snuck its cold way into the streets of London day by day, and Lenox watched it happen from his window. The added scarf around the oyster peddler's neck in the evening, the last hardiest leaves going from the hawthorn trees. Above all the speed of the walkers on the street to their next warm destination. If they hadn't one—the above bless them.

He had little appetite but dutifully drank the beef broth and barley water young Halley had prescribed. The detective had lost perhaps ten pounds. His frame felt unfamiliar. He tired more easily, too.

He took visits longer than his energy wanted to allow from his brother and Graham. But at least he laughed with them. There was a bushel of apples from Sven and a note from Polly. But he was only truly happy when his daughters occasionally stormed in to play hands of gin rummy on his bed.

A silver lining was that he was able to catch up on every piece of correspondence he had ever received. (Aunt Matilda's most recent weekly note: "In excellent form. I see Edmund will likely come back in at the next election and have the devil of work for it! Your Sari has an admirer—keep a sharp eye, Charles. MSL.")

That Sunday, after taking the girls to church, Lady Jane came in, bundled in warm clothes. He was still in the sickroom; it faced the back garden and the streets beyond it. She had a white carnation in her hat—the symbol of support for the women's vote.

"Where this week?" Lenox asked gently, as she arranged his pillows.

"Friern Barnet." She looked over. "Don't say anything."

"I wasn't going to."

Lady Jane was not the typical visitor to this type of little suburb of London, filled with lowly clerks and their huge dependent families, some seven miles north of them here at the heart of society. Most of the clerks walked the full seven miles back and forth each day, some so used to the route they could read the newspaper as they went. The most prosperous-looking shop in those neighborhoods was usually the cobblers.

"You had a look," Jane said. She straightened up before the mirror, came and kissed him, brushed his hair back with her hand, and said, "I think they are the most intelligent women I have ever met."

"I have no doubt of it. You will not admire their furniture, I wager, however."

"That does not matter," she said softly.

"And you will go out with your signs?"

"Yes."

He looked at her. It had been a long week in his life; long, and terrifying, and he needed Jane.

"Charles," she said.

"Yes?"

"I shouldn't have kept it from you. I was wrong. I just—I *had* to do it. I cannot put it any other way. And I couldn't bear the idea of fighting with you first."

He took her hand. "It's all right."

"I love you."

The doctor came each morning and evening from Harley Street. That day was the fifth, and each of the ten visits had ended with the same admonishment: not to leave his bed, to get absolute rest.

Lady Jane was strictly enforcing this injunction, and for Kirk it might have been laid down on Moses's tablets. He sat in the hallway reading penny novels (he thought Lenox didn't know this) in case Lenox tried even to reach too far for the bell. Even McConnell would not yield. It was the latest medical wisdom, he said; total relaxation of the tissues.

But that evening Lenox was restless. He was heartily sick of the room, the bed, the view. He would have liked to sneak down to his study above all, but he knew the way was mined with servants specifically instructed to subdue him if he attempted so much as a step down the hall.

There was a tap on the door. He glanced at the clock—past ten o'clock. "Come in."

It was Angela. He felt a little glow in his heart—and realized that somewhere, in the past weeks, he had come to love her, not out of duty, but a real sense of familial love.

"I have come to ask you a favor."

"If it is within my power I shall grant it."

She came a few steps into the room, upright in her plain white dress, hemmed at the neck with intricate blue lace. "I would like to move into Edmund's house," she said.

"Edmund's!"

"Yes."

He sat up a little, then felt his head bend. "I have failed you," he said.

"No!" she said. "No. I have been more than content here—as comfortable as can be. But I want to learn about the economics."

Lenox raised his eyebrows: surprise and incomprehension together.

The economics was a recondite new specialist subject, much discussed in Edmund's world. The cutting-edge scientific findings of their studies was a proud expertise of several of the lower officials in Parliament who worked with Edmund and Gladstone, bright young Cambridge men—fairly certain, one had confided in Charles, that within a decade they would be able to guarantee that there would never again be a financial depression.

"I see. Can you not learn it here?"

"I want to be around it," she said simply.

Lenox broke into a wide grin, involuntarily. "I'm sorry," he said.

"What?" she asked.

"For a second you were so like Jasper—the way he would say, 'I'm going to climb that wall,' and before you knew what had happened, was over a wall nobody in the village had ever climbed."

She colored, but looked happy. "I came to ask permission."

"You have it of course. He will lord this over me for the rest of my life, Edmund. On the other hand, there is much to recommend it—perhaps you might even in time help him manage the household."

Lenox said this a little hopefully. Edmund had never been overfond of London, and after Molly had died, even less. The tall town house their parents had so loved was empty and unloved now—a place where Edmund could lay his head, nothing more.

Angela would move into the pink bedroom, he reflected, which had been for guests, but which his mother had always secretly hoped to give to a daughter.

"But, Angela," he said, "what about Sari? You have a responsibility to her, too."

Her face said plainly that she understood this better than he could. "Yes, I know. She has—her own life to lead," Angela said evasively. "And doesn't care a fig about the economics."

"Nor should she," said Lenox. "But have you asked her?"

"No."

"She is welcome to stay here, of course, but I assume she will want to go with you."

Hope flared across Angela's face for a moment. "Perhaps she will."

He waited for her to say more, and when she didn't, said, "Very well—I can write Edmund tonight."

"Thank you," she said, and came over and gave him a quick, ardent hug about the shoulders—and in it, Lenox felt the once living body of his cousin.

It took his breath away. Perhaps it was because he was convalescent—but the incredible weight of the long year sank into him in the instant of the embrace. He had much to mourn. But there were green shoots, too. He loved this strange, brainy, shy girl.

"Good night, Cousin."

"Good night, Angela," he said.

It was an hour later—fitful, unable to sleep after this strange conversation—that he snuck out of the house in Hampden Lane for the first time, and slipped into the familiar infinite streets of London.

CHAPTER THIRTY-ONE

As boys of eight or nine, Lenox and Jasper had once tried to steal some Simnel cake from the pantry, when a particularly nasty upper footman named Porkins had walked in on them—or rather, had walked in on Lenox, for Jasper, quick as a fox, had hopped out the window and knelt down behind the ledge outside.

After Lenox had gotten his dressing-down and they were alone again, he'd said accusingly to Jasper, "How'd you think of that so quickly?"

"Uncle Roderick says that you must always know how you are going to leave a room as soon as you enter it."

Jasper's uncle was a famous soldier and adventurer, dark brown from the tropics, scars crisscrossing his hands and lines scored into his face, who had never had an address of his own since boyhood. Jasper revered him.

"Maybe that's why he's always with some new woman," Charles had once suggested. "They don't stay after they find out he hasn't got anywhere to live."

"Yes, probably," Jasper had replied seriously.

"But some women have their own houses."

"Who?"

"Mrs. Blankenship, for one."

This was an old woman of about eighty who lived in a cottage on the Lenox property. "I don't know how she would do for him," said Jasper doubtfully.

"No, perhaps not."

Lenox thought of this faraway day with a smile just after Angela left, for some reason: then he saw that it was because his brain at that same moment was engineering for him the idea that he might just glance out the window and see how to exit this room.

He walked over to the window and saw the long, sturdy double drainpipe descending to the ground.

With a feeling of real recklessness, but driven by desperation to escape, to escape this illness, dreary as a wet Sunday, indeed to escape all the infirmity that he had experienced since Newport, he wrapped his heavy wool coat around him, stuck a cap on his head, and chanced it.

He reached the ground a bit faster than he had expected to. "Humph!" he said, sitting on his behind very suddenly, in a patch of ivy.

He felt himself over, though, and nothing was too far wrong.

It was the work of a moment to sneak the spare key from its hiding spot in the eaves then, and let himself out through the black side gate and into Hampden Lane.

For the next seven nights, Lenox followed the same schedule, resting dutifully during the day, to all appearances a model patient, then waiting until the night, two, three, and letting himself out.

On that first night he didn't walk above a mile, and when it came time to climb the laddered stone around the drainpipe he could barely do the job—hauling himself into the room exhausted.

But the next night he walked a good two miles, and after that the number increased rapidly, three miles, five, and finally ten, ten, ten.

How good it felt simply to walk! It was like regaining a self. He grew used again to the black befogged sky above a London night, silvery violet at its edges; he walked through the ghostly silent enormous pale buildings of Whitehall, sleeping until the entire government returned at eight the next morning; he turned down little alleys and saw the places Skaggs knew, down-at-heel gambling salons, gin parlors, brothels, boxing clubs, everywhere that managed to slink out an existence after the city went to bed.

He had known these places his whole adult life—but in a sense he was seeing them again for the first time. Not since he was twenty-five or so had he had the time, or energy, or inclination to survey this city in the middle of the night.

There was not a moment of doubt in his mind about defying his doctors. He would not have gone on if he did not feel energy seeping back into his dormant cells each night, the warm blood circulating under his skin.

Besides the exercise, too, there was charm in having a secret. Even from Jane! For nobody suspected a thing at home—nobody, that is, except little Clara, who on the third or fourth morning came in with her sister to give him a kiss before going to the nursery, but lingered after Sophia had bolted for just a moment.

"Papa?" she said.

He was reading the newspaper over his coffee, and looked up. "Yes, darling girl," he said.

"Why is there mud on your shoes?"

He looked over his newspaper, frowning. She was holding up one of his brown brogues, and indeed she had found a streak of mud on it.

And he had wiped his shoes clean, too. "I don't know—perhaps they need to be cleaned."

"But they clean your boots every evening, and you haven't been out."

Lenox shrugged, though he was proud of her powers of observation. "I suppose we shall have to sack the upstairs staff."

"You are joking," she said quietly, more to herself than him. She was still holding up the shoe. "Papa, you aren't leaving your bed, are you?"

"No," he said gravely, for he knew how seriously the girls were taking his illness.

"You had better not."

"I won't."

She dropped the shoe and, in her childlike way, seemed to forget about it completely, picking up a little glass jar, then putting it down in the wrong place and zooming out of the room when she realized her sister had beaten her to the good toys in the nursery.

On the very last night of his scheduled convalescence, Lenox walked longer than he had yet—fifteen miles, he supposed, probably longer. There was a brilliant moon in the sky, and he could see London in all of its beautiful lineaments. He moved quickly, and as his heart thumped, he realized, with a sudden shock, that the pain had moved out of his ribs.

He halted, not far from Blackfriars Bridge. He put his hand to his side. A deep breath, another—and then he almost laughed, for he could not find the pain anymore, no matter how he tried.

It must have gone.

That morning, Halley and McConnell came back together and pronounced him fit as a racehorse. It was the first time his friend had been back in a week. "Aren't you glad we counseled you rest?" McConnell said.

"Yes," said Lenox humbly.

"It is never very fun for the patient," said the young, round-spectacled Halley, "but its success is invariable."

"And the good news is that you can go for a short walk today—fifteen minutes or so, perhaps twenty."

"Thank you."

Strangely, in all his many peregrinations throughout the previous week, Lenox had never passed Conduit Street. That day, though, walking in the unaccustomed brightness of mid-morning, he found his footsteps bound for the street—glanced up at the greenhouse, gave a smile to the Coach and Horses.

A strange case. He wondered still who had killed Martell.

He was two or three streets away when a chilly winter rain started to come down, gusting up lightly every ten minutes only to die away, like a tune that can't find a melody. The trees moved about moodily. In the gray flat light the city became a mass of intersecting lines of umbrellas.

Lenox had been walking for just a mile or two, humming to himself an intricate old Bach tune that he had been forced to practice endlessly upon the pianoforte as a boy. He walked with his eyes about ten feet ahead of him and at knee level, as a game with himself; for shoes were the quickest way to place a Londoner.

It was only because he kept his gaze at around this level that he spotted, with a start of surprise, a solitary leftover clue from the Conduit Street case.

It was carved into the vestibule of a tobacconist's on Regent Street.

He was strangely thrilled to recognize the symbol from the house in Conduit Street. He knelt down to be sure—yes, there could be no mistaking it. What did it mean? An architect's mark? The remnant of some long-forgotten society?

He wanted to know. The rain intensified, and he went inside the tobacconist's to inquire.

CHAPTER THIRTY-TWO

"Good morning," said the old gentleman behind the counter. He had a white fringe of hair and wore a green eyeshade.

Behind him was a glass case with hundreds of colorful boxes of cigars and loose tobacco. *Finest Rajah—Tuppence a Cigar—A Shilling the Seven!* said a prominent picture; there were twelve pence to the shilling so this was a free seventh cigar. *Westward Ho—Highest Quality Shag—3 d. per ounce.* Like all tobacconists it sold sweets, too, which were sorted into glass jars, with a stack of paper bags to make your own assortment. These were dearer than the tobacco—a penny an ounce, or four farthings.

"There is a small square symbol carved into the wood outside your door," Lenox said.

The man frowned. "Most people notice the Indian fellow."

Lenox smiled. There was indeed a six-foot oak chief outside the front window, stoically absorbing the rain. "I have seen the Indians before however. Do you know the little carving I mean?"

"Oh, yes. There's one over on Berwick Street."

"Berwick? You are sure?"

"Quite sure! At Cottard's Stationers. No idea what it is, meself. It was here when I came in."

Lenox's pulse quickened. That meant there was the one on Conduit Street two streets west and one on Berwick Street two streets east. His pattern-seeking mind saw the sequence.

"When was that?"

"In '74." Five years before. There was a brass monkey about a foot high on the counter, and the man pushed on one of its paws. A little flame shot up from the brass matches the monkey was holding in his other paw, and the tobacconist relit his pipe. "Like I said, it was here."

"How did you notice the one in Berwick Street?"

"I didn't—the younger Cottard brother pointed it out to me." He gestured to a pennant behind him. "He comes in for two ounces of Dr. Emerson's finest every morning."

Lenox glanced at the advertisement. A hearty-looking doctor with a spectacular mustache offered his pipe tobacco, guaranteed to cure asthma, foul breath, canker sores, diseases of the mouth, and bronchial blockages.

The tobacconist emitted a hacking cough.

"Thank you," said Lenox.

The detective walked the two streets through the rain and found the stationers.

It was a prosperous-looking venture, and there, about a foot or so off the ground just outside its front door, was the same symbol.

"Hello," he said, to a tall fellow in a white shirt and suspenders, sorting through packets of Christmas cards.

"Morning," said the fellow without looking up.

"I came from Whittemore Tobacco—on Regent Street."

The shopkeeper looked up. "My brother goes there."

"It's about the symbol carved into the wood outside your door. Do you know anything about it?"

"Oh—that." The stationer leaned down to his task again. "No. It was here when we moved in. Eight years."

"I see. What was here previously?" Lenox asked.

The fellow looked up. "Why?"

"I am a detective," said Lenox sharply.

This had the effect he desired. "Oh. I see. Well—it was a fishmonger. Gutted by a fire in '69, and we got it on favorable terms. Now our cousin has opened a second branch in Lambeth," he added, with pride.

"And you know nothing about it?"

The fellow shrugged. "Nothing at all."

Lenox nodded. "Thank you."

Outside, he stooped down, ignoring the rain, and felt the carving with his fingertips. It was a strange little symbol—and too purposeful for his liking, too time-intensive. It would have taken a good thirty or forty minutes to score the lines in so precisely and deeply. Someone meant this mark.

Likely it had nothing to do with Martell; certainly nothing to do with Mrs. Huggins. Yet he couldn't help his curiosity.

That afternoon he went to the library of the House of Commons, where his old friend Thomas Carruthers still presided. They had met when Lenox was first elected to Parliament. He had been not more than thirty-five then, and felt very ancient. Carruthers had been eighty or so—and as librarian, in charge of, as the old joke went, the most reliably empty place in Parliament.

But there were a few eccentric members who always did read under the rain-soaked windows—either books from the beautiful old neo-Gothic library itself, or "blue books," the endless reports members were given on matters of state. Lenox had been one of these—he and Carruthers had talked daily.

It had been several years, but as Lenox should have known, Carruthers had not changed.

"How your brother has risen!" said Carruthers sharply when he looked across the circulation desk and saw Lenox, as if they had spoken five minutes before. He laughed, the loose skin around his eyes and neck wobbling with joy. "I'll wager you one thing—I will last longer in this job than he do in that one."

He talked in that way of the previous century—shortening verbs, plenty of *ain'ts*—and his high stiff collar would have been old-fashioned even in Lenox's father's youth, the boyhood style of the 1770s. A different world that was.

"Do you rate him so lowly?" asked Lenox.

"On the contrary—too highly. But what is it, Master Charles? I see a question in your face."

Lenox explained the little square symbol to Carruthers and showed him the drawing. The old librarian pulled up the glasses hanging from a gold chain around his neck.

"No," he said immediately. "It's local you said? No."

He had a famous memory, and Lenox knew the answer was final. "Drat."

Carruthers rang a little bell for his "young lady," a sixty-year-old woman named Maeve who taught library science at Girton. "Maeve knows everything about London," Carruthers said.

"You are far too kind, sir, in fact my knowledge of the—"

"Hush now, Maeve. Charles, show her."

But Maeve, too, was confounded. She apologetically and periphrastically said that she had not seen the symbol; it did not belong to any of the halls, the guilds, the royal seals, the—

Carruthers cut her off and Lenox thanked them both.

But his attention was caught by Maeve, who was new at the library, and evidently a woman of immense learning. "I know a fellow you might be very curious to speak to—the Duke of Aderkenalty," Lenox said, "not to put too fine a point on it."

She raised her eyebrows. "I would be honored, of course."

The duke, whom Lenox knew socially, was a forbidding and absurdly rich old fellow, the tower of his castle in Hampshire so large that it was said you could drive a coach and six from the base to the tower and back again without the slightest inconvenience—but Lenox doubted he had ever met someone who knew as much about London, his special obsessive study, for his people had helped found the city.

Lenox asked to borrow an envelope. He wrote to the Duke, enclosing a drawing of the little symbol and a line about Maeve, and thanked them both.

"Frank this for me, would you?" he asked Carruthers.

"Certainly," said the librarian, turning back to the incunabula he had been lovingly studying. "Come visit us more often, Charlie! I have a good ten years left in this old green chair I tell you."

CHAPTER THIRTY-THREE

When Lenox returned home, he heard voices from the lower drawing room. Peering in from a crack in the door he saw three unfamiliar young men amusing themselves freely, it seemed, for no member of the household was present.

Lenox found his way downstairs to the butler's pantry, where he found Kirk and Lady Jane. "Hello, Charles," said Jane.

"Kirk, I'm glad you're here," said the detective, standing in the doorway. "I don't think I run an exceptionally strict household."

"Sir—" said Kirk.

"And yet I cannot believe that I am expected to wander through a passel of young gentlemen, morning, noon, and night—"

"Oh, sir!"

"Drinking my wine, as if I were Odysseus—"

"Of course he had to offer them wine," said Lady Jane. "These are our visiting hours, Charles."

"And eating my *cheese*," said Lenox, a little viciously, for it was a matter of long-standing fury to him that the one cheese he really liked (a sharp cheddar from the Gorge) was continually being given away to guests.

"Leave him be," said Lady Jane. "Kirk, thank you—you may go. If I do not appear in the next fifteen minutes you may tell them that she is not in to visitors after all."

"Who is not in?" asked Lenox. "Who are these young gentlemen?"

"Did you not recognize Fairfield Warren?"

This was the son of a major industrialist. "No."

"You mustn't do that to Kirk," said Lady Jane, pushing him back into the hallway. "He's getting on."

"He's barely sixty, and he was supposed to retire a year and a half ago," said Lenox crossly.

To his surprise, Jane laughed. She paused and put a hand on his face. "How are you feeling?" she asked.

They were standing in the front hallway now. "Quite well."

"Yes," she said, with a note of cautious pleasure, studying his face. "I think you look well again, too." She sighed. "The three young men—they are suitors."

He was shocked. "For Angela?"

Fairfield Warren was her inferior in birth and connections—but she was an orphan, penniless in her own right. She might do worse, he reflected.

"No," said Lady Jane. "For Sari."

For once in his life Lenox was actually lost for words.

"I know," she said. "It surprised me, too."

"She has only been out in society once!" said Lenox.

"Twice, if you count our party," said Lady Jane. "Anyhow, I could hardly turn them away."

"No." Lenox hesitated. "I suppose I should say hello to them. Will Sari herself come down?"

"I do not think so. She is taken aback—claims not to remember any of them individually, though how can that be true?"

Lenox went into the drawing room. All three of the lads jumped up as if he were about to lead them to the gates of heaven.

"Good afternoon, Mr. Lenox!" one burst out, and Lenox recognized him as a meager-boned little devil named Samuel Goodheart, a member of the Athenaeum.

"Hello, Goodheart."

As he joined the three lads, he tried to spot any similarity between them. But they were all rather different. Fairfield was a hiker and an adventurer who loved Scotland; Goodheart a penny-pinching younger son, worse still from a lower branch of one of the oldest squire's families in England, trying to parlay his thousand-year connections into what he could make of them on the marriage market. The third boy was a vague tall blond fellow who introduced himself as Lockett.

After a few minutes, Lenox saw a way to introduce Sari into the conversation—and he saw all three faces open wide with hope, with anticipation.

So they were here for her. Was this why Angela wanted to move?

After twenty minutes or so the young lady herself appeared with Lady Jane. She was wearing an embroidered daffodil-yellow dress, and looked calm, cheerful; only from having known her these weeks since her arrival could Lenox discern the tremulousness in her speech.

"Good afternoon," she said, inclining her head to the three, and taking a seat on the sofa opposite them.

"What splendid weather!" said the boy Lockett—and Lenox glanced doubtfully outside at the specking rain, but the others took up the theme, mentioning that if *today* was not an example of the splendid weather, it must at least be owned that it had been a milder winter than usual—or if not, in strictest honesty, milder than usual, at least fairly sunny. None of them said, but Lenox could glean, by the young Indian woman opposite them, that it really ought to have been good weather, on her behalf.

He saw with a flash that what really united the three was that they would be disowned by their families for marrying an Indian girl. At least—disowned as an opening gambit, at the very minimum, in the family's protest against the idea. He didn't like that. Sari was not an ax to grind against their families. They would have to protect this girl, he saw. He had underestimated how much.

Lenox was saved from their company by a footman, who announced that he had a visitor from the agency waiting in his study. It proved to be Montague, standing awkwardly just inside the door. He beamed when Lenox came into the study.

"Good afternoon, sir—nearly evening," he said.

"Hello, Montague," said Lenox. Distantly he heard a loud laugh from the drawing room, and frowned. "How are you?"

"Very well, sir. I went to Bluegate Fields after all, sir—though I know it's all over, the case."

Lenox was surprised. "Alone?" he asked doubtfully.

"I know one of the constables there, a sound fellow."

Lenox grew alert—he heard in Montague's tone that he had discovered something.

"Were you accosted, going among the dens?" he said to the eager young man, whose shoes still had raindrops on them. He reminded Lenox of himself at that age, unbridled by time, experience; and he felt a deep pang, not unhappy, at the years fled. "Sit for a moment and tell me all."

CHAPTER THIRTY-FOUR

Montague sat down as Lenox went and poured them two glasses of scotch. "On the contrary, I did the accosting. I spoke to a dozen or so of the men who run the opium dens over in that part of the city. And I showed them this."

He held up the picture of Martell.

"Several of the fellows went very rough when I showed them the picture, and warned me not to come back or it would be my neck—straight in front of Dorrance, too, my friend the constable, who could only shrug."

Lenox sat on the opposite sofa, handing Montague his drink. "Pray go on."

"Thank you, sir. Ah, that's good." The rain had picked up outside, and Montague glanced at the windows, recollecting his thoughts. "The ninth man we tried, however, laughed."

"Laughed!"

"Yes. His name was Lang Tu. A great brawny chap. He recognized Martell at once, that was obvious. At first he wouldn't say a word. Dorrance and I had a drink at the bar—just pressed lemon, you know, they have quite a few refreshments without alcohol because the wives of the men sit there waiting to bring them home. They were playing cards—it seemed quite sad.

"After a little while Lang Tu's hostess led us to a small back room. He was there and asked me what it was worth to know the truth. Well, Dorrance had prepared me for this. I said I hadn't very much money, just ten shillings, which I gave him, as an act of good faith, you see—but that Martell was my cousin. They take family quite seriously over there it seems. Anyhow, Dorrance thought so.

"Lang Tu thought and said, well, it could do no harm, since all the parties were dead."

"Dead!"

"Yes—the parties being Martell and an opium seller named Chang, who was murdered in a tearoom in Clerkenwell Road last year.

"About a week before Martell died, Lang Tu told me, he was visiting his associates, sitting in the noodle house there in Bluegate Fields, drinking the liquor they have made of rice and sugar. They were all talking about death, one of the risks of their profession, and Martell said that if he died, it wasn't a Chinaman—it was either a fellow named Phipps, he had chivvied out of some money—"

Lenox stopped him. "He was sure of Phipps? The name did not come to him this week?"

"No—he knew Phipps well."

"Working on the river," Lenox murmured, sitting back. "It makes absolute sense."

"But Lang Tu went on to say that he remembered the moment because—well, first because Martell died, I suppose, but also because of something Martell said as a joke—that it would be either Phipps or, and he laughed when he said it, a boy of ten."

Montague sat back. That was the end of his intelligence to report—and it was a good deal. "A boy of ten," said Lenox, baffled. "What does it mean?"

"I don't know," replied Montague. "That was all he could remember.

'A boy of ten,' he was sure of that being the phrase. They all thought it very droll, apparently. A week later Martell was dead."

Lenox and Montague discussed this strange turn of affairs for a good while. Could the apothecary have meant it literally? Ought they to check with Inspector Adamson once more that Jacob Phipps's alibi had been legitimate? But, no—where he was at the time had been attested by numerous impartial witnesses in the report.

It was an intriguing, almost maddening hint. A boy of ten years old.

With the five o'clock post, a note came from the Duke of Aderkenalty. Lenox could tell when the letters came in on the tray, for the envelope was twice as large as the others, on paper heavy as linen, with the ducal seal impressed upon it.

```
Dec. 12 79
Lenox—
I do not know the symbol. I have consulted
Pugin and Scott but neither record it and
you may be sure that these later-coming
revival fools would not tolerate it. Of older
London symbolism I would concede to few
(this Maeve woman is sharp I grant you) and
it is not dated to them. Nor did Ruskin know
it, and I had him out of bed to be asked.
But if you tell me there are three instances
in W.4, I must add it to my book. It is
impertinent of you. Best to Jane.

Aderkenalty.
Wisteria House, Pall Mall.
```

Enclosed was Lenox's crude drawing of the symbol, on which the Duke had scrawled, "I have sent out one of my young men to make a better drawing—you will be copied one." There were a dozen architects the Duke employed, most of them building him an immense Palladian folly upon the western shores of Scotland.

"Take a look at that," said Lenox, and handed the note to Montague.

As the lad read it, Lenox dashed off a quick letter telling Adamson of the new phrase, "a boy of ten years old." Then he wrote to the Duke.

When he was done with these notes, Lenox told Montague all about the little symbol—which, he admitted, had become its own mystery to him, independent of the Martell business.

"How can I help?" Montague asked.

"My own plan is to walk the area and look for more of them." He peered outside doubtfully. "Well—tomorrow, anyhow."

"I might go to the registry office and check who owns the buildings," suggested Montague.

"That is an excellent idea. But does the agency not have you on a case?"

"No—Lady Dallington told me to stick with you until this was finished. 'Stick with you,' those were her words."

How good Polly was to him. "Very well," said Lenox. "Let us pursue it. What else did Lang Tu tell you?" he asked. "Would it be useful to recount the story once more?"

So Montague did this, and they were in the midst of discussing it yet again when they heard a thump come from upstairs, followed by a loud voice, and then a soft second one, and a loud, long return. A door slammed. Then the voices started again, and Montague stood up.

"I shall return tomorrow at about midday, having visited the registry," he said.

"Excellent," said Lenox. "I had better go and see what that is about."

Montague took his umbrella in the front hall and went out under Kirk's watchful eye, while Lenox went in the opposite direction. He was halfway through bounding up the stairs when he noticed how easy it was; how since being ill, since his obsessive streak of days walking mile upon mile, step upon step; how since his work with Sven, too, which had given him the strength to recover from this illness—how through all of that! He was better.

But there was barely time to reflect on this, for as he entered the sitting room where they always passed the hour before dinner, he heard another tremendous thump, and Sari's voice, crying, "How *could* you?"

CHAPTER THIRTY-FIVE

All five women of the house were in the sitting room, with its pretty pale green wallpaper. Lady Jane and her two daughters were pressed in surprise against the back of the little walnut sofa, eyes wide. Sari and Angela were about eight feet apart, staring daggers at each other.

From the books on the floor he surmised that Sari had been throwing things at Angela. He had a brief vision of his future—for neither Clara nor Sophia was meek.

Sari whirled accusingly on Lenox, "And you knew?"

Lenox saw that there were large tears in her eyes. "Angela told me that she might like—"

"To leave me," said Sari bitterly. "After a childhood together, after a trip across the world together, she—"

"You are going to be married," said Angela.

"I am not!" said Sari hotly. "And I have told you so a hundred times, a thousand times, you hardheaded obnoxious—"

"You are going to be married soon," Angela repeated doggedly, indeed hardheadedly, "and as kind as you have all been to me, I have no place here."

They all objected to this at once. Angela ignored them.

"Let me finish, please. I know now that I am very lucky in my family connections. It was something my father never told me we had, and I am bitter for it and grateful at once."

There was a silence.

"But I must find my own path." She turned her look back to Sari and a soft smile appeared on her face. "When you are married, my dear, if it is one of the rich ones, you may keep a bedroom for me. And if it is one of the poor ones, I shall sleep in the garden. I have always known the world would want you, Sari. Why wouldn't they? You are the best person in it. But it is time for me to get out of my way."

Sari was silent, her small body racked by sobs. "You are wrong, you are wrong," she said miserably.

"Edmund has no wife, and little society," Angela said, and Lenox realized then that she had perceived Edmund, too, was not just consulting her own wishes. "Perhaps I can help him a little, as a young female relative. Someone to pour tea." She took her old friend's hands. "And the economics, dear one, the economics! Think of how happy that shall make me."

Sari looked at her, as if to say that she understood all of this—it all made sense—but it had nothing to do with them. "How could you?"

The Indian girl burst into tears then and flew from the room—after which Clara, too, burst into tears, and ran out, trailed by her sister and mother.

This left Lenox and Angela facing each other. "Couldn't have gone better!" he said brightly.

She had the grace to smile, though she looked bereft. "I will go to my room now, if you do not mind, Cousin."

"Of course not. But, Angela, are you sure? Why not wait?"

The girl shook her head. "If I stayed, it would stop her, I know it would, her loyalty—and why should I stop her from being married? Why should I deny her what my father and her mother had? Only check on the man she chooses, Cousin. Please."

For the first time since he had known her he saw her face tremble with emotion. She was near tears. Lenox longed to reach out and hold her; and he remembered that he had once in a while felt the same about Jasper, whose uncanny knack with animals had almost made him seem one of them, as if the world had touched him less, nature held on to him a little longer, than most.

He might not have done it a month earlier—but he had been very ill, and impulsively he stepped forward and took her into his arms. She returned the pressure lightly, but he held on tightly, as if she were her father, and he were saying goodbye. He didn't let go, and after a moment she relented into his chest, and soon she, too, was sobbing, long feeling-full exhalations, a silence released.

"We love you, dear," he murmured.

And when supper came an hour or so later, all six members of the household were seated, and in the event it was one of the most laughter-filled, joyous of their meals together; and Sari and Angela's truce, whatever its terms, meant that they had rarely seemed closer, finishing each other's sentences.

After supper Angela and Sophia were playing cards, when Sari approached Lenox and Lady Jane. "If Angela goes, I can go, too," she said quietly.

"We would not forgive you or her," said Lady Jane.

And that was the end of that idea.

It was an unusually cold night, but Lenox felt an itch to be out in the city. On the third floor, he spent a moment sitting beside each of his daughters' beds—his last daily moment with the miracle, the genuine miracle—and after kissing them good night, he withdrew, went down to the front hall, and put on his greatcoat. As he donned it, he saw the windowpane catch a few snowflakes, which stayed still, crystalline, in the cold.

He had lived in this city for most of his life and recognized it, from a hundred small signs he couldn't have named, the scent, the temperature, the humidity, for what it was: the beginning of a blizzard.

Nevertheless he went out, turning right up toward Grosvenor Square. He had no fixed destination in mind, merely wandered. Soon enough he ended up at White's, one of his clubs.

"Hullo, Winters," he said to the stolid porter.

"Good evening, Mr. Lenox."

"Anyone in?"

By this Lenox meant his brother, or one of his half-dozen particular friends. "No, sir," said Winters.

Lenox nodded hello to several people on his way through the richly paneled rooms. In the bar, he asked the barman, LeBoff, for a cup of coffee with whisky. When he received it, he went outside and sat down on the balcony, where he could be alone.

He knew as a fact what some Londoners denied, which was that you could see the sky better in the country—in no context but its own immense blackness, the air around you as noiseless as space. But as he sat on the balcony of his club, wrapped in his scarf and an overcoat, drinking his coffee and watching large flakes of snow fall very slowly but steadily over the London buildings, he felt nearly that completeness. It was so still. He took a long breath, then another, then another. He still could not quite believe that his wound was better. He felt new; the joy of newness.

Some fifteen minutes or so later he heard the door click gently open behind him, and saw that it was Graham.

"Good evening," said his old valet, compact and tidy in his dark suit. "Winters said you were here."

"Graham!"

"May I join you? I asked for tea to be sent out."

Soon enough this came, and LeBoff brought Lenox more coffee, too. They sat in silence for a few moments, staring at the stars. "There is all of that and then there is us, eh, Graham? A million other worlds."

"This one has been difficult enough for me to understand at times, I confess, sir," said Graham, and laughed, his eyes crinkling. It was a rare and amusing sound to hear, Graham's laugh—and Lenox recognized in it some of his own nervous exhaustion. But that made no sense. Graham was the strongest person Lenox knew.

"Why are you here at this late hour?" asked the detective, following his hunch.

"I happened to be passing, and asked Winters if anyone was in."

Lenox nodded. "I did the same."

"I had dinner with several senior members at the Reform," said Graham. "Indigestible food." He sighed. "I fear I am becoming a nuisance. There is talk of me being sent to Ireland. A great honor, you know."

He laughed bitterly.

Now his mood made sense. He was coming from receiving bad news. They were going to try to ship Graham out of the way—useful in opposition, but not quite "our kind," when it came to ruling, his birth against him. Lenox felt a rush of anger.

"Is it settled?"

"No," said Graham, jaw set. "I will fight."

They sat in silence for a long time. At last Lenox ventured that Ireland was not so bad. Graham said he was sure it was so—but was not in a great haste to prove it to himself personally.

"I am already half Irish, I suppose, " Graham said, "for they say there that the trouble with the English is that they never remember, and the trouble with the Irish is that they never forget. I shall never forget this insult."

"I'm sorry, Graham." Then suddenly, Lenox realized why he had left the house. "Graham," he said, "it is late and I know you will decline. But do you have any interest in a bit of a tramp with me? It's about a case—the Huggins case, still."

"I should like nothing better than such a distraction," Graham said, standing. "Let us go at once."

CHAPTER THIRTY-SIX

It was late the next afternoon, about four o'clock, and Adamson, the inspector from Scotland Yard, seemed perplexed by Lenox's continuing desire to know who had killed Austin Martell.

They were at the Coach and Horses. Lenox was in such high favor with Ernest Huggins that he barely took the last sip of his pint of mild before another one appeared at his elbow. Above the two veteran London detectives, a soft yellow lamp dropped its even pool of light, swinging gently whenever anyone came in or left.

"Neither the street nor the world seems worse without Martell in it," the inspector said.

"That may well be."

"The only time I never heard a single kind word about the dead man in a murder investigation."

Lenox had asked Adamson to meet to discuss the case, but he had no idea what Martell could have meant by "a boy of ten" being his murderer, and no interest in speculation about it. Only when Montague's bright, excitable young face appeared in the doorway did Lenox hope for anything from the outing.

"You found a fourth mark?" Montague said without any sort of salutation.

"Yes!"

"I have been studying the problem all day. Lady Dallington—Polly—thinks it looks like a monogram."

"May I see it again?" Adamson asked.

Lenox was going to produce the little drawing he had in his pocket, but Montague in his enthusiasm had already slapped down a larger piece of paper with a rough rendering of the little mark.

"There it is," he said. "Excuse me, I need a pint. Bitter weather, isn't it? Imagine, it used to be spring, not so long ago."

Lenox and Graham had, indeed, found a fourth example of the little mark. It had been extremely fun to be out on the trail together, however briefly. For three decades now, Lenox (and usually with Graham by his side) had treated crime scenes the same way: by circling outward, an inch or two at a time in some cases, until he had found everything scattered into the area by the incident—blood, pocket change, a weapon, whatever it might be.

He and Graham had done the same the night before. First Lenox had shown him the two marks, at the tobacconist's and the stationer's.

"Shall we try Berwick Street?" Lenox had asked.

The streets had been all but empty, large flakes falling in unrushed windborne drifts. Lenox had explained as they walked how the three marks of which he knew were set exactly two streets apart. They tracked their paces up and down the long narrow avenue then, walking through the shuttered stalls of the little market where Berwick crossed Peter Street.

Graham was rarely personal in his conversation, but after they had walked several blocks, he said, "I have seen Lady Jane in the newspapers."

"Yes," said Lenox.

He didn't know what to add. Fortunately, Graham started to talk in a general way—recalling, from their early years in London, the great philosopher and political leader John Stuart Mill's introduction of the subject of the women's vote in Parliament. That had been in 1867, and though the debate in the House of Commons had elicited a storm of reaction in the press, nothing had come of it in the end.

"So it always goes," Lenox said, as they continued up Berwick Street. His eyes were scanning each entryway. Nothing yet. "There is a period of excitement about some new, fairer idea, and then the forces of revolt say it can never be, and then the idea is reintroduced with some of the edges taken off of it, and—by 1979, let us say, a hundred years hence, the Englishwoman of property will be granted a vote."

Graham had smiled at this, his quiet smile, hands in his pockets. "It is no wonder you left politics," he said. "Your estimation of it being so low."

"Perhaps that is true," said Lenox.

"Do you know what Lady Jane's aim is?"

"She—she and her friends, I suppose—would like the woman's vote to be included in the next Reform Act."

Graham raised his eyebrows a little. This would be a difficult task—perhaps an impossible one. But all he said was, "So would I."

"Are you a suffragist, then, Graham?" Lenox asked.

"I suppose I am." He walked alongside Lenox in silence for a few moments. "I have known my whole life that the people who have power did not do much to earn it."

Lenox nodded. "Indeed."

"Of course it was taught to us in school that the authority of God was what made a duke, or a king, of one man, and a peasant of another." Graham laughed self-deprecatingly. "Of me. Or so Lord Winmouth called me at a party meeting last week."

Lenox winced. Winmouth was a scotch-soaked bag of old bones, who had been bullying the less well born since he was in short pants; but he had authority in a room.

"I told him I am. And proud of it."

Graham was worth ten of Winmouth, a hundred—but whatever he might achieve, he could never turn himself into the son of a lord.

They had reached the bottom of Berwick Street, studying each doorway, and stopped. Lenox felt an obscure disappointment: nothing. But Graham was unwilling to give up. Two streets over was Dean Street, and he insisted that they try that.

It was in a little cake shop that they saw the symbol once more. "Graham!"

Graham stopped—Lenox had grabbed him by the arm. "There it is," he said.

They stooped and looked at the carving.

"It only looks ten or fifteen years old," said Graham, who knew a good deal about carving. He came from a family of craftsmen. His uncles had been master masons, and his cousin Monkshade had been a woodcarver on the new Houses of Parliament a half century before. "I wonder what it is."

"We may never know," said Lenox. "But I love a mystery."

He carefully noted down the address, though he hardly could have forgotten it; and in excitement they walked on, though they did not see the mark again all up and down Dean Street, despite traversing it twice.

"I think I have long assumed that women would get the vote in time," said Lenox, as they turned back up the broad avenue, filled with bare trees, leading back to the West End. A few lonely vagrants haunted the doorways, huddled over small kerosene lamps with their tobacco. Lenox thought of Ezekiel Phipps. "It's only that I did not think Jane would take up a position in the discussion."

Graham did not reply but Lenox had known his old friend long enough to perceive exactly what the silence meant, and a feeling of wrongdoing burst in upon him. When had he ever known Lady Jane to take up a cause wrongly? When had he ever said that he would not stand by her even if she did?

"Perhaps I can do more to help her," he said.

When at last they were finished in their search, Lenox had walked Graham home to his very eligible new apartments in Pimlico, then turned back to Hampden Lane. He had slept in the next morning till nine—lunched late—and the day was really starting now, near dark, at the Coach and Horses.

Montague returned with his pint. He drank half of it down in one swoop, then sat, wiping his mouth with the back of his hand.

"They haven't gotten back to me at the registry office," he said. "But look at this. You know the tobacconist's? Guess how the previous proprietor vacated the premises?"

Lenox felt a chill. "How?" he said, though he knew. His instincts about London were rarely wrong.

Montague looked up at him. "Murdered."

CHAPTER THIRTY-SEVEN

The music of the pub's conversation continued unabated. "Murdered," he repeated, almost with relish. So they were really onto something. "Who was he?"

Montague shook his head. "A tailor named Wyatt. He was garroted outside of his shop, now the tobacconist's."

"Was it solved?" asked Lenox.

Montague shrugged. "No idea. I have nothing except the name and the cause of death."

"Do you remember the case?" Lenox asked Adamson.

"No," said the inspector abruptly. He took the last gulp of his beer. "And I must be going. I leave you gentlemen to your leisure."

That last word was pointed; Lenox and Montague exchanged glances after he had gone. "What about the third place?" Lenox asked.

"I couldn't find anything. Yet. But now I have the address of the fourth mark, too." Montague's eyes were shining with the thrill of the chase. "Do you think it a pattern?"

"Certainly it is a pattern—whether the pattern has any meaning . . ."

Just at that moment the Passenger was coming by. Lenox stopped him, inviting him to sit, and repeated the name: Wyatt, the tailor.

"Wyatt! I remember him," said the Passenger. "No accounting for the violence in that district."

It was five streets away, and Montague began to object—but Lenox raised a silencing hand. In a city as dense and territorial as London, five streets could sometimes be two counties' distance. That was the Passenger's prerogative.

"What were the details?"

"Unlikable fellow," said the chap, sitting back comfortably, thumb in the ticket pocket of his jacket. "But a damn fine tailor, with reasonable rates. So I heard anywise. He was late one night doing the books, and when his apprentice arrived at four the next morning, he found him in the doorway, strangled. Piano wire. They said it bit down to the bone."

Montague grimaced. The Passenger looked pleased. "If you think that's bad there's a few tales for you by the hearth, young chap."

"Did he have any connection to Martell?" asked Lenox.

The Passenger frowned. "Oh no, no. The story given out was that he had the week's till on him, and someone saw the chance to grab it for their own."

This had been the story given out about Martell, too, though.

The Passenger went on talking for a good long while after that without saying anything very particular, dilating on the danger of cities at night, the nature of tailors ("too intimate to be quite nice, but the world's got to have 'em or we'd all be nekkid!"), and the subject that more than any other was dominating the conversation of the pub, Ezekiel Phipps.

But Phipps was old news to Lenox; and after a polite interval, he suggested Montague walk him part of the way home so that they could discuss the case.

This they did, Montague indeed bringing Lenox all the way to Hampden Lane. "I cannot sleep yet," he said when they parted. "I will go to Dean Street and begin to look again. Damn them their slowness at the registry office! I want to know more!"

Lenox went inside with the lovely feeling of having—a friend, a protégé? A friend, he thought; this lower-middle-class boy from Lincolnshire being, in remarkably many respects, so much like himself.

Inside he discovered that it was just past the girls' bedtime. He took up a chair in the corner of their room, and read a little *Twelfth Night* by the light of the small lantern that Clara still needed lit throughout the night so as not to be scared. He stole a sip from the untouched glass of milk his eldest daughter had no doubt refused to drink before bedtime, if he knew her. He soon enough dozed off in the chair.

When he woke it was a good hour later, the sky told him, and something was different than usual. It took him a moment to realize what it was: his wound did not hurt. A little sore, but not painful. He smiled.

He stopped himself from getting straight up, from going about the day, to sit with this awareness; and a great darkness lifted out of his mind, for it was a misery to wake out of sleep every time, every time, and feel that pain: defeat before you began, every day at best the bargain of a good day.

He glanced at the clock in the corner. Nearly nine o'clock. Had he been woken by—yes, it must have been the door, for he heard voices two stories down, one Kirk's, one muffled and unfamiliar.

He went downstairs. Kirk was in the front hall. "Lord Carbury, sir," said the butler, looking a little harassed, when Lenox reached the ground floor.

Lenox frowned. "Carbury?"

"Yes, sir."

Jane's dashing young cousin was in the small gray sitting room, studying the street through the window, perhaps pondering just how they had built Rome in a day. He looked troubled, his usually neat hair wild and tall, his face exhausted.

"Hullo, sir!" he said, with a kind of aching ferocity—no echo of his old agreeable insouciance.

"Good evening, Carbury. I see you have already poured yourself a drink."

"Oh, sir! No, Kirk poured it for me."

"I know, I know," Lenox said. The boy's life was such an uninterrupted dreamscape of horses, clothes, gambling, and girls, above all girls, that the detective always gave him a bad time, by way of cosmic balance. But right now he looked as if he had been going through enough. "Take a seat, George. I am glad to see you. How may I help?"

"Oh, sir, you can. I think only you can, in fact."

"Are you finally ready to buckle down and work? Maybe you could be one of Edmund's secretaries."

Carbury's handsome face went doubtful. "Well—no, sir. Though I will. I will work, if I must!"

"What do you mean?"

"Sir!" he cried. "You must speak to her! You must tell her that I love her with all my heart—that I will give it all up for her—the title, my family, anything!"

His family! "Who?" said Lenox.

"Who!" Carbury looked as if he couldn't imagine anyone whose mind hadn't been on the same subject as his own.

Lenox felt anger rising in him; for here was a boy who would set his heart at Sari, win her, and be done with her in a week, as if she were a racehorse he bought, won a race with, and immediately sold off to buy four more. He knew it. The boy could only be here because Sari's name was moving through the clubs, that day's delight. It infuriated him.

And Lenox was about to say something extremely sharp, when Carbury howled, "Who!" again. "Who! Your niece, of course! Angela!"

Lenox was shocked. Carbury paced frantically, hands clasped behind his back. "She is my cousin, not my niece," Lenox said automatically. "You are in love with Angela?"

Carbury looked at him as if he were as thick as a plank. "Yes."

"I confess I thought you meant Sari."

"Her friend Sari? No—I—" He turned away to his pacing.

I must tell Jasper: that had been Lenox's first thought. Funny, for he had often thought it in the years after his mother's and father's deaths. Less frequently now, but never never.

"Georgie, is it a fad? You are always after some girl."

Carbury stopped in his tracks. "I swear I have never felt this way."

They stared at each other. Lenox found he believed him. He did not bother to say—she has very little money, or, she is not at all accustomed to society. He presumed Carbury understood this, perhaps even found it appealing.

But he couldn't resist asking, "Why Angela?"

Carbury, who was often lost for words, spoke as if he had been waiting up all night for someone to ask just that question. "Why the stars! Why the sun!" he said. "Every other girl I have ever met in my whole accursed life till now has been false and striving and seen nothing of me—of *me*, you see?—for a single second."

"And Angela—"

"If she were homely and deformed," said Carbury, with a real fervor building, "I should love the shoes on her feet—that she is as beautiful as an angel, a positive angel, as her name, is only an added—a pleasure beyond that of knowing her character—of—I must know more about her father, Lenox, incidentally—"

"Don't call me that."

"I'm sorry, sir. But do you have his letters? His memoirs? Think how remarkable he must have been!"

"He was a splendid fellow," said Lenox. He was still in shock. "But she is not some innocent, Georgie."

"Sir! She is the opposite!" The boy stood straight as an arrow, as if he could leave his feet and fly to his wishes. "She has the wisdom of a hundred lifetimes, sir!"

Lenox, who had seen Angela puzzle for five minutes that morning over how to use her grapefruit knife, thought perhaps not quite a hundred. But he was not one to stand in the way of young love. "What does she make of your suit?"

"She does not return my letters—but oh, there is the chime of the clock, and here I have been sitting for hours, and now I must be going, damn it all and blast it to hell, but I must—sir, plead my case, you must, sir."

He stormed out in his own tempest, cane and hat in hand, Kirk invisible to him. Lenox and the butler exchanged a glance born of long familiarity. The detective walked back to his study, wondering what would become of this young unexpected ward of his next. Even at this age, he was still surprised continually by the world.

CHAPTER THIRTY-EIGHT

Lenox spent a frustrating three hours the next morning walking north and south along Berwick Street, Dean Street, and the various small and large thoroughfares that linked them, methodically searching for another mark. He found none. Finally he bought a salted hard-boiled egg and a hot seeded roll from a vendor and walked moodily back to Hampden Lane, munching them in disappointed contemplation.

At home, he saw in the hallway Angela's neat little leather cases stacked by the door. For the first time he saw they had Jasper's initials on their straps. They must have been a present when he went out to England.

Then he saw Edmund's head pop around the corner. "Hello, Charles!" he said. "Beastly cold. I say, could I trouble you for a spot of lunch before I take her?"

"Of course."

Angela came down the steps at that moment and saw Edmund. "Thank you for coming to get me. You needn't have."

"Nonsense. But I am going to have a bite of food before we go—if you don't mind? I have been at Parliament since dawn." A stormy look passed over his face. "Some of these fools would already be bargaining for their position in the next government."

Edmund, whose birth and amiability had made ambition unnecessary to him, had too little appreciation of the fact that those men had been bargaining for years for those positions. Not since that morning. It passed through Lenox's mind that he hoped Ed wouldn't be battered—if he really did become the Chancellor of the Exchequer. Good lord. It was a high post. Well, someone in the family had to stir themselves every couple hundred years to keep the family name afloat.

"Is Sari coming?" asked Edmund.

Angela's face fell. "No. Excuse me," she said. "I need a little while, too, if you don't mind."

She left in tears. Edmund had asked the question innocently enough. "What did I say?" he asked, looking almost boyish with astonishment, in his old-fashioned coal-black tailcoat.

"Come and have some victuals," said Charles, clapping Edmund on the shoulder. "I daresay a glass of malmsey wouldn't go amiss either."

In his study after they had eaten, Edmund was reading *The Times* on the sofa, as Charles contemplated the little mark that had so occupied him these last two or three days. He had Aderkenalty's much finer and more detailed copy:

$$\mathcal{K}\mathcal{F}$$

On his desk was a package with an illustrated legend of the hallmarks of silversmiths and goldsmiths in London for the last century, which he had requested from the specialist bookshop. He opened it. "The first silversmiths thought to stamp their work in 400 AD," he read, and flipped several pages ahead. "The most common element among the smiths' mark is the lion of England, followed by the crown, then initials." The trouble was this one looked more like a maze to Lenox. "Occasionally smiths reverse letters to differentiate their initials from makers' with identical initials."

This was more interesting. Lenox took Aderkenalty's drawing. If you separated it, there were two letters: an F and a backwards K. It seemed plausible when you gazed down upon them: ℀. Or was he fooling himself?

There was a knock. It was Lady Jane, who was dressed in one of the slim new sorts of day dress one saw, with a fine row of ruffles down its center, and delicate white cuffs.

"Angela is ready," she said.

"Thank you, dear," said Charles, and both brothers rose.

She stood in the hallway alone, in her new blue cloak, a present from Lady Jane. In the hallway Lenox embraced her, and held her by the shoulders for an extra moment at arm's length. Still too thin, he thought. Jasper, am I failing her?

"You have to be very strict with Edmund," he said.

"What's that?" said his brother, coming in, holding a slim volume bound in brown Morocco leather. "Here it is, Angela—I knew I had left it with my brother. Unopened, of course. There is still not a finer mind that has ever bent itself upon the economics, in my view, than Ricardo's. And I think even Malthus himself would have accorded with that position. Now as to influence, Smith—"

Kirk came down the stairs followed by two footmen, who had the old, battered trunk between them, the one that had been Sari and Angela's whole little life until Portsmouth Harbour. "Miss Sari wished you to take this," he said.

A fiery look flashed in Angela's eyes. "Tell her I shall not. Tell her she must keep it."

Kirk raised his eyebrows just a little. "Very good, miss," he said.

She took the book from Edmund with sincere gratitude, tied her bonnet, and put her arm through his. And it was then, with their backs to him, that Lenox saw he hadn't failed his cousin—at least, not his cousin Angela. She was happy.

No: it was Jasper he had failed. True, the detective had been young, but so had his cousin. Charles ought to have kept up the correspondence—ought never to have slackened in writing because Jazz did—ought perhaps even to have visited, though he knew it was a far-fetched idea, or invited his cousin back, made him understand he still belonged in England, too.

They went outside. It was gray, the streets almost unpopulated because of the fierce snowless cold. A one-legged old veteran, a beggar, huddled in a doorway across Hampden Lane, and Edmund dashed across after he had deposited Angela in one side of the carriage, gave the man a coin, and then got in on the street side of the carriage himself. Lenox squeezed Angela's hand through the window—and then they were off.

Lady Jane was waiting for him in the sunny entryway, looking through her tiny daily appointment book, when he returned.

She smiled. "Now we only need to marry the other one off."

"Jane! Will you be so ruthless when Clara and Sophia are out in society?"

"I suppose I will, if I think it will make them happy—I suppose so," she said, hooking her arm in his, just as Angela had done. "People are their own selves after all. She will love being at Edmund's, and as for Sari, she was born to be in society. She just needs to learn a bit more about it first. If she can become the bride of a rich man, we shall have discharged our duty."

"What of his character?"

"No men are very good, Charles—if he is not a brute and she loves him, we will call it a happy day. At least that is my opinion."

"It is a low aim for women—the people you are out protesting to give the vote to."

"That is why I am out protesting," she said dryly. She kissed him on the cheek, and retreated to her desk in the pink drawing room.

As for Lenox, he could not resist the lure of the case. He ought by rights to have gone into the office yet what he found himself doing was dressing in a double overcoat (rarest of London riggings, but such was the cold), sticking a piece of biscuit in his outer pocket, and hitting the streets.

He loved the light on days like this, the city's spires quiet and stark, the sun never too strong, but diffracting in random brilliance here and there as the clouds moved. And the streets so beautifully clean and empty, as if man had made this place and left it.

He went first to Soho Square, two streets on from Dean Street. He held out little hope. Yet his doggedness had been intrinsic to his character as a detective. This was perhaps in reaction to the scorn of some members of his class at the choice, back in the distant '50s and '60s. Defiance: not always a useful cause for motivation, perhaps, but certainly a powerful one.

And then he saw it.

He was standing there motionless. A happy-looking fellow in a cap and a tunic, precious little for this weather, was driving pigs through Soho Square, and paused to say to Lenox—"What's got you stoppered, guv? Price of beefsteak?"

Lenox looked at him and grinned. "Can't find a decent chop in Westminster any longer."

The fellow tilted his head back and laughed and continued hustling the pigs through the square toward the market up north on Rose Street.

Lenox, for his part, stayed there: what had commanded his attention so absolutely was another mark, at 1 Soho Square, and another, the very next doorway down, at number three, and two doors beyond that one, at number seven. He must finally be close to the heart of the mystery.

CHAPTER THIRTY-NINE

At the gymnastiskaal the next morning, Lenox felt springy. He even forgave Sven with what he considered a certain greatheartedness for saying "Push harder, harder—you cannot even be sixty, sir, yet, can you?"

In the lounge, Lenox passed Wickham Murdock, the officious newspaper baron, who said, by way of greeting, "Is it true you're marrying that talented little Indian off to an earl's son?"

Lenox froze. Murdock was with one of his lieutenants, the editor of the *Daily Clarion*—who snickered. Lenox turned to face Murdock fully. They had been together at one or two supper parties in the past year, because Murdock was welcomed everywhere these days, even the palace. It was what gave him license to make a personal comment.

"Are you asking as an acquaintance or a reporter?"

A little silence fell and an eye or two turned quickly up in the steamy, pine-lined lounge, with its freezing-cold clear windows.

Murdock reddened, an ugly reaction distorting his features. "What kind of comment is that meant to be, Lenox?"

Murdock fancied himself for a lordship, and had long since stopped being involved with the daily operation of any of his newspapers, and had—as the very rich always could—several prominent politicians as his paid vassals and "friends." The implication that he himself was a gutter reporter was a grave insult.

This told in his twitching small body. His power was immense; but he also had two daughters, plain, dull-minded young girls, whom he longed to make good marriages and lives for—the one thing he had not yet figured out how to buy exactly bespoke, for the truly eligible young men would not have crossed the street to save the lives of either of them.

Lenox saw Murdock weighing him now. Lenox, this malevolent little man was thinking, meant Lady Jane. And Lady Jane: the world.

"I would ask you to withdraw your comment, Murdock," said the detective. Even he could hear his voice carried a certain danger. "All else aside, it is beneath you to speak so of a woman."

She was only not off-limits because she was Indian; Murdock's face said that he had taken that as tacitly accepted between the two of them. He glared at Lenox for a pregnant beat. "Apologies," he muttered, and turned and walked away.

Well, another enemy. So be it.

It was warmer that morning, and Lenox felt so invigorated that he walked by Soho Square again, just to look with his own eyes at the seventh version of the little symbol he'd discovered the night before. Montague was this very morning at the registry office, asking about the old addresses and the new.

And indeed, the sprightly young fellow, with his upward-sweeping pale ginger hair, was waiting on the step in Hampden Lane, as if he weren't quite sure which entrance to use.

"Good morning, sir!" he cried.

"Come inside, Montague, come inside," said Lenox—and realized with a little smile, following the young man in, that he sounded old now, that in his own fervent twenties he could have stood three days outside upon such a stoop for a case. It was a jolly joke in a way—life.

In the front hall there were three dozen Delilah roses, which Kirk was attending. "From Lord Carbury," he said to Lenox.

So the lad still had not spoken to Angela—well, it was the most absurd thing for a young bachelor to give a "household" that he could conceive, and since Angela was not here everyone would certainly assume it was intended for Sari. So, all in all, about what one would expect of Georgie.

"Are you being courted, sir?" asked Montague.

Lenox laughed. "Very good."

Montague had a packet of papers in his hand—Lenox had spotted it before anything else, and had been waiting impatiently in the fore of his mind during this whole entrance to find out what it was.

"Coffee and tea, please, Kirk," he called out as he went to his study. "Scalding hot."

"Yes, sir," said Kirk.

Lenox closed the door and Montague said, "I've got them, sir—the first addresses. And it's interesting."

Lenox took the thin folder from him. It had just two sheets of paper, a receipt from the registry office for half a shilling, the cost of looking up the deeds, and a list of the deeds themselves. He scanned it:

```
Jaddo J. by Deed
Dunham by Sale
Francis by Deed
Jaddo J. by Deed
Jaddo by Deed
```

"Jaddo," Lenox said. "Any idea who he is?"

"No, sir, and they had no information there for him except an address, near Lincoln's Inn. Perhaps a fellow in the law, some barrister, solicitor, judge."

Three houses, ten streets apart in London, could not be coincidentally owned by the same man.

"Give me a moment to change," he said to Montague. "And we shall pay a call at Lincoln's Inn."

He was obscurely disappointed that it was not an ⚥—for he had grown rather fond of that theory. But inflexibility of mind was the deadliest trait a detective could have, and he had already filed the idea away with the "boy of ten," the connection to the opium dens, and the rest of the case's details.

In his bedroom he changed from his gym clothes into an informal dark suit that was good for long wear; he had an idea he might need it. He pulled on his best pair of cork-soled boots.

Lenox thought how lucky he was and vowed that if he really was better now, after his American voyage, he would begin to set aright his little universe, which had wobbled this last year. Starting with a trip to find McConnell.

But that would have to wait. Downstairs he found Montague reading from the *Illustrated Saturday Post*, and sipping a cup of coffee. "Ready," said Lenox.

Montague stood with his cup. "Very good," he said.

"No, stay, finish your coffee and I will swallow down a little tea." He took the ebony handle of the silver pot and poured himself a half cup. A splash of milk. A sip, and he sighed, happy for a moment. He sat on the arm of one of the brown sofas. "Odd name, Jaddo."

"Most likely bastardized French, sir," said Montague, "something like 'Giroux' or 'Jadeau,' I would wager. Either that or a West Yorkshireman, but you don't see many of those in London."

"Impressive. How do you know?" he asked.

Montague squinted and looked away, as if quoting. "'It is wise to learn one or two useful subfields of knowledge as thoroughly as an expert.'"

"Who said that?"

Montague blushed. "You, sir!" he said. But he forged on. "You said that you had chosen wound types, London geography, criminal history, and one or two others, but that if you had to do it over again, you would learn something that touched every case, something mundane, like names. I chose names."

Lenox had only given one interview about his profession—by mail, to an old friend in America, a veteran of their Civil War. It was many years before. Somehow the boy must have found that. Could he flatter himself that it was circulated among fans of the art of detection? Perhaps it was not conceited to think so!

"I do not remember saying it, but it sounds very pompous—and thus, I can believe it."

"Oh, no, sir! The number of times my knowledge of names has given me a new turn on a case, you would scarcely credit it."

Lenox took another draught of his tea. "Good then. Now stick one of those sandwiches in your jacket pocket and let's get in the carriage."

CHAPTER FORTY

There were four Inns of Court in London: the Middle Temple, the Inner Temple, Gray's, and Lincoln's, which was where they arrived now. It was an eleven-square-acre warren of barristers' chambers, domiciles, and clerks' offices, surrounded by a tall and rather beautiful wall of red brick—it was said that Ben Jonson, the playwright and close friend of Shakespeare, had laid some of its bricks in his youth.

The porter, who wore a sharp suit and a bowler hat, was an iron-faced man of fifty. Lenox's fine clothes and accent would cut no ice with him.

"Yes?" he said.

"We are hoping to pay a call upon a resident of the west tower. Mr. J. Jaddo."

The porter looked up sharply from his calendar. Behind him were ranged volume upon volume of the black books which recorded the history of Lincoln's Inn, some from as far back as the 1400s. The newer ones had gold embossing on the spines.

"What is your business?"

"We are detectives," said Lenox. "He's wanted for questioning."

The porter gave them a hard look, then sat back in his chair, having made a decision. "There are two of them, the Jaddos. John and

Jacob. Not one. So you're already amiss. But you won't find them here anyway."

"No?"

"No."

"Then where?"

The porter looked at them again. "That is not my business. Good day, gentlemen."

They walked back outside. "Yet he knew," muttered Montague.

It was still frigid, the river gulls doing their business briskly among the rooftops. A sparrow will drop dead of cold without uttering a noise of complaint, his father had once told him. A Lenox the same.

Suddenly he had a thought. "Let's go back."

At the porter's office again, Lenox took out a five-pound note. He held it up in the weak winter light. "We only want to know who the Jaddos are. Nothing else—not to see their rooms, not to pursue their friends. Save us the time."

The porter looked at their two faces, then barked with laughter. "Keep your money," he said, "or put it in the poor box. The Jaddos are in Newgate Prison now. And though you stay a year you shall not get another word out of me."

They left through a beautiful vaulted undercroft. A perfect little gargoyle perched over the exit, leering horribly.

Neither Montague nor Lenox needed to say how alive the scent seemed now, their quarry definitively proven to be criminals suddenly—both of them were striding fast, keen upon their work, so attentive they barely spoke as they got into the carriage and began to roll across the cobblestones to Newgate.

If the Inns could claim a lineage to the fifteenth century, Newgate beat it by three hundred years at least, perhaps more. The building they pulled up to half an hour later stood immense, fearsome, and completely unlovely; men forfeited their lives when they entered these walls.

"That is where they hanged Michael Barrett," said Lenox in a low voice as they got down from the carriage.

"The last public hanging in London," said Montague.

"A gruesome day. It was not clear that he was guilty. But the entire country was terrified."

Barrett had been an Irish nationalist. After the Clerkenwell explosion he had been hanged here for murder; but he had been an eloquent, thoughtful person, and few there that day enjoyed seeing him die.

They entered through an ominous stone arch underneath a flying St. George's Cross. "I have been here many times," Lenox said. "Follow me."

He led them down a corridor past the main porter, through an open yard where a few dozen men were taking exercise on the other side of sturdy bars, and into the director's office: a lowborn fellow named McKee, fat, shiny, and a passionate lover of music, who had started staging concerts in the prison.

His secretary called him when he saw Lenox, and McKee pushed his head out of the door. "Mr. Lenox!" he said.

"Hello," said Lenox. "I am after talking to a prisoner named Jaddo—two prisoners, it may be."

McKee's face opened into true astonishment. "Jaddo!" he said.

"Yes. John or Jacob, I believe."

McKee—never lost for words—just stared at Lenox. "But, sir!"

"Yes?" said Lenox curiously.

"They were both escaped out last night, sir! What it's a Monday!"

Lenox and Montague exchanged a glance. Escapes were not uncommon from Newgate—there were one or two a month, and a dozen failed ones beside. It was possible with the use of a lot of money: for the guards were not a wholesome lot, all told, and could be persuaded to look the other way. Even to turn over a key, for the right price.

But the timing of this escape made it impossible it could be a coincidence: thrillingly, the game was afoot, too.

"May we see their cell?" asked Lenox.

"I don't see why not."

They went across the yard. The inmates liked McKee, and hailed him, some with rough language ("Morning, y'old bugger"), which he ignored. It was a very good job, if you weren't nice about your morals, and not so much work.

"Why is it significant that it should be Monday?" Montague finally asked.

They had stopped at a cell, and McKee had taken out a ring of keys. "Most breakouts being on a Sunday, sir. Church Day, sir. Though holidays is the worst."

"So this happens often?" Montague asked.

"It's a large place, sir."

McKee led them into a comfortable cell with two cots, a small library of books on the sill of the barred window, an oil painting kit on a desk, and a wire birdcage in one corner, open and empty. It did not look like the cell of two men planning to escape.

"When were they missed?" asked Lenox.

"After vespers. It could have been one of twenty guards. But they would have needed someone on the outside, according to my warden, because they went over the low wall—meaning they would have had a boat waiting."

"How long was their sentence?" asked Montague.

"They were three months into sixteen."

Montague and Lenox looked among their things. They were literate, curious men, it was clear. Breaking them out was a fairly drastic measure—they would be re-imprisoned for ten years if recaptured. Of course, it was unlikely they ever would be found again, and they could give false names as easily as any man in the docket. A hungover Oxford acquaintance of Lenox's had once presented himself as "Napoleon Bonaparte" to a disbelieving magistrate after the boat race—a pound fine and he was free.

"What were they like?" asked Lenox.

"I didn't know them well. Here, let me call in Harrier."

This proved to be a guard, who told them, in a cockney accent, that the Jaddos had been London street boys, but half educated somehow nevertheless, and "fearful clever"—had run a gambling ring here in Newgate, and had the "knack," Harrier said, "what makes money flow into people."

"What are they like in person?"

"'Orrifying. We'd knew as soon as they arrived that they had a reputation, like—came up from the age of five on the streets and would slit your throat then, people said. Only trusted each other, no one a jot beyond that, even those as they were friendly with. And oh, in their person you could see it! Both of them with evil eyes—not human."

The brothers had had no visitors, they learned; few friends; and kept very close to themselves. Certainly they could have done the rest of their sentences comfortably: they had dinner in from the pub every night ("A chop, a follow chop, a penny newspaper, a pint, and a pipe," Harrier reported their identical orders to be) and female company when they wanted it. It was accepted at Newgate that money could be brought to bear on nearly any aspect of prison loneliness or deprivation.

Their crime had been forgery, apparently. Neither Harrier nor McKee knew more.

"Thank you," Lenox said, handing a coin to Harrier, who disappeared the coin and then disappeared himself down the hall, not needing to be asked twice.

McKee walked them back through the Yard. "What have they done?" he asked.

Lenox shook his head. "Hard to say," he replied. "We must go to Scotland Yard if we wish to find out."

CHAPTER FORTY-ONE

Only the Yard would have the precise criminal record. Lenox still had a few strings to pull there, though the place had changed in recent years.

Its massive redbrick shape stood motionless in the December air, like an antipode of Newgate's stone one. As always there were busy huddles of people in and around the entranceway, planning prosecutions, defenses, explanations for the police.

Lenox led them from his carriage to a side door: RECORDS. Here a desk of clerks waited, sipping tea and chatting, shuffling through papers. Lenox knew several of them.

"We are after a criminal record," he said to Evans, the fellow he knew best. He handed over a slip of paper. "Jaddo, by name."

"Fix yourself a cup of tea," said this competent chap, standing up. Lenox had bought him many a lunch over the years in exchange for information. "Ten minutes or so unless there is a problem."

Montague and Lenox retreated to a corner of the drafty room and talked over the case in the kind of involved detail that reminded Lenox of conversations in the past with Graham, with Dallington. The clerk took more like twenty minutes than ten, but that was all right, for there was an infinite amount to tease out, the little carved mark, the opium dens, the docks, the Jaddo brothers, the Phippses, Soho Square, Austin Martell.

The sun was beginning to wane in the west, a whitish light filling the sky. It would snow that night if Lenox wasn't mistaken.

"Jaddo, sir," said the clerk, approaching with a file.

Montague and Lenox took their prize to a small table, and scanned it greedily together.

"*Forgery on the deed of a house in Carlisle Street belonging to W. Trammell*," read Montague out loud.

"Off Soho Square," said Lenox.

They read the criminal case. The victim, Trammell, had been clever in tracing the Jaddos, or they wouldn't have been caught—he had noticed his name on a document that set the value at the house of ten pounds, with all movables included, a comically low price.

"Look," said Lenox, pointing to the bottom of the page.

His finger was under the penultimate sentence in the report, part of a postscript. *Trammell was killed by misadventure in June, after an accident near the Hammersmith Bridge tube station.*

Montague and Lenox exchanged a glance. "Nasty business," murmured the younger man.

They drove by Carlisle Street to see the small yellow house that had sent the Jaddo brothers to prison. To Lenox's surprise it did not have one of the carvings; he had been expecting one.

It had been a good day's work nonetheless. "If there is nothing else I will go bother them at the registry office again," said Montague.

Lenox glanced at his watch. "Good," he said. "I shall check in at home—please send word if you find anything. Or come by Hampden Lane, of course, noon and night."

It was twilight, and the detective walked the mile home. He went slowly, testing his body, his legs, his breath, his temples, for the weakness of the last year. He could not find it—he was tired, but in the healthy old way, in a way that now almost felt like alertness, fair earned soreness.

At home he spent a profitable half hour in playing squeak lamb with Clara, who was by the end of it jumbled into a soft little ball of laughter, climbing her father's face and shoulders.

"We shall have to send you to the farm to be a little lamb," said Lenox.

"That is not true," said Clara.

"No," he conceded, "probably not."

"Do lambs have school?" she asked.

Lenox frowned thoughtfully. Clara was always trying to sort the world out like this. In some ways she was brighter than Sophia, but in others slower; the advantage was doubled by age; and it was hard for her, her father often saw, to struggle into her own self when such a clever and correct one loomed older than she.

"Lambs have to clean themselves and their crofts, that's all."

"But not mathematics, or spelling."

"I did hear of a pig once that could spell."

"No, you didn't, Papa," she chided gently.

"Well—it could stamp out letters with its hoof, they said. But I think you are right, and it is not likely. Do you think piglets could draw?"

A slow grin dawned on her face, which was just an inch or two from Lenox's own, her little heart beating sturdily on next to his; full of future, full of time. Drawing was her great skill—she was the best in the family, the best since Molly had gone, as Sir Edmund often told her. Her drawing of Lenox House stood in a frame a few feet away, next to a little Giorgione drawing that had been part of Lenox's mother's dowry.

"No," she said. "Not like us."

"Perhaps they haven't been given paints, though."

"They could paint a mess."

"Like Mr. Turner," said Lenox. They had been to the galleries not long before, Jane and Sophia, too—Sophia mortally bored, Clara agog with interest.

At that moment Kirk entered with the evening papers. "Run along," Lenox told his daughter, giving her a kiss. "It is nearly suppertime."

She sprinted out without being asked again, and Lenox picked up the newspapers.

The first was the evening edition of *The Telegraph*, and there was nothing particularly interesting there; but the second was *The Clarion*, and with a sense of first shock and then anger, Lenox saw that Wickham Murdock had exacted his revenge for that slight at the gymnastiksaal.

Peer's Sister Disgraces Long Lineage
Humiliation for Houghton Earls in public display for women's vote
Mental sickness mentioned as possible cause

The article that followed contained nothing new, nothing news either—only poison. Lenox read it through twice, then threw the paper into the fire.

Lady Jane came in just after the clock struck five. She was holding a copy of the paper, too. "Have you seen this? Ten people or so have written round to tell me about it."

Lenox was behind his desk now, writing letters. "I have, darling," he said. "Put it out of your mind."

"Oh, it is far from my mind," she said, and Lenox saw it was true. "Most of them are congratulating me. But I would not want it to weigh on yours."

"Only for you," said Lenox. "I am writing a few people now, as it happens, about this Murdock. I think he has gone too far."

"Not on my behalf, Charles," she said. "I expected this."

She stood, proud and unblinking, looking at him, and he saw that his own skepticism, too, was being confronted here. He came around the desk and embraced her. She laughed, hiccupped, a little something akin to a cry—a release at being held by him, evidence perhaps that it had affected her a little, at least.

But she threw her paper into the fire just as he had done, though she couldn't have known it, and laughed. "There. Now that is over. I have told Kirk to tell the newsman to stop bringing in *The Clarion*."

"I just canceled all of his papers," said Lenox.

"You need them for work, darling."

"They have them at the agency."

She went off to see to the girls' supper, and Lenox spent several hours in serious work then; and had to glance at the clock to see the time when there was a knock at his study door. Nearly nine o'clock.

"Mr. Montague," said Kirk, announcing the young slender detective.

"Registry office, sir," said Montague, nodding his thanks to Kirk and coming directly in, a little more comfortable in the presence of a gentleman. "I had to hound them but here you are. They found seven of the eight."

"Good work," said Lenox.

He looked at the list.

```
9 Soho Square    Jaddo J. by Deed
7 Soho Square    Elias by Sale
427 Bateman Street  Kimbrough Jaddo by Sale
14 Carlisle Street  Francis by Deed
9 Greek Street   Jaddo J. by Deed
21 Neal Street   Elias by Inheritance
```

Lenox's eyes widened as he read this, and then as he scanned it once more, a smile appeared on his face, a little smile, and he felt something rest in his heart. He glanced up at Montague.

"Good work," he said again, holding the paper up, the slip of paper that told so much. "There are questions left—there are more questions than there were before in a way—but you have solved it."

CHAPTER FORTY-TWO

Though she'd moved to Edmund's, Angela had declared that she would return to Hampden Lane for breakfast each morning—her time with Sari.

As she ate, the girls quizzed her about Christmas in India. Sari sat off to the side, quieter than usual, and Lenox took a seat next to her at the round table, where Lady Jane was reading through her morning letters.

"Did you have plum pudding in India?" Sophia asked.

"Oh, yes," said Angela seriously. "But only once a year—on New Year's, not Christmas."

"What about Father Christmas, does he go to India?"

Angela nodded, spooning a little sliver of soft-boiled egg from its shell. "Certainly," she said.

Sophia nodded with sober happiness. "Good."

"It's not even mid-December, girls," Lenox said. "You cannot possibly already be thinking so much of Christmas. Why, in my day, we never thought of it at all until—"

"We *know*, Daddy," the girls said together, and at that even Sari let slip a little smile.

Back then Christmas had been nothing too important—perhaps an extra pie, a stocking with a piece of fruit and a shilling, certainly no presents. The thing that had been most memorable was the interminable length of the church service.

Nowadays, of course, since Mr. Dickens's story had appeared some decades before, you saw Christmas "trees" for sale on the street on December fifteenth, which people over forty agreed was unforgivably early to start thinking of the holiday; the poor put into lotteries for fat geese they could never afford on their own but hoped to win for Christmas dinner; others, a little more prosperous, the fellows at the Coach and Horses for instance, paid a few shillings a month in a turkey subscription, so they were guaranteed the sacred bird.

And people tucked presents for each other into the tree, wrapped in tissue paper. Lenox rather liked that part.

The breakfast dishes were cleared and Sari and Angela were in the corner of the little room, talking intimately over their cups of tea, a truce established, when Kirk appeared at the door.

"Lord Carbury," he said.

Lady Jane glanced up. The girls had run off with their governess. "For me?" she asked.

Lenox had not found the right time yet to tell her of Carbury's declaration. "For Miss Angela, my lady."

The young lord appeared in the doorway behind Kirk, gaunt, with dark circles under his eyes. He stared at Lenox's young cousin, with her long fair hair, as if no one else was in the room, indeed as if no one else was on the planet.

"I have found you!" he said.

He looked at all of them reproachfully, non-helpers in his search.

"Me?" Angela said, puzzled.

Carbury's face softened into love. He strode a step to her, then stopped himself, conscious of being too forward. "Yes, you," he said. "Why have you not answered my letters?"

"Georgie, you know full well that this is not appropriate," said Lady Jane. "And if it comes to it—"

"I thought they were for Sari," Lenox heard Angela say, more to herself than anyone. She was confused.

"No, Jane!" Carbury cried. "No!"

Lady Jane put down her reading glasses. "Excuse me?"

"My whole life I have been listening to you, people like you! Mother, Father, it doesn't matter! I won't do it a moment longer! Your mindless opinions of me—your judgments—the endless harping!"

The room stood silent; Carbury was trembling. It was true that it would have been more polite of him to call during regular hours—but Lenox knew that he had tried to visit during normal hours without knowing that Angela was gone, and that therefore his love had starved for the past few days, feeding on nothing but its own anxieties and hopes.

"Me?" said Angela quietly again, more to herself than the room.

Carbury strode forward and fell to one knee. "Since I laid eyes upon you," he said, "and then since I heard you speak—the way your mind—how you *say* things, Angela, how you understand them better than I do—"

Lenox stood. "Perhaps we had better give the young people the room," he said.

But he was the only one who moved. Sari was gripping Angela's hand tightly, and in her face Lenox saw a strange blend of shock and happiness. "Angela, you do not need to listen to anyone's suit at this hour," began Lady Jane.

But Angela stood up and walked toward Carbury. His hands were out to her, and tentatively, she extended one a few inches. He took it, gripping it with both of his, and stared into her eyes.

"Are you sure you mean me?" she said, in a voice so quiet it barely broke into the stillness of the room, the silence of the sunlight falling at white angles over the floorboards.

"As sure as I am of north, or night, or day," said Carbury. Nothing he said entirely made sense, yet no one could misunderstand a word of it. "If you want to move to India—if you want to live in the city—the country—only tell me that I may hope!"

Lenox and Lady Jane glanced at each other. This was a new man. Lenox had once heard him say he planned to start seriously considering marriage at forty-five.

There was an awkward moment, and then Sari, from some irrepressible instinct, stood up and fiercely embraced Angela.

"I cannot marry for eighteen months," said Angela, looking down. "I am in mourning."

"Hang it, I would wait a hundred years! But—then—do you mean—may I hope?" he asked, in wretched expectation.

Angela was still looking down. "Perhaps we could go for a walk in the park," she said, and the smallest happiness ghosted through her expression. It was a look of Jasper's. "Though it is very cold."

"I will bring a fur for you," said Georgie wildly. "Hang it, I know my mother just bought an ermine—she will tell me where."

"George!" said Lady Jane at the idea of this extravagance.

"But I am not grand enough for you, or your family," Angela said, in a voice filled with pain.

"Slow down," said Lenox—for he would have stood his family's roots here against any upstart duke's, had been raised every instant to feel that.

"I am an orphan from India," she said proudly, fighting her shame. Lenox honored the effort.

"Grand enough!"

Carbury gave Angela a look that said he would go on loving her even if she intended to make insane statements, such as this one. Lenox had rarely seen anyone so hard-fallen. The whole tenor of his idle young being seemed to sing for the first time with the happiness of purpose, as he held tightly to her fingertips. He started to babble about grandness, about London, about her eyes—until Lady Jane and Lenox both began, rather alarmed, to cut off his warm tributes, and even Sari intervened, smiling, and asked if Angela could help her with her wardrobe before leaving.

But George had received an answer to make him happy, and it was as docile as Clara's little lamb that he followed Kirk to the front door. He looked a man reborn, with goodwill for everyone on earth, shaking Lenox's hand over and over before he went, promising to return early and often.

The house remained in a state after this for a good while: Angela and Sari disappeared up to the little pair of guest rooms, while Lenox and Lady Jane sat and talked for an hour, marveling at the thing, and speculating about how Georgie's family would react. His older brother Lawrence, who stood to become the next duke, was a mongrel beef-witted lord, as Shakespeare had identified the genus; one of the least adventurous-minded people Lenox had ever met, a dullard with strong convictions of his own superiority; a bad admixture; and he would be angry that Carbury had not married for the specific glory of him, of the "family."

This prospect at least made Lady Jane happy.

But they asked each other, too, whether this was one of Carbury's fads, whether he would stick to it—barely knowing the girl, as he did!

After breakfast Lenox went to his study. It had been a delightful surprise, but his task now was the case.

Kimbrough: Sir Francis Kimbrough. That was the name. These Jaddo brothers were doubtless involved up to their necks—for the inexhaustible Montague had now uncovered violent crimes in three more of the houses they had researched, all within the last five years—but it was Kimbrough who mattered. Lenox had worked for too long to believe in chance further than he could see it, and to see that name, Kimbrough, after the man had introduced himself at the gymnastiksaal the week before, was enough to show him the truth.

All of which was of course subordinate to the fact of his initials: ⸫F.

CHAPTER FORTY-THREE

It was to his friend McConnell's house that Lenox went, however, at a little past eleven. It was one of the grandest in London, situated at the center of Mayfair; the Scot had come from a family of workingmen, doctors and lawyers, but his intelligence and rare looks had won him one of the most coveted women in the land as a bride, high born and immensely rich.

It had cost him his sanity. For one thing, Toto's family had insisted that he step back from his work: a doctor worked with his hands, placed his hands on people, making him, to some snobbish minds, no more than a workingman.

It had taken him fifteen years to overcome this prejudice within his own bosom. Only since returning to practice at the Great Ormond Street Hospital—London's first destination for indigent children who were sick—had he seemed his happy gallant self again, freed from the devil of drink.

Yet, apparently, those old woes had returned.

Lenox knocked at the door and was greeted by the familiar Carstairs. "Thomas in?" he asked.

"No, sir, Mr. Lenox," said the butler formally. "You are welcome to wait in the Fragonard Room if you wish."

Lenox shook his head. "That's all right. Tell him I was here, would you?"

The detective made to leave but, as he had once before, crossed the street and hung low in a doorway, thinking of an old friend who many years before had taught him how to disappear into such spaces. Time! It went, and went; and the residue of it was lessons, in love, in regret, in the great mystery of crossing years inside of a body.

The doctor did not appear at the second-floor window this time. But about ten minutes after Lenox's knock, he did himself one better and came out through the front door, tall and rangy as ever, hair flowing down to his shoulders, long black cloak nearly touching the pavement.

He strode east for half a mile, and Lenox followed him from a street or so behind, ambling carefully, hands in his pockets. There was a bright sharp sun that offered no warmth. McConnell's walk was purposeful—and at a little black door in Beak Street, unmarked and much-scarred, he stopped and went inside.

Lenox took up a station at a tobacconist's across the street, giving his friend fifteen minutes or so despite the cold: because he knew that what lay inside was the first drink of the day.

Then he went across and opened the door.

It was a little gin bar, not so different from the one where they had interrogated Phipps. Inside it might have been morning or midnight. There were stubs of candles along the bar and at the rickety tables. A few sad sots drank alone. McConnell was one of them, staring into a glass, already empty.

He glanced up when Lenox entered—a look of confusion came into his face, then fury, and then one of despair. "Fancy meeting you here," he murmured, as the detective approached.

Lenox sat down opposite him. The barmaid came over but Lenox waved her off—to which she protested by bringing McConnell another glass unasked. Apparently he was a regular.

"That was a dirty trick," said McConnell into his hands.

"I know," said Lenox gently. "But I need your help."

"Are you sick again?"

"No—Halley has worked a charm."

McConnell laughed bitterly. "Then it is about you. Would I stop drinking for you, but not my children, Charles? You're arrogant." His anger started to build. "An arrogant, smug, self-satisfied—"

Lenox shook his head. "No. I need to know what you can tell me about Sir Francis Kimbrough."

McConnell's mouth fell open with surprise at the randomness of the request. He took a sip of gin, thinking, and after he had swallowed it Lenox saw the telltale softening around the eyes and temples: an addict released from anticipation, just moments from the tripping glorious hour or two of euphoria, before the black pain began to seep in once more at the edges.

"Kimbrough," McConnell said.

"Yes. Kimbrough."

The doctor knew a specific stratum of society with which Lenox was less conversant: young, modish, beautiful, sometimes scandalous.

"He's an affable fellow," said the doctor, sitting back and looking in the air. His powerful mind began to organize facts. Now that the topic was not his drinking he looked happy. "Almost never speaks. Arrow thin, with a permanent browning to his skin. Makes sense because he was in Africa so long. Clear intelligent eyes, like a hawk. Dresses well. Humble. Solicitous of women, a friend to them as far as I can tell. He spent his early twenties as an explorer—he was the first man to walk the Nile alone, or a portion of it, and collected infinitely valuable samples for us. Now he is retired, and if my medical eye does not deceive me, will suffer from a worsening case of pleurisy all his life. But he is exceedingly bright and young for now. Still studies Africa and is very well liked. Silent as a tomb.

"But of course he cannot be a criminal. Why do you want him?"

Lenox narrowed his eyes. "Why could he not be a criminal?"

McConnell looked at him strangely. "He is a baronet, with ten thousand acres up north. Hettie Kaye, you know, tried desperately to marry him, and she had the Prince of Wales waiting by her door each morning with flowers a year or two ago."

"Is he often in society?"

"Yes, enough to keep his place, certainly," said McConnell, frowning. "He has a gift for making himself liked. Though I should not have said he had many very close friends. That circle is not full of close friends—close enmities, perhaps."

"Have you been to his house?"

"No. It is not a block from here, though—the tall gray one on Golden Square." Lenox knew that. It was his next destination. "There has never been a word about his character, I can tell you. Not a breath. Have you met him? He is no fool. Used to have a small beard, like one of the Elizabethans, but he's shaved it, and dark curling hair—and I know that he rides very well."

"What are his interests?"

McConnell took a deep drink and signaled to the barmaid. "He collects maps. I only know that because he once asked where I got one at our house—I couldn't remember where. He was gracious. Always asks about one's self, now that I recall—never talks about himself."

"Clubs?"

"Mostly the Beargarden. Never gambles, but plays billiards for money, I know. Sometimes quite a lot of money. In with that Lord Laughton set, you know. I saw him at Ascot, too. He did not come to London till twenty or so, I recall now, and his schooling was all up there, up north, so no one knew much about him. Didn't come south to one of the public schools, which is odd."

"University?"

"No. That whole set thinks university is a curate's business, as you know. Africa was his university. I should have said at the start—he is always at the Explorers Club, of course. But if you wish you can spend a week there without exchanging a word with anyone. They are all such odd ducks."

Lenox nodded thoughtfully. "Mm."

McConnell had finished his new drink with alarming swiftness. He held his glass up to the barmaid again. "You must congratulate me, incidentally, Charles."

Lenox's pulse quickened. He knew this was his friend's way of bringing up the great topic that stood between them. "Why is that?"

"My experiment with the algae cells worked at last."

Lenox widened his eyes. "That is remarkable, Thomas. That is wonderful."

And it was. Toto, for one, had for years spoken of "Thomas's algae" as a quixotic nothing, a lark. But McConnell had been working on various recondite matters connected to the Atlantic Ocean's "biology"—that fashionable new word for the branch of natural philosophy involved with living creatures—for a decade, sometimes day and night, sometimes only on weekends, but always with a focus on the cell. Evidently he had succeeded.

"Yes, I know. I ought to be the happiest man in London. It will be the making of me at the Royal Academy, and I know they will ask me to speak in Paris, which is the highest honor I could ever have hoped for from this work. LaGarde has already written me the most sincere, enthusiastic letter about it all."

"Yet you are not happy?" said Lenox again.

McConnell laughed. He drank the last drop of lemon gin from his glass, and pushed away his long, flyaway blond hair, which had set so many hearts aflutter in certain distant seasons. "I can certainly say I am not."

Lenox let a minute pass in silence, then two minutes. He knew better than to try to chase down the start of the drinking. Enough to know it had started.

"Could you stop if you had time to yourself?" asked Lenox at last.

McConnell's new gin arrived. "Me? Eh? Oh—yes, I suppose. If I go up to my little shack in Scotland, and let Mrs. Campbell take care of me, I suppose . . ." A fleeting look of sadness passed McConnell's face. "Anyhow. Toto cannot spare me here, nor the hospital . . ."

"Are you mad? Toto would be delighted if you went."

"But we have so many parties this week alone, I—" McConnell looked up and met Lenox's gaze for the first time in a drink or two. "She knows?"

Lenox nodded.

"For how long?"

"I'm not sure. But she knows."

It was pitiable that McConnell thought anyone could have missed it. He threw his hands in the air, laughing now, buoyed by the drink. "She is still angry with Jane for protesting. I think she feels hurt."

Toto did not believe in the vote for women. "You are worth saving," said Lenox gently.

McConnell laughed bitterly at this, and waved to the barmaid for another drink. "Not true," he said. "Ah, here, the bottle comes around to us. Have a drink, Charles, it won't kill you."

CHAPTER FORTY-FOUR

Lenox abstained, McConnell did not. After another hour or so the detective had learned a tremendous amount about Kimbrough. All of which only added to his curiosity about the fellow.

McConnell was drunk at the end of this time, actually drunk. He lapsed into silence now and then, but more often he talked: for the last half hour or so of patients he had lost at the hospital. When he started to lean out of his chair, Lenox said, "Hi there, Thomas, eyes up. Listen, will you walk by Kimbrough's with me?"

"Eh? Oh, why not?"

Lenox waved to the barmaid. "Cup of coffee, please, to take away. What is his bill?"

"Two shillings."

Lenox passed her two and six, and in a moment she was back with a paper cup of the black coffee, bitter smelling and hot, which stood boiling in a small pot over a kerosene heater, there to ease the dipsomaniacs back into normal life when they departed.

McConnell accepted it and staggered up with Lenox's help. "One of our detective adventures!" he said, a slur in his pronunciation somewhere for the first time, and some of the coffee came over the lip of his cup.

"Yes," said Lenox sadly, and put a hand under his arm. He had a thought, and turned back to the barmaid. "Do you sell bottles?"

"Two kinds, same size, sixpence gin or shilling gin."

"Give me the shilling gin," said Lenox. He exchanged a coin for the unmarked stone bottle and put it in his coat pocket.

The cold and daylight braced McConnell a bit, and as they walked toward Kimbrough's house he spoke soberly about his discovery, the exhausting work—without sabbatical from the hospital—that had led up to it, the moment of happiness when his microscope revealed the structure of the algal chloroplast, and the sunken fatigue afterward.

Lenox thought he understood the course of the drinking from this picture of events.

Golden Square was built around a beautiful small garden, with different trees growing slant and slip at its edges, and the solemn gray and red houses standing in even attention around their wildness.

"There's Kimbrough's," said McConnell, pointing.

It was finely maintained, no expense spared, Lenox registered: flowers on the sills, new paint on the eaves and doors and windows, a thick blue velvet rope pull outside the servant's entrance. He scanned high and low, but could not find the little mark that read ℀.

McConnell was sitting on a bench now, slumped a little, attracting glances. Lenox turned. Right. Time to act. He hailed a carriage and bundled McConnell into it, over the doctor's sluggish objections.

When they were about halfway to Hampden Lane, McConnell started to say something angry, in a confused way, and Lenox gave him the bottle of gin. The doctor took a little sip, sighed, and leaned back into the corner of the cab.

At Hampden Lane, Lenox asked the driver to stay, handing over a sixpence as deposit. "He is sleeping, sir—a most estimable gentleman, a doctor to orphans."

"Is he! Cor," said the driver—who had seen a drunk before.

Lenox went and knocked on the house's lower door. This was something he didn't do above once a year. An angular and well-meaning young maid named Cecily opened the door and then stood up in surprise.

"Sir!"

"Could I have a footman, Cece?"

"Yes, sir," she said, but didn't go. "Does it matter which, sir?"

"No."

"Right."

She disappeared into the kitchen and appeared pulling Johnstone physically as he complained, until he stopped long enough to see Lenox. "Oh, sir!" he said, as surprised as Cece.

"Unless you are busy for the next few days, I need you to take my friend Dr. McConnell to Scotland."

Johnstone stepped outside. "Very good, sir."

Lenox smiled. Game lad. "You had better get a coat. Cece, you and cook get him a cold supper ready, one for the doctor, too."

"Yes, sir," she said, and vanished.

When Johnstone came back he had a small ruck and a hat and coat on. "Do you know the doctor?" asked Lenox.

"Oh, yes, sir."

"I doubt he will kick up at you." Lenox said. "You can let him drink till he gets there if he gets obstreperous."

"Gets what, sir?"

"If he causes a bother. The stop is Caithness Rockery. Only one line goes there from Edinburgh and no one gets off. Here is my Braddock's. You can read it?"

Johnstone had been born and bred in London, and he could read a Braddock's fifty times more easily than his Bible. No doubt to his mother's ongoing chagrin. "Certainly, sir."

Lenox reached in his pocket. "Here are a few notes to spend on tickets and anything else you need, or McConnell's name will be good to buy on credit after Edinburgh. So you know it's eight hours on the Caithness Rockery line by slow train. He will likely sleep. Keep him good and drunk until you are on that line, but once he is on that line he will be docile. I will wire to Mrs. Campbell. Her nephew will be there waiting for him. His name is Diarmid and he is large and simple."

"Caithness Rockery, Mrs. Campbell, Diarmid, large and simple, yes, sir," said Johnstone, looking all in all rather thrilled.

Lenox thought a moment. "What is your day off?"

"Wednesday afternoon, sir, and Sunday."

It was Thursday. "Then get him there and take the Saturday off with the Sunday. That is a whole weekend." Lenox gave him a few coins. "See Edinburgh if you haven't, or come back here if you prefer."

Johnstone's eyes darted to the door. Perhaps he thought of returning to see Cece. Or someone else—one never knew one's servants. "Thank you, sir," he said.

"Then get in the carriage. You can catch a train in ten minutes if you hurry."

"My—"

The door flew open and Cece appeared with a hamper. "Here you are," she said.

"Thank you," said Johnstone gruffly.

It was Cece after all! "Thank you both," said Lenox. "Go, Johnstone."

Johnstone fair sprinted to the carriage, and Lenox watched it go, then went in through the kitchen to keep everyone on their toes—cottage pie for dinner, he saw, as he nodded with a friendly face to the servants—and found his way upstairs.

He poured himself a glass of water, stood in the warmth for a moment, a little tired, and thought what he ought to do. Some lunch, and then catch up on his letters, and then speak to Montague, really hash it all out, decide how to proceed to Scotland Yard.

He went into his study—but a chill ran through him when he entered, for there, sitting by the fire, was a young gentleman in a well-cut gray suit, at his ease, who slowly rose, and bowed slightly toward Lenox, as if he was forgiving him for being late for their meeting. He had remarkably intelligent eyes. It was Kimbrough.

CHAPTER FORTY-FIVE

"Good evening," he said.

"Good evening," said Lenox. He was grateful to witness in a fleeting fraction of a second that he was sharp in his response; not dulled, as he had been so much of this cursed year.

He walked a pace forward and pulled the curtain back. A young constable was out front.

Kimbrough spoke, hands behind his back. "Yes, I was able to circumvent your security measures. You must not blame the young officer. I am a London street boy, and accustomed to tight spaces in London. I came in through the window. The servants hadn't a chance either."

Lenox turned back. "Do not flatter yourself that he is placed there to prevent this intrusion," he said slowly.

In his mind, he was recording those words: street boy. Kimbrough had been born and raised in the north. He was the opposite of a street boy.

Yet his mind flew irresistibly to Martell's last words to the denizens of the opium dens, the stray comment about who might murder him: "*or a ten-year-old boy . . .*"

Kimbrough took his seat again and waited, as if it were Lenox who had set the meeting.

The detective, buying time, went to his liquor stand, poured himself a scotch, took a sip, savored it, looking into the glass, and then sat back onto the edge of his desk, drink at his side.

"We have fifty acquaintances in common, Kimbrough—are you mad? Are you—"

"No," said Kimbrough.

"No?"

"None of that. None of that cant about our status in society, Lenox. We are past that sandbar. And the petty morality of the thought is beneath you."

Lenox said nothing. He studied Kimbrough. "Why did you speak to me that day—about Jane?" He used the name with calculation, to humanize himself to this person—who might well be a madman.

"For two reasons," said Kimbrough. "One, because it is the sincere truth. Her cause is the right one."

Lenox, rebuked again, waited. But Kimbrough said nothing. "And?" the detective eventually asked.

"Because I have my ear to the ground in that part of London. As soon as the Coach and Horses knew you were on the Martell case, I did—and I have followed your career, so I know that you are dogged enough that you would find me eventually. I am not a man who likes to wait. I thought I would offer you the advantage—the honor—of my acquaintance."

Lenox knew that Kimbrough wanted to talk. He wouldn't have said he was a street boy otherwise, however offhand it might have seemed. This fellow was bright, but not bright enough to have eluded in his character's development that most predictable criminal's trait: wanting to boast.

But what was his crime—his deception? His game? Was he mad? Was he actually Kimbrough? An impostor? Yet there were the initials: FK. And he had a baronet's manner. It was ineffable but inimitable.

All of this flashed through Lenox's mind in the length of a blink. "It was not an easy path from Martell to you."

"No," said Kimbrough. "But an inexorable one, if you saw the mark upon the door, had a look at the registry office—I have been following that young Montague, admirable fellow—and found the brothers . . ."

"We were close on your heels," Lenox admitted. His heart had slowed to its normal rate again. Now he was wondering how to get this man out of his house.

"Yes, I watched you and your wretched vile drunk companion staring at my door. Outside of visiting hours. It was then that I came here."

In that description, *wretched vile drunk*, the power of the conversation flipped back to Lenox—for McConnell was a saint, if you looked further than an inch deep; and the detective remembered the main and only meaningful difference between Kimbrough and himself, which was that he had never hurt anyone on purpose. Or not without regret. It was an instinct that Jasper had had in much greater quantities even than Charles, from their birth onward.

Whether Kimbrough sensed the change or not was immaterial. Lenox did. "And do you mean me violence?" the detective asked neutrally.

"What? No."

"You expect me to take that for granted?" Lenox turned to his desk and picked up a sheaf of papers. He read aloud. "A murder in Beak Street. Martell, of course. A drowning at 5 Soho Square. The unfortunate accident with the stack of building bricks in the new nursery at 9 Soho Square, resulting in the death of an estimable tailor. On New Street a—"

"Enough."

Lenox threw down the sheet. "'Enough!'? You stand in my home and tell me enough! And expect me to believe you above violence? Please, sir, step out of your own point of view—it is the quality of mental greatness."

"Enough!" Kimbrough had briefly been discomfited, it was true, but at the words "estimable tailor" apparently Lenox had overreached his case, for the baronet's expression had visibly changed to one of disgust. "You know nothing of the incidents to which you refer. Nothing."

Lenox glanced down at the papers in his hands. "Let me hazard a guess. Racketeering, a little forgery, some violence. Have I got it about right? All criminals think they are original; none yet has been."

Kimbrough's eyes sparkled now. He had his confrontation. "I am extracurricular to your system of economic life, that is true. That makes me a criminal in your eyes. To me you are the criminal—you, and all your kind."

"You can surely concede hurting others is wrong. I have heard high praise for your character, Kimbrough."

Kimbrough smiled his very slight, restrained smile. "I can. What I do not concede is that I cause more suffering than you."

"Excuse me?"

"You are at the crest of a nation which governs an empire of inequities and outrages perpetrated upon the lowliest humans—that is, those without military might like our own. Soon enough your brother will be the fourth or fifth most powerful person in the land. You have parties, oh yes, and jolly larks, and fancy yourself remarkable for putting your nose in a few sordid crimes. Out of nothing but rank curiosity, I would guess, though you dress it up as your morality.

"On my own view, sir, I redress what I have seen to be the evil of the world. A butcher in Camden loses his income because he was once a brute to children, and probably to his wife and children at home, and chiseled every passing vagrant out of an extra coin, cheated every non-Christian of a fifth of their bill because he could get away with it—that small comet of evil is extinguished; well, what of the continent of Africa, Mr. Lenox? What of your own debts?"

Lenox shook his head. "You participate in both orders, yours and mine, and benefit from mine when it suits your interests while returning to yours when mine is inconvenient, because of law or custom."

"I prefer to say that I reject your world as efficaciously as I can."

Lenox paused. "And what about Austin Martell? Was he in your world or mine?"

Kimbrough frowned. His hands rested on his knees.

Lenox saw his moment. He came a few steps forward to the couch and sat on its arm, one foot off the floor, his back to the door, about ten feet across from the armchair where Kimbrough sat.

"Tell me," he said. "Tell me the long story."

"May I have a drink?" Kimbrough asked.

Lenox looked him in the eye and shook his head. "No. You have not earned that courtesy from me." He pulled a whistle from his pocket. "But I will not signal for the constable as long as you have an explanation to offer me. I admit, I am a curious man."

CHAPTER FORTY-SIX

In Lenox's childhood, nearly every man one met was clean-shaven, like Kimbrough. Perhaps an errant bishop might have a long white beard, or an unusual farmer a thick matted dark one, but that was it.

Then, in the 1850s, officers and soldiers had returned from the icy cold war in Crimea with dashing beards grown for warmth, deeply romantic and strange to those who witnessed their homecoming, an effect so strong that even now, thirty years later, it was rather odd to see a gentleman without any facial hair at all.

Lenox had been one of those who saw those beards in the streets of London, out shopping with his mother or lunching with his father and brother, and found in them a whole mystery of heroism and faraway adventure; he himself had never, in his adult life, been without at least a short beard longer than a day or two.

Kimbrough's naked face seemed to speak to his honesty; and indeed Lenox felt that he was dealing with an honest man, however strange that might be. Was it the residue of his title, his reputation? No. It was in his eyes. Here was a man who would never tell much. But when he did it would not be false.

"The first thing to know is that I was a very late child," Kimbrough said. He stood, and in defiance of Lenox, poured himself a brandy and water. "My father was sixty when I was born, my mother nineteen—an old marriage for a baronet, and a very scandalous one, for she was a maid in the house. She died having me, and I was my father's only child.

"As you can imagine, this disrupted the plans of my cousin, Clarence Kimbrough, who was ten years younger than my father and had lived in the expectations of inheritance for many years. My birth was a bitter blow to him. He is central to the story, Clarence—that is why I bring him up. I called him uncle, but he was no such thing.

"My father was a dull, dutiful sort of person, very devoted to his ledgers, always measuring the value of the timber on the estate, counting the plate. It was the kind of grasping hoarding character I have set about rejecting in my own life."

Lenox doubted this but said nothing. Kimbrough remained by the lacquered liquor stand, and took a sip of his drink.

"But my mother was magic. Everyone who has ever known her told me that. I have sought them out now, you see, in the leisure of my adulthood . . .

"Until the age of six I was brought up as Kimbrough men have been in Northumberland for a thousand years—that is, to be stupid, entitled, arrogant, unambitious, powerful, reactionary. Every baronetcy is the same. Whether or not you see it, your own, too."

"Neither my father nor brother match that description," Lenox said shortly.

Kimbrough inclined his head, a mere politeness. "As that may be, in Northumberland, far from London, there is not a much greater power than the local squire, the local magistrate, and my father . . . he conformed to that pattern, old fellow. It is hard to expect greatness of anyone handed so much.

"When I was six he died of a heart attack. I went to bed one night with him alive, and woke up to find him gone.

"It was then that my troubles truly began. We had never had a large family, and it fell out that Clarence was my guardian and really the sole person with a remaining interest of any kind in me.

"From the age of six to eight we lived in the castle together. Clarence gambled and drank and shouted at the servants. He forgot about me except occasionally to berate me for existing—for he would have been baronet otherwise. I grew quite wild. I became interested in animals. I explored every inch of our estate, and my friends were the deer, the birds, the foxes. Later in Africa it served me well.

"Otherwise I was abandoned. The gentleman in town who had been teaching me was sacked, and one by one the servants of my father's day, the ones who had loved me and raised me, were fired on different pretexts. Eventually we had a cook and Clarence's valet and not much else.

"Then they must have talked in town, because a crank old fellow named Winckledon who had been sacked from Eton for drinking, came to teach me for six months. He was tremendously bright, but never sober past eight fifteen in the morning. The lessons got more incoherent as the day went on then and by teatime he would be whipping me for missed answers. But he was an old friend of my uncle's, and they liked to drink together.

"Then one morning, just after my eighth birthday, everything changed. Uncle Clarence woke me in the middle of the night, shook me roughly. Then he opened the door and showed me something awful—Winckledon, lying face down in a pool of blood. It was the most shocking sight of my life.

"Now that I am grown, it seems obvious that the teacher had died by misadventure. Perhaps in a fight with Clarence, even. But you must remember that I was a boy who knew nothing—had never had a mother at all—had not heard a kind word in a year or two, and not many then. My knowledge of the world was nil.

"And so it was easy to believe when Clarence told me it was my fault. He didn't explain how. But I believed him. He said I had twenty minutes to pack. I took the small cameo portrait I had of my mother, my few good clothes, and a pocket Bible, for I felt I ought to. There were many times in the next two years that I wished I had the chance to pack that bag over again. But I suppose I did the best I could at the time.

"While I was doing that I dimly perceived that he was doing something about the body. I suspect he drove it over to the gorge, not ten minutes from the house, and that it lies there still.

"When he came back he rushed me into the cart, which our old pony Blossom was hitched to, and from there we went to the coaching inn five miles down the road. We caught a post bound for London. Clarence had covered the lower half of his face with a kerchief, and bade me to do the same before we traveled. We ate some sort of breakfast—a sausage and a piece of rough bread, a dip of water from the butt—and then we were traveling for seven hours, and not a word was I to speak.

"When we got to London he told me the awful truth at last. I was ready to believe anything of course. I was still so shocked at the sight of my schoolmaster, in all that blood, in that quiet room.

"There were men trying to kill us, he told me—bad men, enemies of my father. They had killed Winckledon. I believed him utterly! I had known only death, really: my mother, my father, now this. Everything else was merely an intermittence. Death I understood.

"For my own protection he said I must hide in the city. He brought me to a low sort of inn near Hackney, a filthy place. A woman named Mrs. Bacon was the owner of it, a slatternly, loud person. I would later become terribly afraid of her. My uncle told me that he had secured me a room at great personal expense and that he would write me soon to let me know what to do . . .

"I only learned when I was twenty or so what happened next. Clarence told the few curious people left in Northumberland that I had been sent to school in the south, and then stripped the place absolutely bare—sold the old Plantagenet goblets, two van Dyck portraits, every stick of timber on the property, immensely valuable, grown over a hundred years, every memento, every keepsake, every handkerchief. Every horse, every donkey. Without my corpse to show he could not sell the house or the land but after three years they were all that stood there. Never I think in England has a family's history been incinerated so completely by one of its own members.

"In the meanwhile he had what I am sure was a very gratifying debauch. I have pieced together some of that, too, much of that. You see—perhaps we are both detectives, of a sort. He had a cottage on the estate that he preferred to the large house, and it became notorious, filled at all hours with gamblers and prostitutes. There were violent deaths like Winckledon's. I could pass a few hours elaborating on the details—but in the end it was only one sordid and evil man's idea of fun, which cannot contain much of interest for a person, like you, like me, with thoughts in their head."

At last the baronet paused. Lenox already thought he understood some of it now. But he waited, without speaking.

"Are you not curious what happened next?" Kimbrough asked.

"Very."

"It will come to the part you care about soon enough," said Kimbrough bitterly, and drained off the brandy and water, of which he had only taken small measured sips so far, as if in tribute to his malevolent drunkard uncle.

CHAPTER FORTY-SEVEN

I lasted two months at Mrs. Bacon's. I was miserable every minute of it. She gave me a meal at midday, hard cheese and hard bread usually, but otherwise I had no food. I was scared to leave the inn. After two months she demanded my rent—and when I didn't have it, and told her my uncle would pay her, she laughed, and put me out on the street. She warned me not to come back. Strangely I was happier after that. I was scared, but at least I wasn't . . . *immobilized*, at that awful inn, avoiding life, always hungry, trying not to be noticed.

"The first ten or fifteen nights were hard, I grant you. I slept under the Waterloo Bridge for three nights, and thought I had found a home, but then I was attacked and my mother's portrait and my change of shirt were taken. I don't know why they left the Bible. I still have it.

"I began to creep my way slowly about this—this beautiful and infinite city, this cruel city. I found that one could sleep fairly well in certain parts of Hyde Park. I still visit them. It was summer, luckily—my first break—and I had until the fall to find some way to keep body and soul together."

"What did you do for food?" Lenox asked. It was his first question; he couldn't help himself.

Kimbrough smiled. "Begged. Stole when that didn't work. London became my mother. This house—I suppose you could walk its rooms in the dark?"

Lenox thought. "Yes, I suppose, with a bump or two."

"So it is when you are a child in a city. Or at least the boy I was. I was a walker. From my observations, a trait we share."

Lenox nodded; a little chilled.

"A child is a machine for understanding new things. I could walk every street of central London with my eyes closed, I sometimes thought. I knew what each shop was, who the owner was, if he was kind or crank, what could be scrounged where, whom to avoid, which pubs had the worst men in them . . . for there are bad men! This is what even Dickens only barely understands, the sheer number of bad men!

"Everything Mayfair to Shoreditch on this side of the river, though—that was my bedroom. Other than the City."

The City was where the bankers and lawyers lived and worked. "Why?"

"Every street boy knows there's no charity to be found there. It is free of our kind. But keep me to Pall Mall, Lenox, or set me loose along High Holborn Street . . . sometimes I look back upon those days with a kind of wonder, and wish I had the novelist's power! For it was all so real, you know—those chestnut vendors you never see anymore who would slip me a small bag for breakfast—the lights outside the theaters, where the men and women in love could be so kind, so gallant, though every time you asked it was risking the stick of a police officer.

"The police! Our sworn enemies. We marveled at how they acted so kind to *your* type—smiling, subservient, veritable apes . . . but they were the other kind of apes behind your backs, grunting and taking and beating, Lenox. You work with Scotland Yard fairly often, do you not? And so my estimation of you falls; I apologize, it is not civil, but neither were they.

"I always felt myself apart from the other boys. This was in part because I remembered who I was perfectly clearly. But more importantly,

I was terrified. My uncle had said that we had enemies everywhere, and I didn't for a second think to question the idea.

"But the Jaddos were different. Jacob and John."

"Different?" said Lenox, picturing the bloodthirsty monsters that he had heard described at Newgate.

"For one thing they had grown up with a mother. She was dead by the time I met them, but they had had a mother—and what a mother! She became a mother to all three of us in a way, because they shared so many of their memories of her with me. She was a poor, fallen lady, but the world is filled, Lenox, with remarkable people, at every station; rather fewer in the more powerful ones, that is all. She had been a woman of the streets, and they lived in the most derelict building in the Dials.

"But what a home she had made for Jacob and John there. No matter what she had to do they ate two meals a day; had a present on their birthdays; a warm breast at night. But she was most remarkable for how she educated them, for really I do not think the class of men running Oxford and Cambridge can have produced a more brilliant natural teacher than she, who embroidered into their souls every myth and folktale of England, the stories of the Greek gods in a long, flowing epic from night to night, hundreds of lines of poetry she kept in her head . . .

"Jacob and I fought the first time we met. He was nine, I still eight. There was a loaf of bread at issue. He won and then he grabbed me by the hand and trotted me, bleeding, back to his older brother for a clean-up. They shared their bread with me that night and from the next morning on we were inseparable . . . I resorted to every sort of way you can make money in this city as a boy with no strength, no wits, no connections: searching the shores of the river for boats of coal, selling pure to tanneries, picking up cigarette ends. Illegal ways, too, soon enough."

"I heard the Jaddos were violent," he said.

Kimbrough's face blackened, and then he caught himself and

laughed shortly. "When you are a street boy, you belong to any vicious person. Let me say that again, Lenox, since you have had a life uninterrupted by violence and hate, as far as I can gather: when you are a street boy, you belong to any vicious person, to no kind person, to no one with goodness or warmth anywhere in their heart.

"That estimable tailor you mentioned, he buggered me every time he could catch me."

Lenox felt himself redden, and damned the involuntary reaction.

"You are shocked and embarrassed. You think I shouldn't mention something so vile. But why should I be ashamed, Lenox? It is his shame, not mine; his secret, not mine, is it not? The Jaddos never doubted who they were for a minute. Once every six months or so they would demolish the biggest, meanest boy they could find, and thus they were left alone. I was, too, for the most part."

"But then they started slitting throats."

Kimbrough nodded. "By the same logic. Once a year or so, to make sure everyone was scared of them. One of the first was your . . . what were the words? Your *estimable tailor*.

"As we got to know London better and better, as we begged and scrapped to keep our lives going another day, we got to know all the shopkeepers and pub owners intimately. The cruel ones, the ones who beat us, or set the police on us, or buggered us—for that was what half these vicious men were after, half the priests, too, maybe more—we vowed our vengeance on them."

"The little mark . . ." Lenox murmured.

"Yes. I was the one set on revenge. You have a great deal of time when you're a street child. I spent hours and hours skulking in those doorways, scoring my little monogram deeper and deeper into the wood with my penknife. Because I wanted to remember. I never wanted to forget. The labor it took to make each of those marks, the hours and hours, was a promise to myself: the person at this house who hurt you will have their reckoning. Every child is also an artist, you know. It is only as adults that the habit is mocked out of us. I made those marks with an artist's soul. I smile when I see one still. The Jaddos, for their part, had inherited a sacred reverence for *property*, from their mother, so that as soon as they had an extra shilling it went in their mother's small leather case, their memento of her—and they were innocent of nothing, poor boys, by the age I met them, but that remained their one innocence, their religion, *property*."

"That is why they own all these buildings," Lenox said.

Kimbrough smiled. "I had to sign on to one they really wanted very badly. Only my name and title could do it; and it is how I was caught, by you, or perhaps by this enterprising Montague. Sentiment."

Lenox laughed, hollowed a little. "Sentiment," he said.

"It mutates form between the classes."

Lenox was close to seeing it all now; and closer to liking Kimbrough, which was a strange sensation. He walked to the liquor stand to fill his drink. Then he turned to the baronet. "And Martell?"

CHAPTER FORTY-EIGHT

"For a little while we had a fourth friend," said Kimbrough, and pity passed over his face. "Linus Tettleton, an undersized milk-colored little fellow, barely eating when we found him in Green Park, whimpering and mostly starved, two black eyes. But he was unexpectedly clever—unexpectedly funny. And innocent, above all innocent. He followed us around like a puppy for a few months, and got a little fatter.

"Martell liked to take these boys and hook them on opium. He tried with us, but we had each other, you see. Linus—he had us, but he couldn't trust in that, he had been so battered by the world, had given up so much, that I imagine the relief of the opium was everything to him. I have seen strong men of your class, men untouched by childhood suffering, succumb to the same drug.

"Martell turned Linus out as a boy prostitute. Had him carry the most dangerous parcels into the East End, short on money. One night Linus's body was found near the Thames. Great joke among the boys. For there were hundreds of us, our own little Eton or Harrow. And not one left with a beating heart such as you would recognize.

"I killed Martell myself. It was one of the finest nights of my life. I had told him, when I carved my mark into his home, that it would happen, and he laughed in my face. But I was fourteen by then and not so easily dismissed. With Jacob watching out on Conduit Street, I told him it was for Linus. Really it was for myself."

So the motive had never been opium, or money, Lenox thought. It had been revenge.

"How did it all end then?" he asked. "How did you come to be this, instead, again, Sir Francis?"

"I was passing along the Strand one day and saw a tiny headline at the bottom of a newspaper: *Clarence Kimbrough Dead in Newcastle Brothel. Heir Sought.*

"You can imagine the intensity of my interest in that. Part of me still believed Clarence's stories about my family's supposed enemies, but I was getting older, smarter. At last I chanced it. I went into the solicitor's listed in the article, and by that night—my God, it happened so fast!—I was staying with a distant cousin I had never met, Molly Kimbrough, in Chaste Lane. She was a sweet old spinster. The only person from my family I ever loved. She died five years ago."

"You must have been relieved."

"I don't know what I felt," Kimbrough answered. "I was numb, I believe. Six years is an infinity of time in a boy's life you know—much more than half of my living memory—all I knew, a world from which I thought I would never escape . . . to suddenly be cosseted and . . . no, I have never forgotten what it meant to be down and out . . .

"Literally overnight, my life changed in every way: privation to plenty, and all the education I could ask for. The law began in its grinding way to appoint me to the status you see now.

"But I knew different. That whole time I missed John and Jacob, too. I thought I was happy. Not until I was nineteen and went to Africa was I ever really honest with myself about it all, did I look myself in the face, and there were some dark days, the truest solitude you can imagine, alone on a different continent, with no one alive who loves you. John and Jacob were all that kept me from death in those years.

Still I courted it with ninety percent of my soul every minute. But that is a different story . . .

"You may imagine how I had developed strange, secretive, deeply idiosyncratic ways in my years on the streets. In retrospect I should have simply demanded that my friends come live at Kimbrough Lodge with me, be educated . . . but instead we arranged for a way that I could send them money every week, as much as I could scrimp. But they barely needed me. They had their first house, and though they were faithful friends, letter writers, I knew they didn't need me.

"I was sixteen then. Everyone at Marlborough smelled the wrongness in me from first second to last. The masters especially. Those schools are no good for a boy without protection. Three of the masters tried to bugger me; one managed it, and he had to convalesce in the country for a month afterward because I fought him so hard. I am pleased to say one of his eyes is still sightless, and may the other rot in his head."

There was a long and strange silence then. At least an hour had passed. Rarely had Lenox learned so much so quickly of any other person.

"And now, I ask you," Kimbrough said at length, "to give it up. To leave me and John and Jacob alone."

"You cannot possibly ask me that," said Lenox. "You broke the Jaddos out of prison—why, two days ago, Kimbrough!"

The baronet didn't deny it. "I could not let them incur any risk when I was responsible."

Lenox shook his head. "No. The extent of the crimes is astonishing. And for all I know you are telling me a quarter of the truth at most."

Anger flared hot in Kimbrough's face. "In fact I have not said a word of a lie to you. But if that is your attitude, then I propose this," he said icily. "You leave me alone and I will give you my solemn word not to kill you."

Lenox laughed. "So that is your final card. Violence."

Kimbrough looked around the room. "It is a hard world, old man. If you have yet to learn that in your travels through it, count yourself very lucky. Have you ever missed a meal? Maybe for failing a Latin exam. Have you ever looked at an adult and calculated the likelihood they were going to hit you in the next moment or two? What's the longest you ever lived on a penny?"

Lenox had no answer.

Kimbrough snorted. "It's time to grow up, man. You're fifty."

"Will you leave by the window or the door?" the detective asked drily.

And yet—what could Lenox do? He was stuck, and they both knew it, standing there, staring at each other. There was no proof connecting Kimbrough to the murders. The houses had been legally bought. And he was a man of overwhelming influence, of high connections.

Lenox was thwarted.

He rose. "You tell me to grow up. I tell you the same: grow up."

"You have heard what I say and dare to speak to me that way, as if I did not grow up before ever I was allowed to be a boy?"

"Yes. Because I have something that you do not: a family."

"I could have you two families by noon tomorrow for a hundred pounds."

Lenox shook his head. He was the older man, and he saw that his judgment, for all Kimbrough's self-certainty, held his attention. "No, Sir Francis. As I come to know you, I see that you will never have a family, not like I have, or the man who shines your shoes—what you could have out of this life—love—unless you give it all up completely, Kimbrough. All this crime.

"You ask if I will harass you further. I don't know. But for yourself: change. Go to the country. Go abroad. Square your conscience with the Jaddos and go. You have enough now and you are not lost. Stop stealing."

"Ha."

"Stop fighting for what you imagine to be your cause, Francis—fight for yourself, for your soul, first."

Kimbrough laughed acidly. "Always the refrain of the rich."

Lenox nodded slightly. "You are right. That is true. But it is not the whole truth, though you would wish it so. And what next, anyhow?"

"Excuse me?"

"What will you do now that these smaller vengeances have been exacted? What is your next plan?"

Kimbrough shook his head, a smirk; and Lenox, who had seen so many faces in calculation, saw how his eyes lidded slightly, and he was at a blockade in Kimbrough's consciousness that even Kimbrough himself might not see; and certainly a secret, too, for this planning mind had not ceased its roving.

"It is not vengeance. It is justice." He looked around the room. "And this is a nation badly in need of a dose of anarchy. Though I cannot expect you to see that."

"You live very richly yourself, and among the rich, do you not?" said the detective.

"What could be more advantageous to my aims?"

"You let them think you care for them, I am sure, these friends of yours."

"I tell them no lies."

"Will you marry?"

"Sir!"

It was Lenox's turn to laugh; he had finally shocked his intruder, who realized the irony of his position even as the word left his mouth.

He rose; as if to say, well-played, and stood there, in his exquisite suit, lean, fledged, built to cut through life by the cruelty of those who had raised him. It was the pity of the world. His face was closed to the detective now.

Lenox thought long what to say, and then decided. "I am so terribly sorry, Kimbrough."

The baronet was taken aback. "Sorry?"

"I am sorry for all that you endured, Kimbrough. It was not fair. And you are right. I have not been through a hundredth of it. It is the world. I know that. It is just that I do not think it makes you right."

The imperturbable young man stared, stared; and then sat back in the chair, a new blankness in his expression.

Lenox could tell in that instant that he had never told a fifth of this to anyone, a hundredth; but had been desperate to, and had been ready to face cruelty in response. Just not kindness.

Lenox went and poured him another drink. "I have some questions," said Lenox. "Is your day taken?"

"What else would you like to know?" Kimbrough asked.

"Everything."

"Everything?"

"I want to hear about it all again," he said. "This hidden city you and your friends discovered—created—mapped. It is what I have never been able to know myself, as hard as I have tried. I cannot know the police as you knew them. The shopkeepers. The viciousness, the kindness, too, for I am sure it must have arisen, once in a very long while. I want to hear it again, Kimbrough, if you can bear telling it. With every detail you can remember."

CHAPTER FORTY-NINE

At last in that cold December it snowed. For a few hours the city had gone ghost-gray, and then suddenly the blizzard had begun, and suddenly it was brilliant sparkling white, every surface and jut catching some pattern of the accumulating snow.

It was the twenty-first, four days after Lenox's confrontation with Kimbrough. In two mornings he and Jane and the girls, with retinue, would embark on the train to Markethouse to spend Christmas at Lenox House.

Dallington and Polly were at Hampden Lane for supper. Polly, who was close to the birth now, though she was still working from home, was radiant, Lenox thought—the future shined in her face, amidst the candlelight.

Dallington was staunchly in favor of young Carbury. He was a romantic. "Do you think she shall have him, in the end?" he asked.

"I do," said Lady Jane.

"She shouldn't marry the first person who asks," Polly said.

"All but a little of her attention is on Norwegian fishery statistics at the moment, as far as I can ascertain," said Lady Jane, taking a discreet bite of the lovely soup—cream of potato, one of Lenox's favorites. "She is in earnest about waiting her mourning period and told Sari that she will see what Carbury says then. I don't think she quite believes it's real still."

"George has not wavered," said Lenox. He had thought much about this subject. "Still, I am glad there is an enforced delay. Let him prove constant."

"Doesn't Sari have suitors, too?" asked Dallington.

"Yes, rather too many for my liking," said Lady Jane. "I think I shall take her down to the country for a few months after Christmas with the girls."

Lenox raised an eyebrow. He had not heard of this decision. But Jane looked quite sure.

"She is an innocent," Lady Jane said, "while being at the same time so fluent and intelligent that she could be mistaken for another of these girls who is watching their eighteenth London season, even if they are in their first. Next year can be hers. And Angela will be out of mourning."

"And what about your husband," Lenox asked, "is there room for him in the luggage?"

"But do you want to spend three months in Sussex?" asked Dallington. "Come back to work!"

Polly said nothing, only looked at him expectantly—which told her agreement. And it was true that three months in the country sounded dire to Lenox.

"Leave him alone, you two," said Lady Jane.

When supper was over, Lady Jane and Polly went to the nursery to discuss baby clothes; Lenox and Dallington walked through the snowy streets, a digestive stroll. The young lord was bundled in a heavy black coat. He was older now, his brilliant wrecked youthfulness transmuted into something quieter and steadier, injured but capable. He had become a man.

They came to their club, where they smoked a cigar and played a game of billiards with several fellows. One was a regular at the gymnastiksaal, like Lenox, and took advantage of their break in the game to complain vociferously of Sven, who had started forcing him to drink the juice of beets.

There was a stir in the club, something imperceptible, at about half nine, and news rippled through the rooms that the Prince of Wales had stopped in for a drink.

Lenox finished his game of billiards, but kept an eye on the door; and when the Prince descended the stairs, Lenox went to him and asked, as he rarely had, for a quick word.

What he asked was that the Prince of Wales, as a personal favor to him, cut Murdock out of his social circle. The Prince, who barely knew the magnate, had immediately agreed to this request. He hadn't asked for an explanation; Lenox was lucky to have known him so long. He had never liked the fellow anyhow, he said.

"Is it true you're a suffragist now, by the way, Charles?" the Prince asked, guffawing. They were on the steps of White's, and a large retinue of Pall Mall celebrities was waiting impatiently for him to go to the casino. "That's what they're calling them, you know—jolly good, I think, clever. What's the word for that?"

"Neologism, Your Highness?"

"That's the one. Well, march on, though Mother hates these women voters, you know—despises them." The Prince laughed again, and clapped Lenox on the shoulder. "For my part I think they have quite a lot of spirit. A woman voting! Fancy it. See you soon, Charles. Don't take any tin pennies."

It was interesting to hear from Wales himself that the Queen despised the women's vote. Perhaps they were not so far off, then; for the Queen was old, more and more she felt like the past to him: Clara and Sophia, the future, much of their lives to take place in the dim-dawning new century that was not so far away.

It was with this in mind, the next morning, that Lenox hatched a secret plan.

It had been a busy day already. He'd gone and found Montague at the office, where the young fellow was working on a new case, full of youthful verve. After they had consulted for some time, Lenox went into his office, with its small windows offering their beautiful view of St. Paul's, whited over now with snow, birds rising from its spires and settling back onto them in unequal rhythms.

On his desk, he had a set of papers laid out that were for his eyes only. Even to Montague he had not shown them. They were a map of Soho Square and environs, and a chart next to it; for though Lenox was uninterested in Kimbrough's arrest, he was extremely interested in his crimes, and he was tracing them all now, having solved a dozen or so.

The East is a career, Disraeli had famously said. For Jasper it was a life. As Lenox shadowed Kimbrough's peregrinations with pencil and paper, he thought of the two young men—both with qualities of such goodness, both derailed by circumstance. For the first time, in a sense, the detective, who had always seen the good fortune of his life, really internalized it: not just the money, the position, his family, not at all, though those were what others would call his good fortune. None of that really. Rather: to have had a chance. Not to have been so harmed by life early that there was never hope.

A chance. That was what he must fight for other people to have.

It was with this in mind that he started to prepare his secret plan for the afternoon. He took some ink and an oversized sheet of paper and began to work; occasionally stopping for a sip of room temperature tea.

When the clock struck one, he glanced up. Already a little late. Hurriedly, he did up his jacket, threw on his gloves, rolled up the paper, and left the office.

"Will you be back?" cried Montague to his retreating figure.

"Tomorrow morning!" Lenox called behind, already leaving.

As he walked London, he found his heart was pounding, his cheeks numb and tingling at once. When had he become so unlike himself! This was what he wanted to know. He had never asked a favor like the one he had asked of the Prince of Wales the night before; Murdock would be sick with anger. Good.

Lenox came within view of St. Paul's and looked around expectantly, until his eyes fell on the little group for which he was looking, three women bundled in clothes, with a little girl.

It was she who attracted the eye. I WISH MAMA COULD VOTE, her sign said. Next to her was Jane, holding up her sign, OUR BODIES, OUR MINDS.

"Charles!" said Lady Jane, when he approached. She was genuinely shocked. "Charles, you cannot ask me to leave. You cannot think—"

"No," he said, and put a hand on her forearm gently, to stop her.

He unfurled his own poster so that she could see it. VOTES FOR WOMEN, it said, and he fancied the scrolls he had drawn underneath brought a certain élan to the image.

She looked at him searchingly for a moment, and then some pure vein of happiness opened in his wife's eyes. She kissed his cheek. Lenox held up his sign.

CHAPTER FIFTY

They arrived at Markethouse Station by train in great numbers (Charles and Jane, the girls, Angela and Sari, three servants) and found that Edmund had forgotten to send so much as the dogcart to meet them from Lenox House.

"The poor fellow has his head wrapped up in Parliament," said Lady Jane.

"Parliament's not sitting," said Lenox crossly.

"You know his work doesn't end because of that. Molly would have remembered."

Lenox felt a pang. Edmund's wife had been an unworldly woman, happy in her skin, always ready to laugh. Edmund had loved her ardently—and the only thing Charles could compare her death to, as he looked back on it, was watching his brother go through one of those terrible falls from a horse you saw in the country sometimes, his brother's full physical absorption of the violent loss.

It was because of Molly, in part—because of the part of him to which Molly appealed, which gently rejected everything flinty or worldly or sophisticated—that he had never sought power. Now she was gone, and he did. Was it unhappiness? Perhaps a different kind of happiness, in strength. Not a compensation for the loss, but a distraction from it.

The town square was in fine fettle. The Lenox Arms looked fairly bashed in and broken, and its sign hadn't been painted in a decade—but it was the comfortable wear of a busy coaching inn. The tree at the center of the green had been festooned with white angels made by the schoolchildren and the holly trees were red; and smoke busied itself into the sky from every chimney around the green, the costermonger, the bootmaker, the papermaker, the draper, the bakery, the small city hall.

"Master Charles?" said a voice.

Lenox turned and saw old Remington, a handsome dark-haired fellow of sixty, town cooper. "Your brother sent me—the cart is broken at Lenox House."

"Oh!" said Charles, forgiving Edmund instantly.

The next two days were tremendously busy. There was the village fete ("Why is the Virgin Mary smoking a cigarette?" Sophia whispered to him, pointing at Mrs. Reaubuddy, the smith's wife, in the wings of the stage) and there were presents to be handed out by Charles and Edmund at the almshouse and there were horses to be unstabled and ridden and there was food to be overeaten and there were the girls to find their way into mischief; and, in short, it was Christmastime.

Practically the first moment Lenox had to breathe again was at around five o'clock in the evening the day before Christmas. In what they had always called the long living room, there were two trees, a large pine in one corner, presents laid delicately in its branches, and, eight tall portraits away, at the opposite end of the room, a small one festooned with every ornament and oddment Clara and Sophia had been able to lay their hands on: strings of cutout ponies, silver bells, strands of bright hard red berries.

Lenox was by the large tree, near the fire, breathing into his side evenly. He felt a pleasant warmth where the wound from Newport was; receding by the day, that traumatic moment. He held a cup of tea. Through the windows he could see the snow falling gently over the long miles of grassy hillside that swept west from Lenox House. A herd of woolly sheep ate on a steep incline, grazing out the last grass. Birds flew by the thousands in the distance every so often, like moments of the soul's grace; for it had never been a hunting house, though Sir Edmund obliged the county by hosting the opening of the season.

He was lifted from his thoughts by a sort of squeak from the other end of the room. Angela was in a little soft armchair by the small tree, with a silver goblet of wassail. She loved a drink—just one, usually, two on Saturdays, and it always turned her glassy eyed and very suggestible to anything funny.

Lenox got up and went down the same long Turkish rug, threadbare in many spots, that he had crawled upon as a baby.

"What are you reading?" he asked.

Angela looked up, and smiled to herself. "Oh! Just—but it is a small joke, not worth repeating." She held up the little leather book, which was an introductory guide to London by a rector at St. Martin-in-the-Fields. "It says here that sandwiches are named after a man—an earl!"

This was followed by such a mirthful shake of the head that Lenox found himself laughing, too. "Yes, it's true," he said.

"I just found it—I don't know, funny!"

Lenox sat down. "Did you know," he said, "that in chess— Do you know how to play chess?"

"Yes."

"Did you know, then," he went on, smiling a little to himself as she had, "that checkmate doesn't really mean anything—it is a soundalike of a Persian phrase, *shāh māt*, which means, very simply, the king is dead."

Her eyes widened. "Do you know any others?"

He laughed. "Oh, Jane would say you are foolish to ask me that. I am forever telling her them. I'll tell you one I just heard again. Do you know the word *quarantine?*"

"We had them in India often. Ten people in the house next to us died one year when I was very young. And I know what you mean—it is from the Italian for forty days."

"I shall have to dig deeper I see. Sticking on Italian, then, how about the origin of the word *palace*?"

She shook her head.

"From the famous *palatine* hill in Rome," he said, emphasizing the word carefully. It was just what Jane could not stand, and he felt a grin form on his face. "It is most blatantly there in the word *palatial*."

"Sari could not give a fig about it either," said Angela.

"I remember you reading on the train while she looked through the window, and I thought—here are two very different girls, though they are so close!"

She blushed, and Lenox saw with a complicated emotion that she was accustomed to feeling ashamed or embarrassed—that this was a legacy of her upbringing by Jasper, along with the good ones. Was it because she had been shunned in the community? Because Jasper had been? Because he had given up on the manners and customs of his upbringing—gone native, as people so often said, with a shudder, about unfortunate mostly forgotten relatives dotted far away in the impossible-seeming vast places of the empire?

"When we got off the ship that day," she said, "I think both of us expected nothing but coldness. My father's history was not— unchecked," she said, forcing the word out proudly, "and everyone in Bombay, sometimes I thought every last one, every major's wife, every fine lady in the city, told me that I would be shunned if I appeared in London with Sari."

"I did not know that," Lenox said softly.

"Oh yes." She laughed bitterly, a little *ha* to herself. "And I was happy to take the risk. So it was almost alarming that you were so kind, you see, Cousin. But now we are getting used to it. Or rather, I am. Sari was always more hopeful. It is her lovely nature that she should be so even in the face of experience."

"I—"

"And this whole time, I have above all said to myself," she went on, cradling the silver cup of wassail and looking into it, "that I shall never leave Sari or disown my father—or what he was, what he became—not if it meant dying in the streets."

She said this last bit so quietly but fiercely that he saw she had envisioned just that possibility.

"You could have trusted your father when he chose me," Lenox said.

She glanced up at him. "Whatever you imagine when you picture my father," she said soberly, "you must imagine a very altered man, these last twenty years."

He nodded slowly. "I know," he said. "I am sorry."

"Don't be sorry!" she said. "He was still the same, far deep down. A wonderful father. A wonderful man. He was never impatient with me once in my life—and I have been a dunce since the moment I was born. No! You cannot convince me otherwise. I know it—I have never been clever like the other girls, or pretty, or able to say just what I think."

There was a silence, and he thought she might cry. But at that moment the two little girls erupted into their room, their cheeks frosty cold-looking from the outdoors, and somewhere long behind them Edmund, calling at them to slow down.

They came over to the little tree and told Lenox and Angela at great length about the snowman they had made ("Began to make," said Sophia, more precisely). Edmund came in, and after a few moments he and Sophia were distracted by an old toy horse they had been assembling, while young Clara had put her thumb in her mouth and laid her head on Angela's lap, allowing her cousin to stroke her hair.

They sat there in silence for a little while, until Lenox said, "My younger daughter would never so love a dunce—or someone unbeautiful or unclever."

She rolled her eyes—another first in their relationship.

He waited a moment, then said. "*Dunce*—do you know that one?"

"I'm sorry?"

"Dunce—there was once a very great philosopher, many thought the greatest philosopher, named Duns Scotus. Which only means that his name was Duns and he was a Scot—Duns the Scot, in Latin. Well, a couple hundred years ago some of the young arrogant fellows about London and Paris started to think the old ways were not all that useful anymore—as young people always will, I have lived long enough to learn—and they turned against Duns Scotus, started to call each other Duns as a mild insult, a joke. Duns, as in—"

"Dunce," she said, her eyes shining with satisfaction, still smoothing Clara's dark hair down.

Lenox paused. "As for your father, I am loyal to him, too, I hope you will always know, and I honor his memory with you."

"Thank you," she said, quietly but with feeling.

Then the girls' governess came in, and as if chiding herself, Angela swiftly transferred Clara to Lenox's lap and stood up, took her goblet to the sideboard, tidying up, busying away the conversation. But he knew she had heard him. In his heart, he said goodbye to Jasper.

CHAPTER FIFTY-ONE

The family returned to London on the third of the new year—though Edmund had left early, for the vote was coming soon.

On the clear, warmish afternoon of their return, Lenox sat at his desk. The house was in its familiar whir again. As for the detective, he had not felt better since he was thirty.

He went through his Christmas correspondence, some one hundred and fifty notes, by his count. One was a desperate entreaty from Aderkenalty, begging him for further information on the little symbol. Another was from Ernest Huggins, on thick card stock, and on more delicate blue paper, a note from Mrs. Huggins, with a homemade knitted scarf for him, maroon, and a thanks for the shortbread that Jane, who never ever missed a trick, had apparently sent.

At about three there was a knock at his study door.

It was Graham. His whole aspect told of misery, and Lenox rose to his feet, more alarmed than curious. His old friend's indomitable, smallish frame had never looked so diminished before.

"I am defeated," Graham said.

"Defeated?"

Graham pulled a small folded map from his pocket, and gradually began to unfold it. With unusual candor, lack of discretion even, in his voice, he said, "I have been invited to take the well-paid position, two thousand per year—"

Lenox whistled, for it was indeed a great deal of money.

"Of Under Secretary for North America. This would involve an immediate trip of five weeks to the western part of the United States."

Lenox saw it all now. "To return after the election."

Graham set down the map on Lenox's desk and sat back, sadly. "To return after the election," he affirmed.

Lenox pondered this for a long time in silence. "It is because they think they will win," he said at last.

"Precisely," said Graham.

They didn't need to say anything else—Lenox could follow step by step his old servant's chain of logical inferences. Graham was useful to an opposition party, but might prove less so to one in power. Then, birth would take over; men who had been at Winchester together would pass the laws, those at Eton together contest them; there would be no space for Graham.

But he was too well-connected and industrious to ignore—hence the offer of this sinecure. Graham was one of the poorer men on the benches of Parliament, which was an unpaid job; nearly every other member was independently rich. Only with such a secretarial "promotion" did the boon of a salary come, making it a convenient way to sideline people.

"It will not be forever," said Lenox.

"No," said Graham.

But he looked done in.

"For one thing Gladstone cannot live that long," said Lenox.

Graham smiled slightly, which Lenox took to mean he had hit the target—it was that canny old operator who did not want Graham, scourge of conservatives, to disrupt the negotiations with his aristocratic friends from the other benches. Otherwise, of course, if he possibly could have, Edmund would have saved him. The leader had spoken.

"You will take it then?" said Lenox.

"Yes, I suppose I must," said Graham, glancing out the window at a noise. His alert gray eyes had not aged, but his reliable face had, a little. "I have reflected upon it from every angle and do not see a better course. Even if self-interest did not compel the choice, my remaining would make me only a nuisance. When I come back I will be a new factor."

"Nowhere is memory shorter."

Graham nodded. "That is what I must rely on—and the men who dislike me, the four or five cabinet members you could no doubt identify, will change their song if I am useful again in some way."

It meant Sir Edmund really would be Chancellor of the Exchequer. That somber thought, the greatness his brother would attain, its meaning for the family history, lurked somewhere in the back of his brain, more a feeling than a thought, bound up in his parents and the house in Sussex.

On an impulse, he said, "Graham, I shall go with you, if you will have me."

"Excuse me?" said Graham—who was never surprised, never.

Lenox looked at him levelly. "I will go with you."

Graham laughed outright. "You cannot."

"Surely they will let you bring a pair of secretaries at Her Majesty's expense—one must be young Atwater, of course"—this was Graham's most valuable young assistant, a raw-boned fellow from Oxfordshire—"but I do not see why I should not be the other. Or I could pay my way."

"No, you shouldn't have to—I have been allowed six secretaries in my party and berths on the fastest packet ships we have! I suppose it is flattering that they so badly want to buy me off." Graham smiled. "But as for you—what about Lady Lenox—Clara, Sophia."

"They will be in the country!" said Lenox excitedly. "That is why it is perfect. Jane wants to take Sari there for a few months, to keep her out of the season. And of course I should go mad in Sussex for that long. I would start interrogating the cows after a week."

Graham laughed. "Yes," he said.

"And my last trip to America deserves a chance at redemption."

Graham glanced down at Lenox's side involuntarily. "That is the other question," he said. "Are you strong enough?"

Lenox glanced at the great beautiful scar of the Rocky Mountains on the map, running north–south down the side of the United States; Graham had outlined its lineaments carefully in red pencil, and Lenox could see all those delicate places where the land suddenly rose up. The high gray peaks, covered unevenly halfway down with pure white snow, the blue sky above it, the pine smell—the cowboys they would have to hire. Native Indians even! Imagine it!

"Yes," he said with great certainty. "I am strong enough."

Graham shook his head, doubt on his face. "I must go back to Parliament." He hesitated for a moment, and Lenox saw doubt and also just a little hope in his eyes. "But do you really mean it?" he asked. "Would you really go?"

"After all the service you have done me, Graham—I will speak with Jane tonight, and wire you. But the answer is yes."

Graham put out a hand, and they shook, an oddly formal moment. "Thank you."

Then he left, and Lenox was alone.

He went to the window. It had begun to snow again, and his eyes moved restlessly over the familiar buildings across the way, each bearing so many secrets, so many stories. When he thought of Kimbrough now it was with gratitude: for Lenox once more looked at the world and felt the mystery racing through it. Inside him was something irrepressible, something like curiosity, like love.

It had been a hard year, there was no denying it. Perhaps in midlife, a man owed some debt to self-discovery. Its collection could not be avoided. But he was better. He had paid.

He watched the snow fall and fall through the beautiful late daylight, until at last the sound of one of the girl's laughter somewhere far off in the house brought him out of his reverie. And then, involuntarily, a great smile broke over his face; he loved them so much, his little family, and all the years he had spent worrying about the world, trying to redress its wrongdoings, solve its crimes, fix its troubles, all of that counted for less suddenly than the laugh of his daughters. Was humility always so near to grace? A tumbling noise told him the girls were chasing each other, and he felt a warmth, a happiness, indeed a wholeness, that had never been entirely there since his wound. He checked the carriage clock over the fireplace and saw that it was nearly suppertime. He set down his teacup, rolled the papers left onto his desk into a neat bundle, and closed the door of his study behind him, headed out toward all the adventures ahead.

ACKNOWLEDGMENTS

My first thanks as I send this book into the world go to my steadfast friend and editor, Charles Spicer, along with his assistant, the cheerful and capable Hannah Pierdolla. Thank you both so much for making this book what it is—though I must quickly add that its faults remain my own.

Andy Martin and Kelley Ragland provided invaluable guidance and leadership at Minotaur, which remains the best publisher in the business. The team there has been simply exceptional: James Sinclair, Mac Nicholas, Paul Hochman, Alisa Trager, John Morrone, and David Rotstein. Working again with Sarah Melnyk and Martin Quinn has reminded me that they are not just wonderful at their jobs, but wonderful people. How fortunate I have been to get to know them over the years!

The readers of this series are why I still write it. Thank you for every last note, message, post, every kind word! They mean more than you can know.

To my mother; to my sister, Isabelle; and to Peter, Rosie, Julia, Sarabeth, Henry, Jamie, Teddy, Remi, Wes, my thanks for so many happy times, and so many to come. I love you more than words.

To my departed Lucy, most wonderful of dogs, stout and brave and funny and sweet, thank you for teaching me as much about love as any creature ever has. And to Emily, Annabel, and Alexander, my irreplaceable ones: eternal gratitude, eternal love.

ABOUT THE AUTHOR

Charles Finch is a novelist and literary critic, author of the beloved Charles Lenox mysteries, following one of the earliest private detectives in Victorian London. The books have appeared multiple times on the *USA Today* bestseller list. He has written numerous essays, articles, and reviews for *The New York Times*, the *Chicago Tribune*, *Slate*, *New York*, and *The Guardian*, and was honored with the 2017 Nona Balakian Citation for Excellence in Reviewing by the National Book Critics Circle. He subsequently served on the boards of the NBCC and the arts colony Ragdale, and was a judge for the 2021 PEN/Faulkner Award. He lives in Los Angeles with his family.